HOW HE GOT THE GIRL

BY AMANDA SCHIMMOELLER

Royal Hearts Series
A Royal Obligation
A Royal Competition
A Royal Arrangement
A Royal Promise
A Royal Possibility

Sweeter Than Fiction Series
I Knew He Was Trouble
How He Got the Girl

HOW HE GOT THE GIRL

AMANDA SCHIMMOELLER

2
SWEETER THAN
FICTION

ISBN: 979-8-9926045-1-1 (paperback)

Cover Design by Melody Jeffries
Edited by Caitlin Miller
Proofread by Alicia Whitaker

Visit www.authoramandaschimmoeller.com for more information.

For anyone who has ever wished for a second chance.

CONTENT WARNING

While the overall tone of this story is lighthearted, there's a
brief mention of the loss of a loved one.

But rest assured, a happily-ever-after is guaranteed.

CHAPTER ONE

MALLORY

I love the holiday season as much as the next person, but this pushes the limits of my affection.

"And a happy new year." I draw out the song's final word with Christmas-spirited jazz hands that my friend, Daisy, insisted were part of her family's caroling *routine*.

The elderly couple in the doorway applauds our mediocre—and cringe—efforts.

"Wait just a minute, dears." The woman disappears inside her home. Her husband awkwardly waves before shutting the door.

Even though I think it's over-the-top, I'm willing to oblige Daisy's family holiday traditions because I need a distraction from the fact that I'm not home with my own family for Christmas. I planned on returning to my parents' house in Louisville, Kentucky, once the college semester ended, but the day I was supposed to travel home after my finals, a giant blizzard hit eastern Tennessee, leaving me trapped in my apartment.

Daisy's family saved me from a lonely, blue Christmas. They live in a suburb of Knoxville and graciously invited me to spend the holidays with them. I should've known to expect the unexpected when her older brothers picked us up from our apartments on four-wheelers since our cars were snowed in, but I was simply happy to partake in the holiday spirit.

I just didn't realize how *spirited* caroling with Daisy's family would be.

Apparently, it means embarrassing myself by singing in full Mrs. Claus attire with choreographed routines. But hey, at least the velvet dress I'm wearing is my favorite color: pink.

The front door opens again with the man holding a tray of to-go cups. The woman hands them to us.

"It's much too cold for y'all to be outside without something to warm your bones. I thought some homemade hot chocolate oughta do. It's an old family recipe." She hands Daisy a cup. "Sorry, I'm out of lids."

"It smells divine." Daisy smiles warmly.

The woman extends a cup to me, and I inhale the mouthwatering scent of the sweet, rich chocolate mixed with creamy milk.

"It does," I hum in agreement. "Thank you."

Once Daisy's parents and brothers have received their cups, we wave goodbye to the couple and head down the driveway to the next house.

My friend spins on her heels, holding her free hand out at her side to balance on the snow and ice covering the ground. "That was good, Mallory, but we need a little more gusto in the next song."

I'm not the kind of girl who holds back her punches. I'm the friend my besties call when they need blunt honesty. A fierce protector. The ride or die to help them bury a body.

Okay, maybe I wouldn't go *that* far, but I would totally egg someone's house or something a little less *criminally involved* than burying a body.

But, in this case, I feel like my opinions on providing more *gusto* in my caroling performance wouldn't be helpful or necessary, so I bite my tongue and swallow my pride. Well, as much pride as one can have while wearing a pink velvet Mrs. Claus dress.

"Gusto." I purse my lips and nod slowly. "Got it."

"We sing from the diaphragm," Daisy's younger brother says, striking a muscular pose.

"From the gut." Her other brother clutches his stomach for emphasis.

"From the *heart*." Daisy's mother shoots all her children a look. Her father looks like he'd rather be at home doing *anything* but this. "Just have fun." She squeezes my arm as we walk up the next neighbor's driveway.

"Y'all really do this every year?" I ask Daisy.

She nods. "We drive to a different town around Knoxville every winter to spread the holiday cheer around eastern Tennessee."

Daisy steps forward and knocks on the door while I take one glorious sip of the hot cocoa. It's the perfect mix of creamy and sweet—I can taste that it's homemade with love rather than a basic store mix. My eyes flutter shut as I hum in delight.

An older woman answers the door and clutches her hands to her chest. "Come quick, honey," she yells behind her, before looking back expectantly. "There are carolers."

Daisy turns and counts us into the next carol like a choir conductor. "A five, six, seven, eight." She gets back into position beside me, immediately serious and in character. I mirror my friend's motions, raising my arms and lowering them as I wiggle my fingers—mimicking snow falling—while we sing the opening lines of "Deck the

Halls." My level of enthusiasm doesn't match that of Daisy and her brothers, but I'm giving it my best attempt.

I'm singing my third fa-la-la when a man steps into the entryway. I was expecting it to be an older man after she called out "honey," but the guy watching us sing is definitely *not* elderly. He looks to be around my age, maybe a few years older. His dark hair is styled messily in a way that looks intentional, and scruff covers his jawline. When his eyes find mine, I'm immediately drawn in by the striking blue pools staring back at me like waves pulling me deeper into the ocean. But his smile is the real star of the show. He smiles with his whole face, beaming brighter than the Christmas lights strung across the city.

It's official.

He's the most handsome man I've ever seen—and I'm not exaggerating in the slightest. His face should live in a "Most Handsome Men of Our Generation" Hall of Fame alongside Henry Cavill, Glen Powell, and Zac Efron.

I don't realize I've stopped singing until Daisy elbows me. Hopefully, I haven't been staring at him too long. Maybe he didn't notice. I glance back to find him looking at me with a knowing smirk. Mr. Hottie totally knows I was staring. *Wonderful.*

Heat floods my cheeks. He probably thinks I'm decking my brain's halls with images of him…and he wouldn't be wrong. I think his face will forever be ingrained in the forefront of my memory. One doesn't easily forget a face like his.

Daisy nudges me for a second time and shoots me a sideways glance.

Oops, I did it again.

I jump back into the song. At least I have this elaborate routine to focus on rather than the handsome face in front of me.

I'm laser-focused for the rest of the song. Cool as a cucumber. No more tomato-faced Mallory here.

"Fa-la-la-la-la, la-la-la-laaa." I hold the last note, throwing in extra pizazz so that Daisy and her brothers can't say I wasn't singing with gusto or from the diaphragm or gut—whatever that means.

The older woman claps before turning and grasping Mr. Hottie's arm. "Wasn't that wonderful, Griffin? We've never had carolers at our door before."

I slowly drag my eyes back to Mr. Hottie—er, Griffin—taking deep breaths to calm my stupid racing heart.

He nods and leans against the doorway, making his arm muscles flex against his long-sleeved shirt. The cotton material goes taut around his biceps.

There's no hope for my racing heart now.

If I die, at least my final view was this fine specimen of a man.

Griffin blows out a low whistle. "You're right, Granny. And if caroling brings women as beautiful as these ladies to the door, obviously I've been missing out." His smirk is downright criminal—straight to jail for his ability to make women swoon.

"The men aren't hard on the eyes either." The older woman grins.

One of Daisy's brothers covers a laugh with a cough.

Griffin reaches into his pocket. "It's not much, but here's what I have on hand."

I have no idea what he's talking about until he approaches me with a handful of change. Before I can tell him we're not collecting donations, Griffin steps forward and plops the coins straight into my lidless, half-full cup of hot chocolate.

The pennies, quarters, dimes, and nickels falling into the cup send the liquid sloshing over the side onto my mittens. I hiss as the hot chocolate quickly soaks through the material and burns my fingers. Instinctively, I drop the cup. It hits the shoveled sidewalk, spilling the rest of my drink and sending change rolling everywhere.

He stares at my mittens, his eyes wide in abject horror. Without saying a word, Griffin steps into the front yard, bends down, and scoops up a handful of snow before pressing it to my hands.

The snow is freezing, but my body shivers for an entirely different reason.

"Are you all right?" he asks, his eyes full of concern.

"I am now," I breathe.

Daisy covers her mouth beside me, and her brothers snicker behind me.

I purse my lips. "I just said that out loud, didn't I?"

His mouth tilts up into a grin that sends my heart on another high-speed chase. I'm not sure what the destination is, but I think Griffin's muscular arms are a good guess.

"I'm happy to help you be *all right* any time, beautiful."

I'd usually be creeped out by any man calling me beautiful, but there's a genuine presence about him that makes his words sound endearing. And his slight Southern drawl doesn't hurt anything either.

"I'm sorry about your"—Griffin looks at the spilled drink on the ground—"hot chocolate?" The higher inflection in his tone makes it sound like a question.

"Only the best cup of hot chocolate in the world," I say, trying not to sound overcome by his nearness.

"Griffie, I can't believe you ruined that sweet girl's drink." The lady steps forward and swats his arm. "It's freezing out there. And now she has wet gloves to boot."

"Yeah, *Griffie*." I emphasize the cutesy nickname with sass.

He steps back, bashfully rubbing the back of his neck. "I thought you were collecting donations." When he looks back at me, there's not a trace of bashfulness remaining, but a cocky smile in its place. "I guess that means you'll have to let me make it up to you."

I quirk a brow. "What did you have in mind?"

"I know of a local café with the *actual* best hot chocolate in the world. Let me buy you a cup tomorrow?"

I force my face to remain impartial. The guy deserves to sweat it out—at least a little—before he knows that my answer is a resounding *yes*. I would be a fool not to at least see if there could be something here, especially when he seems to make every nerve in my body come alive.

After a few beats of silence, I meet his gaze. "Make it two cups, and you've got yourself a deal."

His smile widens. "I would've bought you three. Meet me at The Cozy Bean tomorrow at one."

"Works for me."

I'm staring up at him, locked in the blue pools of his eyes again, when Daisy's head pops between us. "We should get home unless you want your hands to freeze."

I hear the retreating steps of my friend and her family walking down the driveway. Reluctantly, my eyes leave Griffin to look at my hands. My gloves are soaked through, and my fingers are getting colder by the second. I pull the gloves off, and Griffin reaches out and takes them.

"I'll get these cleaned for you."

"Thanks." I dip my head to hide my blush as I slide my hands into my coat pockets. If only I could transfer the heat on my cheeks to my hands.

I bend down to retrieve my now-empty cup from the ground, but Griffin stops me with a hand to my arm. It's an innocent touch, but it sends my body buzzing.

"I'll clean everything up. It's the least I can do." He drops his hand as if my velvet dress burned him. I see his hand flex at his side. Maybe I'm not the only one who feels this chemistry between us. "I'll see you at one."

I peer up at him through my lashes, offering him a soft smile. "See you then." I offer a quick wave to his grandma before shoving my hand back in my pocket and walking as fast as my short legs will take me down the driveway.

When I reach my friend's family, they burst into a fit of laughter. Daisy doubles over and clutches my arm. "That was hilarious."

"I can't believe he dropped coins into your hot chocolate," her younger brother says.

Daisy's older brother holds his arms out wide, getting everyone to settle down. Then he holds his arm bent at the elbow and pretends like he's sprinkling salt on a dish before saying, "Plop."

Everyone breaks into laughter again, and I join them this time. When I'm not getting my hand burned by hot liquid, it's actually pretty funny to think about what just happened. And if I got a date with a handsome man out of it...even better.

"Okay, but seriously. Did anyone else feel like a third wheel back there?" Daisy's younger brother asks.

"Yeah," the older brother drawls.

Her mother sighs. "I thought it was sweet."

"Me too." Daisy smiles at me. "Please tell me you're going tomorrow. That man was smitten with you."

I shrug. "I'm sure he's smitten with all the girls."

"He wasn't looking at *me* like he wanted to press me up against a wall and kiss me until I forgot my name."

"You read too many romance books." I shake my head.

She scoffs. "There's no such thing as too many romance books. But you have to go. He could be your soulmate. Plus, that was the cutest meet-cute ever."

"Relax. I don't understand any of the words coming out of your mouth, but I know that I would be an idiot if I didn't meet him tomorrow."

She blows out a breath, the puff of air lingering between us in the cold like a cloud. "Good. I expect you to thank me at your wedding."

"Don't you think that's jumping the gun?"

"No," her family responds in unison.

I purse my lips. Well, okay then. "I'll be sure to thank you *if* we get married."

Daisy smiles, as if satisfied with my response.

Although I'd never admit it out loud, hope swells inside of me for what could be—which is crazy, because I'm not the kind of girl who believes in love at first sight or soulmates.

But what I do know for certain is this: tomorrow can't come soon enough.

CHAPTER TWO
GRIFFIN

IF THERE IS A Guinness World Record for the world's biggest idiot, I'd gladly accept the title.

I rub my eyes as if I can magically erase the memory of what I did last night. Unfortunately, I didn't wake up with wizarding powers, and the vision is still seared in my brain.

I may as well wait for the Easter Island heads from *Night at the Museum* to show up and call me a dum-dum. It's not like I don't deserve it.

My only defense is that I thought her family sounded so professional while caroling that they sang to collect donations for charitable causes. I understand now how that logic wasn't *logicing*. But I was so wrapped up in the beautiful woman in front of me that I couldn't focus on anything besides her eyes—like looking into her cup before dropping a handful of change into it.

I feel awful that I burned her hands. Hopefully, the snow I pressed on them was enough to help. And I pray that the hot chocolate I'm buying her today will make up for everything.

My fingers pull at the bottom of my bomber jacket as I wait for her to arrive. I glance at my watch—it's 1:12. Maybe she's standing me up.

I suppose I deserve that after burning her.

The bell above the door chimes, and my head whips in that direction. Nothing can hold back the smile on my face as I watch *her* walk in. There's a slight flush on her cheeks, and her soft curls are tousled, both evidence of the harsh winter wind. But I've never seen anyone more beautiful or captivating than her.

She spots me and lifts her hand in a small wave before making her way to me at the table near the register. "Sorry that I'm late. Linda hates the snow, so I had to wait for my friend to drop me off."

"It's not a problem." I smile good-naturedly. "Dare I ask who Linda is?"

She shakes her head, sending her wild waves fluttering around her face. "Linda's my car."

"You named your car *Linda?*"

"Yeah, because she never listens." Her lip quirks up at the corner, and her eyes take on a playful glint.

I stare at her blankly. Am I missing some kind of joke?

Her mouth falls open. "You've never seen the 'Listen Linda' video?" When I shake my head, she pulls out her phone. "It has millions of views—you have to see it."

She passes me her phone, and I watch a video of a young boy telling his mom—Linda—to listen. I laugh, handing her phone back as a 10 percent battery warning pops up.

"Do you see why I named her Linda now? I adore my girl, but she loves to not work at the most inopportune times, even when I sweet-talk her."

I chuckle. "You sweet-talk your car?"

"You don't?" She raises a brow.

"I can't say I ever have." I run my hands across my stubbled chin. "But I suppose there's a first time for everything."

When we reach the counter, I gesture for her to talk to the cashier, but she steps to the side. "Order for me, *Griffie*?" The playfulness in her tone mixed with the steely look in her eye only pulls me further into her orbit.

I can already feel the power this girl has over me, and I'm in trouble.

Deep, deep trouble.

"Of course," I grunt, sounding like some kind of cave-man. Who even am I? Next thing I know, I'll be pounding my chest and throwing her over my shoulder as I carry her to a table. Turning to the cashier, I say, "We'll take your hot chocolate flight and one signature hot chocolate, please." I give them my name and pay.

"A hot chocolate flight?" Her eyes are wide with excitement as we walk to a table near the window and settle into our seats.

"I figured, why buy you two hot chocolates when I can buy you four?"

She grins. "You're really trying to make up for yesterday."

"What can I say?" I shrug. "I try not to make a habit out of ruining a beautiful woman's drink, let alone burning her hands."

"I don't make a habit of meeting strangers for hot chocolate."

"I wouldn't classify us as strangers." I lean forward on my elbows and get lost in her brown eyes. They're light, like hot chocolate with the perfect amount of milk. In a word, they're stunning. That, plus her brown hair that falls past her shoulders in wild waves is the perfect combination—my kryptonite.

"What would you classify us as, then?" She runs her fingers through her hair.

"I'd say you're someone I'd love to get to know."

She dips her head as her cheeks turn the same shade of pink as the sweater she's wearing.

I hardly know anything about this gorgeous woman—I don't even know her name—but I do know that I want to learn everything about her, and that's more than I've ever been able to say about girls in the past.

I live a fast-paced lifestyle, and I have big dreams. I'm used to meeting a lot of women in my day-to-day life, but I've never really invested in getting to know them when I know that I'll be on my way to the next thing soon enough. But there's something about this woman sitting across from me that has me wanting to cancel all my plans just to stare into her eyes and count each of the freckles that lightly dust her cheeks.

"You don't know anything about me."

"Hence why I want to get to know you. I—"

"Griffin." A barista calls my name from the counter.

I smile. "I'll be right back." Pushing up from my seat, I head to the counter, carefully balancing her hot chocolate flight in one hand and my mug in the other.

I set the board of drinks in front of her and warm my hands with my own mug as I sit across from her. "Prepare to be amazed."

She takes a small sip from each miniature mug in front of her, maintaining a poker face.

When she sets the last mug down, I lean closer. "Well, what do you think?"

She stares me down until her eyes begin to sparkle with mirth. "You were right. Nothing can beat this hot chocolate."

I blow out a puff of air in relief and take a sip from my mug. "Which flavor is your favorite?"

"Snickerdoodle. No contest. The white chocolate with the cinnamon notes is literal perfection."

I set my cup down and smile at her. "I'll be right back."

After purchasing a large mug of the snickerdoodle hot chocolate, I return to our table, setting it in front of her.

"You didn't have to do that." She leans forward and inhales with a soft smile on her lips. "But thank you."

"I said I would buy you two cups—I'm only holding up my end of the bargain."

And I want to make her happy. Being the reason this woman wears a smile on her face is my new favorite thing.

I lean back and take another sip of my drink. "You want to know something utterly devastating?" I continue before she can tell me no. "I know your car's name but not yours."

"Oh." She laughs and extends her hand. "I'm Mallory."

I take her hand—loving how it fits in mine—and give it a gentle shake. "Mallory," I echo. The name feels fitting for her. The sound of it coming from my lips sends a shiver up my spine, a feeling I can't shake that we were meant to meet.

Call it divine intervention. Kismet. Fate. But I know that, somehow, we were both *exactly* where we were supposed to be yesterday.

She raises a brow. "*Your* name is Mallory, too?" Her expression remains neutral, but the twitch of her mouth gives her away. Taking on a Southern accent, she says, "I don't think this town is big enough for the both of us."

I grin. "I like your sense of humor." I give her hand a soft squeeze before releasing it. "I'm Griffin, but you already knew that."

"I think I prefer your grandmother's nickname for you."

I chuckle. "She's called me that since I was a kid. It doesn't exactly sound manly now that I'm an adult, but I could never tell her no."

Not that she'd listen to me, anyway.

"So, tell me something I don't know about you, Mallory."

"You mean everything?" She smirks. "Unless you're a creepy stalker who already knows everything about me."

"Whoa." I hold my hands up. "You're the one who showed up at *my* doorstep, remember? How do I know *you* aren't stalking *me*?" I shoot her my million-watt smile—at least, that's what my granny calls it.

Mallory hides her smile behind her mug, taking a sip of her drink. "Touché, Griffie." When she sets the glass back on the table, a ghost of a smile is still on her lips. "Let's see, I'm close with my family."

"I like them. They seemed very enthusiastic." I smirk at the memory of their caroling performance last night.

Mallory shoots me a skeptical look. "Okay, are you actually stalking me? How do you know…"

"I saw them last night." She still stares blankly at me like she has no idea what I'm talking about. "You know…" I shimmy my shoulders. "Fa-la-la."

"*Oh*, that's my friend Daisy's family. I'm staying with them until the snow lets up and I can get back home."

My shoulders fall. "You're not from around here?" That doesn't bode well for my plans to get to know the beautiful woman across from me.

She shakes her head. "I'm from Louisville, Kentucky."

"What brings you to Knoxville?"

"I'm a senior at UT."

If she started college right after graduating high school, that should only make her two or three years younger than me.

"What are you studying?" I ask.

"Early childhood education." My brows lift, and she tilts her head. "Why the face?"

"You're not like any of the teachers I had in elementary school."

"I'm not sure if I should feel insulted or—"

"It's a compliment, trust me." My lips pull up at one corner in a crooked smile. "I would've had a major crush on my teachers back then if they looked anything like you."

"Thanks, I think?" She shakes her head before narrowing her eyes. "What do you do, Mr. Hotshot?" Before I can answer, she holds up a hand, cutting me off. "Wait, let me guess. You're a lion tamer in the circus."

"It can feel like all eyes are on me in my job, but no."

"All eyes on you..." She takes a sip of her drink and then taps her full bottom lip, making my heart rate spike. "Are you an ophthalmologist?"

"I love your deductive reasoning there, but you're moving in the wrong direction."

"Marketing manager?"

I shake my head. "I did go to business school, but that's not it either."

Mallory purses her lips and looks out the window for a heartbeat. When she looks back at me, her eyes are alight. "I know! You're a face painter at kids' birthday parties."

"You're getting closer with the entertainment industry."

She sighs. "I give up. What do you do?"

"I'm an actor."

"I should've known." Mallory taps her pink nails on her mug. "Would I recognize you from anything?"

I rub my hands on my jeans. It always feels a little awkward talking about my dream career, especially when I've been trying—and failing—for years to achieve it. Unless holding up a tube of toothpaste, saying, "You handle the razzle, we'll bring the dazzle. Dazzle the world with your smile when you use DazzlePaste" in a commercial counts as my Hollywood debut.

Yeah…didn't think so.

"No." I clear my throat. "But I have an audition tomorrow."

"What for?"

"A romantic comedy movie. They want an unknown actor. I've been trying to catch my big break for a while now, so I hope this will be it. Honestly, I'm just grateful for every opportunity to audition. Each one gives me motivation to grow my craft."

Mallory leans back in her seat, looking impressed. "I'm more of a fantasy girl myself, but I hope you get it."

Her honesty is as refreshing as an ice-cold glass of lemonade on a summer day. "That's my dream role. Being the lead in a fantasy movie would be epic, but I'll take anything that gets me into the industry."

She lifts her mug into the air. "To getting your dream role one day."

I clink my mug with hers. "To one day," I echo. "Is being an elementary school teacher your dream job?"

Mallory nods. "Although I think I'd enjoy any job where I get to help teach and grow the next generation."

"It's one of the most noble and important professions."

"People say that kids are brutally honest, but I like it."

"Something tells me you're pretty blunt, yourself."

She shrugs. "Sounds like you've already got me pegged."

I might know snippets about the beautiful woman in front of me, but there's so much more I want to know. It seems cruel that I'm meeting her when I'm on the cusp of my big break into the industry, something I've been working toward for years. But if I land that role, I can cross that bridge when I come to it.

For now, I only hope that Mallory gives me the time of day to learn everything that makes her who she is.

CHAPTER THREE

MALLORY

"I HAVE A FEELING there's a lot more to the woman behind the biting words." Griffin's eyes meet mine while a playful smile tilts his lips.

The way he's looking at me makes me feel like he can see right into my soul. It's as if he's searching for the answer to who I am—like he wants to uncover everything there is to know about me.

Although I don't know anything about the man except that he rights his wrongs, knows the best place to get hot chocolate in eastern Tennessee, and is trying to catch his break as an actor—even if the fact that he wants to be an actor feels like a potential red flag—I can't help but feel the same way. There's a feeling deep in my gut that has me wanting to peel back all the layers of this handsome man and discover who he is at his core.

I shoot him a flirty smile. "Just like there's more to the man behind the pretty face."

"You think I'm pretty?" His grin is more genuine than cocky.

I never thought I'd consider dating someone long-distance, let alone an actor. Heck, he could even be preparing for his audition right now. But it's the little things like his lopsided smile and how he pressed snow to my hands immediately after burning me that make me feel like I can trust him regardless of the flirty persona he puts off. Deep down, I think I'll regret it if I don't try to see if there's something between us.

"I think you already know that you're pretty." I pull my hands farther into the sleeves of my sweater, like a turtle retreating into its shell, before taking another sip of my snickerdoodle hot chocolate. I wasn't exaggerating when I said it was the best cup I've ever had. It's warming my soul, and Griffin calling the teaching profession *noble* is filling my heart right alongside it.

"I like your fiery spirit." Griffin takes a sip of his drink, his smirk barely visible behind the mug.

"I like your face," I deadpan.

"Tell me something I don't already know." He winks.

Winks! I don't think I've ever had a man wink at me before, but Griffin makes it look effortless. I'm pretty sure if I tried to return the action, it would look like I have something stuck in my eye that I'm desperately trying to get out.

"I think you're going to land that movie role," I say instead.

"Really?" His eyes widen slightly as if I caught him off guard.

"Yeah, you'll fit right in with the rest of Hollywood since you seem to be oozing confidence."

His shoulders fall like a deflated balloon, and I wonder if I took my jesting too far. I've been known to do that a time or two...or a hundred.

Griffin is smooth—like creamy peanut butter or soft-serve ice cream. I'm the exact opposite: a blunt girlie.

That saying about honesty being the best policy? Yeah, that's not always true. I like calling things as they are, but I've learned over time that not everyone feels the same about the truth. That's why I love working with kids; they never fail to tell you how it is with the bluntness of a butter knife.

I've tried to work on myself over the years because I don't want people to think I'm a horrible person. But sometimes, my mouth moves faster than my brain can process what I'm saying. At least my besties since sixth grade—Kelsey, Alyssa, and Shayna—know me well enough by now to call me out if I go too far. I'm thankful they've stuck by my side over the years. Not everyone has.

I think it's the main reason I've never been in love. Some guys like what some might call '*mean flirting*' in the beginning. But no boyfriend has ever stuck with me for the long haul. I'm holding out for someone who loves me, sass and all.

With the way that Griffin's demeanor just changed, I'm wondering if he's just another man that I'm too much for.

When his eyes meet mine, I hold my breath, waiting for him to say, *This was fun, but I need to be...anywhere else but here. See ya never.*

Surprisingly, his mouth tilts into a lopsided grin, although his eyes don't have the same twinkle they held moments ago. "If only confidence were all it took to land a movie."

I let out a long breath, finally feeling like I can exhale again. "Is there something holding you back? A reason you're not landing roles?"

"You mean aside from the casting directors?" He runs a hand along his stubbled chin. "I think I'm scared to try. And by try, I mean *really* try."

That wasn't the answer I was expecting from the confident man in front of me.

"Why's that?"

"If I put my all—my whole self—into getting a role in the audition process and end up not getting the role, I'm not sure how I'd recover."

"I've never auditioned for anything in my life, not even a school talent show, so you can take what I'm about to say with a grain of salt. But I think if you're walking into an audition with the mindset that you need to hold back, I'm sure the casting people can see that. I don't know anything about the Hollywood industry, but I'm not sure many people are willing to risk the success of their movie on someone who only dips their toes in."

He nods along with my statement. "That's fair."

"Maybe they're looking for a star who's willing to dive right in without hesitation. So, I guess the question you might want to consider is this: Would you rather risk it all and land your dream role, or hold yourself back and potentially regret that you didn't show them what you can do?"

He blows out a low whistle. "Has anyone ever told you that you have a way of saying things they're thinking but are too scared to admit out loud?"

"More times than I can count." My laugh is dry, and I hope he can't hear the hesitancy behind it.

"I hope this doesn't come across too strong, but I've never met someone like you before." Griffin clasps his hands on the table. "Everything about you is refreshing."

I've hardly spent any time with this man, but I already feel *seen* by him. I know I'm not everyone's cup of tea with my blunt honesty, but he seems to like me more for it.

"Like the fact that you can put me in my place but seem to love the color pink." He gestures to my sweater, and I smile.

"I like to think that I can be feminine *and* have rough edges."

Griffin nods. "I believe you can do anything you put your mind to or be anything you want to be, Mallory."

His eyes are kind, but his tone is serious, as if he's urging me to believe the words he's saying.

"You should believe that same sentiment about yourself."

He pulls his lips into his mouth and is quiet for a moment until he meets my eyes again. "You know what? You're right. I'll give it my best shot during my audition tomorrow. It's not like I have anything to lose."

I ball up my hand and extend it across the table. He knocks his fist against mine. "You can't succeed if you don't try."

"To trying." Griffin raises his half-full mug of hot chocolate toward me. "Regardless, if we fail or succeed."

I lift my mug, clinking it with his. "Cheers."

After finishing off my drink, I set the empty mug on the table and wrap my arms around my middle. "I want to know more about you. Tell me, Griffin, who's the man behind the wannabe actor persona?"

"You don't pull any punches." He laughs. "Let's see. I was born and raised right down the road in Lover's Grove."

I hold up a hand as my mouth falls open. "Your town is legitimately named Lover's Grove?"

"Yep." The smile on his face is wistful, like he's told the story a million times but never tires of it. "The founder of our small town was so in love with the woman he met just before founding the town that he named it Lover's Grove as an ode to her."

"Please tell me they got married."

Griffin nods. "They were happily married for fifty-four years and lived in the town until they both passed just two days apart from each other. It was like they loved each other so much that they couldn't live without the other. People say that when you meet your soulmate in our town, you're bound to be tied together forever. Legend says the town has a way of pushing people together."

"Have you never been in love then? Or do you not believe the town's folktales?"

"I think the older women in town have a horrible habit of playing matchmaker and forcing people together. But that doesn't mean there isn't any truth behind some of the crazy love stories I've heard." He runs a hand through his brown hair, leaving it perfectly messy and making him even more attractive. "As for me, I had puppy love in high school but never *true* love. The kind where I meet a woman that makes loving her easy, and everything else fades into the background."

If a handsome, charming man like him can't find love, there's no hope for the rest of us. "I'm sure you'll find her."

"You never know, she may just show up at my door in a pink velvet dress singing Christmas carols." He makes direct eye contact with me as he says this, making my cheeks match my sweater. "But I had this nightmare that I'm going to bungle it by ruining her drink and burning her hands in the process."

"It sounds like you'll have a dilemma on your hands," I say, playing along with his little game.

"One that I'll do anything to fix. I can't disappoint all of Lover's Grove, after all."

"Was that your house that we sang at?"

He nods. "My parents' house. My apartment lease ended in October, so I've been staying with them for the last two months while I've auditioned."

Usually, the thought of a man living at home would scare me away in about 0.2 seconds, but his reasoning seems sound. There's no point in his paying for an apartment that he'd have to leave if he landed a big movie role.

I can't help but think that maybe all the tales about Lover's Grove may not be fictional. Maybe there's some merit to them if it brought me to this man's front door.

"Does your grandma live with your parents as well?"

He nods. "We share a wall. She knocks four times every evening to say, 'Good night, Griffie.'"

My heart is melting. And my heart doesn't melt. But this man...he's something else. The more I learn about him, the more I like who he is.

"You knock back, *right*?" I deadpan, even though I'm teasing.

"Do I knock back?" he scoffs. "I'd have to be soulless not to."

I wipe my hand across my forehead. "Whew, good. I don't have to fake an emergency then. What else should I know about you?"

"How long do you have?"

"My day's wide open."

Even if it weren't, I'd cancel all my plans to spend more time with him.

CHAPTER FOUR

GRIFFIN

THIS IS THE BEST date of my life.

It only took a few minutes for me to realize that Mallory was a special girl—the kind you either wife up or compare everyone else to for the rest of your life if you're dumb enough to let her go.

Even though I felt like an idiot last night, I'm not stupid.

Hearing Mallory tell me that her day's wide open has me smiling like a giddy fool. She could easily say she has plans with her friend to get to. Instead, she's *choosing* to stay here with me.

I don't want to count my chickens before they hatch, but if I were a betting man, I'd say that Mallory's feeling what I am, too—at least to some level.

"It all started on a beautiful summer day twenty-four years ago, when I came into the world."

She balls up a napkin and throws it at me.

I laugh. "I'm kidding. Okay, other things you should know about me… I could eat chicken wings every single day and never get tired of them. I thought superheroes like Iron Man were real until I was thirteen. I sing in the shower, loudly and unashamedly off-key. I cry every time I see one of those dog commercials with sad music playing in the background. And I firmly believe that a hamburger is a sandwich."

"Okay, you had me going there until you called a burger a sandwich." Mallory clicks her tongue. "That might be a deal-breaker."

I hold a hand to my chest. "Did I say it was a firm belief? What I meant to say is that I'm completely open to changing my mind about the matter."

For the right person. The words are on the edge of my tongue, but I don't dare say them out loud for fear of sounding crazy since I literally just met this woman *yesterday.*

"I was kidding, but good to know you're open-minded."

"It's one of my best qualities," I tease before leaning back in my seat. "Enough about me. I want to know about *you.*"

"I'm obsessed with the color pink, which I know you already noticed, but it's worth stating twice. I can never drive past a McDonald's without stopping to get a Dr. Pepper. My favorite artist is Taylor Swift, and I met my three best friends at one of her concerts in the sixth grade. I've loved ice skating since I was little, but it's been too long since I've done it. My comfort show is *The Vampire Diaries.* I won a local pie-eating contest when I was ten, and have never eaten a bite of pie since."

"Yes to Dr. Pepper, but I'm sad for all the pie you're missing out on."

She grimaces. "I can't look at a slice without feeling nauseous."

"I've already eaten enough pie for a lifetime." I smirk, trying to lighten the mood. "The real question, though, is are you Team Stefan or Team Damon?"

"Team Damon," she answers immediately. "I love a good character arc."

"That's the right answer."

She raises an eyebrow. "You watch *The Vampire Diaries?*"

I press my lips together, realizing I just revealed my guilty-pleasure show. "I told you I like fantasy," I say, hoping it sounds convincing.

"You said you want to *star* in a fantasy."

"Okay, fine." I reach my hand across the table and wrap it around hers. It's tiny in comparison to mine, and the feel of her smooth skin sends a shiver up my spine. Everything about being around her feels good and natural. It feels *right*. "I've seen every episode."

Multiple times—but she doesn't need to know that.

I lose all sense of time as I continue to get to know Mallory. We talk about anything and everything, and I learn even more random facts about her, like that she thinks a slushie is something you eat, not drink. I even elicit a few laughs out of her that I wish I could hear over and over again.

When my stomach rumbles, I pull my phone out of my pocket to check the time, only to find the battery's dead.

"Do you know what time it is?" I ask.

Mallory pulls her phone out of her purse. "It's six-thirty."

I let out a low whistle. "I can't believe we've been here five and a half hours."

Her stomach growls, and she presses a hand to it. "I didn't think it had been that long, but apparently, my stomach does."

"Are you down to grab dinner?"

"I'll agree on one condition." Her eyes glitter with amusement.

"What's that?"

"We have to get chicken wings."

"Easiest yes of my life." I stand and extend my hand, helping her to her feet. "I know just the place."

I grab our mugs and drop them off in a bin labeled *dirty glassware and utensils*. When I walk back to our table, I help her put on her winter coat—which is, of course, pink—before shrugging on my own. Which reminds me…

"Oh, before I forget." I reach into my coat pocket and pull out her gloves that I laundered for her.

Her fingers brush mine as she takes them from me. I do my best to keep breathing normally.

Mallory appears unaffected as she slides the gloves into her purse. "Thank you."

"You ready?" I indicate the window, where snow is steadily falling outside, making it look like we're living in a snow globe.

Mallory surprises me when she intertwines her fingers with mine, making my heart pick up speed. "Let's go, Griff."

I've never liked the sound of my name on anyone's lips more.

I open the door for her with my free hand, and we step outside. My shoulders tense from the brisk air.

Mallory stops walking, tilting her head toward the sky with closed eyes and a content smile. Small snowflakes land in her curly hair, making her look like a snow princess. I tuck a rogue curl under her hat so it doesn't cover her eyes. The backs of my fingers brush along her jawline, and her eyes dart open, meeting mine.

"You're beautiful." I smile.

"I think it goes without saying that I find you handsome." She bites her bottom lip, and my heart begins to race in my chest.

"It's nice to hear you say it." It's a wonder my voice remains steady when I feel anything *but* that.

Mallory tilts my world off-kilter. She's beautiful, but she's sassy in a way where I never know what will come out of her mouth next. She keeps me on my toes. She's everything I could ask for, and all the things I never even thought to look for in a partner. And I know all of this just after one date.

One life-changing date.

My gaze drops to her mouth.

Kissing her is a terrible idea when I might be moving across the country if I do well in my audition tomorrow. Not to mention that we just met *yesterday*.

But it feels like I've known this girl for my whole life. There's no ignoring the gravitational pull I feel between us.

I wrap my arm around Mallory's waist and lean down, leaving mere centimeters between our faces. She sucks in a sharp breath, and her eyes flutter shut.

I can't help but stare at her for a moment longer. I love the rosy tint of her cheeks from the wind, and the way the snowflakes melting in her hair make her waves even more untamed. Everything about her appearance right now shows her fiery personality, and I couldn't be more drawn to her.

I move a hand up to gently cradle her face before running the pad of my thumb along her cheek and jawbone. A trail of goosebumps follows everywhere my finger touches, and I can't wait any longer.

Before I can second-guess my actions, I close the remaining distance between us and press my lips to hers. They're soft and supple, just like I imagined. The way they slowly move against mine sends my stomach fluttering like the snowflakes falling around us. I thought a kiss in the snow would be cold, but my whole body is buzzing with warmth from the feelings Mallory is sparking.

If I thought she tilted my world off-kilter before, it's off its freaking axis now, rolling full speed down Mt. Everest. I don't think there's anything else in the world that can compare to this feeling. Anyone else who could compare to *her*.

CHAPTER FIVE

MALLORY

HE'S KISSING ME.

He's *kissing* me.

He's kissing *me*.

The press of Griffin's lips to mine is sweet, like my snickerdoodle hot chocolate. For a man who comes across as charismatic and confident, he's surprisingly tender in the way he's treated me the whole day—especially now.

His mouth moves against mine, slowly nipping and exploring as if he's a modern-day Indiana Jones trying to chart a map of my lips to find hidden treasure.

Griffin's scruff brushes against my cheek, tickling my skin. I always thought I preferred clean-shaven men, but I'm fully team five-o'clock shadow now.

My hands slide up to his chest, and his heartbeat pulses beneath my palm. The rapid rhythm matches my own.

If I told my friends that I was kissing a man I just met, they wouldn't believe me. I don't do this kind of thing. I'm slow to trust and quick to provide reasons why someone isn't right for me.

It may sound crazy, because I don't even know this man's last name, but I think I know more about him than any guy I've ever dated. So, it doesn't technically feel like I'm kissing someone I just met. But it *does* feel like I'm kissing someone I'd love to spend a lot more time with. It's an unusual but good feeling. There's a comfort there that I only have with my family and closest friends.

A small gasp escapes my lips as he deepens the kiss. My fingers clutch the collar of his jacket, and he tugs at my waist, pulling our bodies flush together.

Someone across the street lets out a wolf whistle, and Griffin groans as he reluctantly pulls back. I giggle and press my forehead against his chest to hide my blush, feeling like a teen being caught making out under the bleachers at a high school football game.

"I love the sound of your laugh." He gently tilts my chin up until my eyes meet his.

We stare at each other for a moment. I can't get over how beautiful his eyes are with the snow falling around us. They're like a bright blue sky that brings you immediate joy after days of thunderstorms. I'm usually a cloudy-skies girl, but his eyes may have me changing my tune.

Griffin smiles down at me. It looks genuine and un-forced, like he couldn't hide it if he tried. "Hi."

The whispered word makes me giggle again. I'm not a giggly girl either. Giggles and being a realist don't typi-cally go together, but around him, I guess that's what I'm reduced to.

My stomach growls again, and it's his turn to laugh. "Let's get you fed, beautiful."

He holds my hand as we walk the rest of the way to his car and then opens the passenger door for me.

"What a gentleman." I smile up at him.

"I'll be sure to tell my mom and Granny they raised me right."

Once Griffin gets in the driver's seat, I say, "All the women of the world thank them."

He places his hand on the back of my seat to back out, but pauses to shoot me a playful grin. "I only need *one* woman to know how much of a gentleman I am."

I suck in a sharp breath. "Is that so?"

Griffin leans over and kisses me softly on the cheek, his scruff tickling my face again, as he puts the car in reverse. "Mm-hmm."

The low rumble of his voice sends a shiver racing from my head to my toes.

"Cold?"

I nod, unwilling to reveal that *he's* the reason for my shivering. Mr. Hottie certainly doesn't need the ego boost.

He turns the heat up and drives out of the parking lot, carefully maneuvering onto the main road coated in a dusting of snow.

I wrap my arms around my middle while my thoughts run rampant, trying to process everything that's happened in the past day. It's felt like a whirlwind, but I think it's one I don't want to forget.

Griffin nudges my arm with his elbow, pulling me from my thoughts. "What are you thinking in that beautiful mind of yours?"

The truth slips out before I can think twice about it. "I never kiss on a first date, let alone someone I just met."

"Neither do I." He laughs. "Well, I guess, except for now." I glance over at him and watch as his grip turns white-knuckled on the steering wheel. His voice is softer as he asks, "Do you regret it?"

I take a second to think it over. "No, I don't."

"Good. Me neither." He smiles. "It doesn't feel like we've only known each other for a day, does it?"

"Not at all."

Griffin surprises me by taking my hand again. He pulls it to his lips, pressing a gentle kiss to my skin. "Thanks for letting me make up for my massive flub yesterday."

"I'd gladly let you do it again if it means I get an endless supply of those snickerdoodle hot chocolates."

"I'll give you as many as you desire."

My heart thumps. "Don't make promises you can't keep."

"I only make promises I can deliver on." Griffin rubs my thumb before settling our clasped hands on my leg. We sit in comfortable silence for the remainder of the short drive.

I've already been vulnerable enough with him that I know he has the power to break my heart, so I hope he's being honest right now. Otherwise, I'm in for a world of hurt.

Griffin, ever the gentleman, drops me off at the door while he parks the car. I step inside and pull out my phone, shooting a quick text to Daisy to let her know where I am.

ME

Girl, the date has been amazing! He just took me to Wings and More for dinner. If you could pick me up from here later, that would be great!

Immediately after I hit send, my phone screen goes black. Shoot. I knew I should've charged the battery this morning, but I wasn't expecting this date to last the whole day. Hopefully, she got the message. If not, I'm sure Griffin wouldn't mind dropping me off later.

The chime above the front door rings as Griffin steps inside, shaking snowflakes from his brown hair. He smiles as he moves to my side and speaks to the hostess, who seats us immediately at one of the few available tables.

The restaurant has a fun, farmhouse vibe with red-and-white gingham picnic tablecloths and galvanized decor on the tables and walls, giving the place a rustic charm. If how packed it is in here is any indication of the quality of the food, I think I'm in for a delicious meal.

Griffin orders a platter of sticky honey wings for us to share that he swears will leave me never wanting to eat another flavor of wings, along with fries and Dr. Peppers.

My heart warms. He remembered my favorite drink. "You're a good listener."

He grins. "It's not a McDonald's Dr. Pepper, but I hope it'll do."

Our food is delivered in record time. My stomach grumbles again when I behold the giant stack of wings. "These smell amazing."

"They are." He picks up a flat, and I do the same. It's not exactly the kind of food I'd usually pick to eat on a first date, but Griffin makes me feel like I don't have to worry about getting sauce all over my face and fingers. "Bon appétit."

I take a bite, and my taste buds instantly go wild. It's sweet from the honey but has spicy notes that provide just the right amount of heat, followed by the tang of vinegar.

"Perfect, right?"

I answer him by finishing off that wing and grabbing for another.

Griffin smiles. "This is my favorite place for a reason."

"Is it where you take all your dates?" I dive into my next wing.

"You're the first girl I've ever brought here. Well, aside from my mom and Granny."

I raise an eyebrow. "Really?"

"You act like I'm a player." He frowns. "Truth is, I'm always onto one thing or the next, and I've never made time for dating."

"So this is where you *would* take all your dates."

"Only the special one."

His word choice doesn't go unnoticed. He didn't say he'd take the special *ones* here, just the special *one*. As in, a singular person. From the way his eyes sparkle when he looks at me, there's no question that he's referring to me.

There he goes again, saying things that make me think of a potential future with him—this guy I just met but feel inexplicably drawn to.

To avoid all my confusing emotions, I grab a few fries, dipping them in ranch before shoving them in my mouth.

Griffin laughs a full-belly, eyes-crinkling laugh. "You're truly something else, Mallory."

I finish chewing and narrow my eyes at him. "Is that supposed to be a compliment?"

He shoots me a crooked smile. "Oh, it's definitely a compliment."

I sip my Dr. Pepper, hoping it will cool the blush tinting my cheeks. Spoiler alert: it doesn't.

Once we've finished most of the wings and fries, I lean back in my seat. "I think if I eat another bite, I'm going to need to be carried out of here."

"I can help with that." He winks.

I roll my eyes. "Nice try."

"It was worth a shot." Griffin waves our server over and gets the check, never even giving me a chance to offer to pay.

"Thanks for dinner and the hot chocolate."

"It's my pleasure." He signs the receipt, and I move to stand, but his next words keep me rooted in place. "Before I forget, I have a question for you."

He sounds serious, and my heartbeat picks up speed. Is he about to ask me to be his girlfriend or—*gasp*—his wife? Okay, I'm kidding about the last part, but everything else about my time spent with this man has felt fast, so I have no clue what to expect here.

"Yeah?" I squeak out, sounding just as anxious as I feel.

"Can I have your number?"

I sigh in relief. "I think I can manage that." He pulls out his phone, glaring at the black screen. "I'll have to put my number in your phone, since mine is dead."

I grimace. "My phone died right after we got here."

Griffin looks around the table before reaching down and grabbing the small paper napkin that his drink was set on, along with the pen he used to sign the receipt. He extends them both toward me. "Problem solved."

I write down my number and hand it back. "This is so old school."

"I know. It feels like I'm back in middle school, having you check yes or no to being my girlfriend."

"Whoa, slow your horses, Griff. Let's start with my number," I tease, pushing to my feet.

Griffin crosses the table to my side. He leans in so his breath is a whisper against my ear. "Trust me, this is only the start, beautiful."

CHAPTER SIX

MALLORY

ONE WEEK LATER, I've finally made it back home to Louisville, but I feel numb. And I don't mean from the cold.

I'm numb from the waiting.

The yearning.

The undelivered promises.

I should've known better. I should've said no from the very beginning when Griffin asked me out. Maybe if I had, I wouldn't be here staring out the bay window in my parents' house with a scowl.

The blue sky mocks me. Doesn't it know that it's rude to remind me of a certain pair of eyes I'd like to forget? I want to sulk in the clouds, but no. Instead, I get this unwelcome reminder of everything I thought I could have but lost because I decided to be vulnerable and trust a man who turned out to be a stupid, lying *boy*.

"Mal, your friends are here," my mom yells from the front of the house.

I'm not in the mood to hang out, but time spent with my besties is always the best cure for sadness. Alyssa, Shayna, and Kelsey have all been here for me at the hardest times in my life. They're the girls who pick me up when I can't carry on anymore.

I wrap my bubblegum-pink knit blanket around my shoulders and trudge to the living room. The second I round the corner, all three of my besties hurry over and pull me into a group hug. From that simple action, I'm nearly reduced to tears. I sniffle, squeezing them back.

"I'll be upstairs," my mom says. "There's stuff for hot chocolate and decorating sugar cookies in the kitchen. I know it's a little belated this year, but I couldn't let y'all miss your cookie-decorating tradition."

"You're the best, Momma Porter," Shayna calls after her.

We each grab a few cookies from the cooling rack by the stove and sit at the table in the dining room, which is decked out in a plethora of icing colors and sprinkles.

My friends chatter excitedly while I focus on the masterpiece before me. I slather yellow icing on the snowman-shaped cookie and add brown hair and blue eyes before squirting red icing over the whole thing. It actually feels cathartic. Ten out of ten would recommend.

I glance up to find all my friends staring at me. Alyssa and Shayna's eyes are wide as they glance at my creation.

Kelsey looks like she's holding back a smirk as she leans over and takes the red icing bag from me. "Okay, what gives?"

I blink. "What do you mean?"

"You look...stabby."

"How does one look stabby?"

Alyssa eyes my cookie version of Griffin. "I think the crime scene in front of you is Exhibit A."

"It's he-who-must-not-be-named."

"Voldemort?" Shayna ices the last petal on her flower-themed snowflake cookie.

I shake my head. "Hot Cocoa Man."

"Who's Hot Cocoa Man?" Kelsey asks.

"The guy I haven't told y'all about." I always tell my friends everything, but I've been too embarrassed to bring Griffin up.

"You met a guy and didn't tell us?" Shayna squeals.

"What did he do to deserve that massacre?" Alyssa gestures to my cookie. "I mean, masterpiece."

"He took me on the absolute best date of my entire life and then ghosted me."

"He *didn't*." Kelsey presses her lips together, setting down her icing bag and biting off the head of her snowman cookie. "Give us all the details so we can hate him with you."

So, I do. I tell them everything. From meeting him while caroling with Daisy's family to plopping change into my cup of hot chocolate and offering to make it up to me the next day with the world's best cup of hot chocolate.

I share all about our date and how the hours flew by like they were only minutes. How I felt like I could be vulnerable with him because he felt different than all the men I'd ever dated before. How he was handsome and flirty, but still seemed genuine. How he said he couldn't wait to see me again.

"Then he paid for our dinner and asked for my number. But both of our phones were dead, so I had to write it down for him on a paper napkin. Then Daisy came barging into the restaurant with her brothers like they were security guards." I laugh at the memory of Griffin's terrified face as Daisy's brothers stood intimidatingly over him. "She freaked out after my phone died and she couldn't get a hold of me. But my text to her had at least gone through, so she knew where to find me. Anyway, we all shared a good laugh about it, and Griffin walked me to their car and gave me a chaste but sweet goodnight kiss. The last words he said to me were, 'I'll talk to you soon, beautiful.'"

"Then what?" Shayna asks.

I shrug. "We left, and I kept checking my phone, waiting to hear from him. Only, I never did."

"What a jerk," Kelsey growls.

"He doesn't deserve you, Mal." Shayna rises from the table and gives me a hug.

"It's his loss." Alyssa sends me a sympathetic look.

"What does he do? I'd love to give his company a bad review on Yelp." Kelsey's brow furrows. We all gape at her. She shrugs casually. "What? It's what Mal would do for us, so I thought I'd return the favor."

I shake my head at her antics. "You're the best, but I don't think it'll work here. Griffin's auditioning for a new rom-com movie that he hopes will be his big break. So maybe he was just starting the audition early, seeing if he could convince a girl he was interested when he clearly wasn't." I pick a piece of lint off my blanket. "I guess he's a better actor than he gives himself credit for because he sure played me."

"Ugh, I hate him already. I hope the casting director throws him out like the trash he is." Kelsey bites off the head of another snowman.

That almost makes me laugh, but a sigh slips out instead.

"I know it might be a sore subject, but do you want hot chocolate?" Shayna offers with a sad smile.

I grimace. "Y'all go ahead." The drink didn't do me wrong, but Hot Cocoa Man did. I'm not sure I can disassociate the two.

My friends hesitantly load their mugs high with whipped cream and mini marshmallows while shooting each other glances and then looking at me.

I'm fine. I'll *be* fine.
I just never want hot chocolate again.

CHAPTER SEVEN

MALLORY

THREE YEARS LATER

I hate winter.

I hate the bitter chill that leaves me wondering if spring will ever come. I hate having to fake smiles around my extended relatives on holidays who repeatedly ask when I'm getting married and having kids, even though I don't have a boyfriend. I hate the shorter days and lack of sunlight. I hate flu season and ice on the roads.

But, most of all, I hate winter because it reminds me of Griffin.

"All right, besties. It's time for happies and crappies." Alyssa runs a hand through her blonde hair.

It's nine at night, but she looks like she just got ready for the day, not a curl out of place. Meanwhile, I'm sure my naturally wavy hair looks more like a bird's nest after a full day of teaching.

I settle on the couch between Shayna and Alyssa while Kelsey sits in the armchair beside us. I'm so thankful we all kept our promise to come back to Louisville and live together after our college years. I'm not sure what I'd do without my besties-turned-roommates.

Every Friday night, we have girls' night. Typically, we watch a movie or do something fun in town if the weather allows, and we always try to do a weekly check-in with our happies and crappies.

"I'll go first," Kelsey volunteers. "My happy is that Tyler took me on another date to the local animal rescue, and I'm *this close* to persuading him to adopt one of the dogs." She holds her thumb and pointer finger just a few centimeters apart.

Kelsey thought love was a sham until she started dating our neighbor, Tyler, a few months ago. They've been inseparable ever since. It fills my heart to see her this happy, even if it makes me feel a little sick.

I used to believe love existed…until Hot Cocoa Man.

"I don't have a crappy this week." Kelsey sighs dreamily. "I'm just really, really happy."

"She's been bitten by the love bug," Shayna squeals, dancing next to me on the sofa.

"Before you break into song, I'll go." I pull a fuzzy pink blanket onto my lap. "My happy is that it's finally winter break." My friends all let out a little cheer for me, knowing I've been counting down the days until my three-week break. I love my students, but everyone starts getting a little stir-crazy as the holidays approach. "And my crappy is that Linda has been acting up again."

My *real* crappy is that winter reminds me of Griffin, but I don't want to burden my friends with that thought. Not when I've done my best to convince them—and myself—that I'm over him.

"Oh, Linda. Poor thing hates the cold." Kelsey shakes her head.

"She really does." I turn to Alyssa. "What about you, Lyss?"

"I've been waiting to tell y'all." Alyssa leans forward. "I have enough clients now that they offered me a full-time chair in the salon."

I reach over and hug her. "Congrats, Lyss."

"That's amazing." Kelsey gives her a high five.

Shayna reaches across me to squeeze Alyssa's arm. "We always knew you could do it."

She pulls out four Kizito cookies—a staple dessert in Louisville and our celebration treat of choice for special occasions—and my mouth instantly waters. Alyssa hands each of us our favorite flavor, mine being white chocolate chip. My favorite used to be snickerdoodle, but that changed three years ago, and I have no plans of ever going back.

"To you being the best hairdresser there ever was," I say, and my other friends nod in agreement. As I bite into my cookie, I can't help but smile. It's delicious, and just what I needed to start my winter break on a good note.

"I can't focus on any crappies this week when I just feel like celebrating," Alyssa says around a mouthful of her cookie.

"Not even the fact that I saw on social media today that Austin is dating a supermodel?" Kelsey raises an eyebrow over the cookie. It looks even more ridiculous since the cookie is pretty much the size of her head.

All of us have been waiting years for Alyssa to admit that she's in love with her best guy friend, Austin Bradford—the star shortstop for the Louisville Mustangs. She swears they're only friends, but we're not convinced.

I don't have social media, so I have no clue what she's referring to, but the blush on Alyssa's cheeks tells me she knows exactly what Kels is talking about.

"Austin hasn't said anything about it, so I'm sure it's just the tabloids doing what they do best: gossiping." Alyssa tucks her hair behind her ears, only to untuck it moments later. "I wouldn't care if he *was* dating a model, though. He deserves to be happy." She gestures to Shayna, looking ready to end the conversation about Austin. "Your turn, Shay."

"I'll get my crappy out of the way first." Shayna takes out her knotted pearl headband and runs her fingers through her dark-brown hair before placing it back on her head. It's her signature look, something quintessentially Shayna. I honestly can't remember many days I've seen her without it.

Even though she's one of my best friends, Shayna is the complete opposite of me—the eternal optimist whose personality shines brighter than the sun.

"My parents told me they're going skiing in Colorado for Christmas. They're taking Reagan with them and offered to take me too, but this is a busy time of year at Shirley's Florist, and I can't leave her alone to deal with all the orders. So, it looks like I'll be here alone for Christmas this year."

"No, you won't. You'll come to my family's celebration. You know my mom wouldn't have it any other way," Alyssa says matter-of-factly.

That's one of the things I love the most about my friends: none of us ever has to be alone because we're each other's family.

Kelsey shrugs. "I'd offer for you to come spend it with me and Tyler's family, but it looks like you're covered."

I nod. "Same."

"Y'all are the best," Shayna coos, her ever-present smile brightening. "Okay, now for my happy. You know how I told y'all a few months ago that Shirley was going to retire soon and leave me her store?"

We all nod, intrigued.

"She set a retirement date. March sixth. That means your girl will officially be a flower shop owner in a little under three months!" She says the last words an octave higher, her shoulders lifted in excitement.

I reach over and squeeze her hand. "Congrats, Shay. That's amazing."

"You're going to be the most kick-butt flower shop in town." Kelsey pumps a fist in the air.

Alyssa gets up and pulls Shayna to her feet, right into a big hug. They rock back and forth until Kelsey and I join.

Once we retake our seats, Shayna grabs the remote and turns on the television. She opens our streaming cable network, and the handsome, smiling face of none other than Griffin Reynolds appears on the screen.

You know what else I hate aside from winter?

Actors.

Actually, one actor in particular. I suppose I shouldn't lump them all into the loathing category. I'm sure there are plenty of lovely people in Hollywood.

But Griffin Reynolds is *not* one of those people.

He's the worst kind of person who just up and ghosts a wonderful woman after they've had the best date of their lives.

The interviewer's smile is so exaggerated that it looks disingenuous. "Tonight, on the red carpet, we have a real treat, folks. Griffin Reynolds is here with his costar, Brittany Clearwater."

My friends all turn to me, and I'm sure my face is as pink as the fuchsia blanket on my lap.

Always the empathetic and sweet, positive friend, Shayna pauses the show. "Do you want me to change the channel?"

I shake my head. "No." My voice is barely a whisper. "I need to get over seeing his face everywhere. I can't avoid it forever."

"Griffin, tell us. How does it feel working with someone as talented and beautiful as Britt? I bet it makes those kissing scenes a little bit easier. Am I right?" The interviewer nudges his shoulder, and the enchiladas I had for dinner roll over in my stomach.

"Definitely." Griffin smiles brightly.

Kelsey throws a piece of popcorn at the screen. "Boo."

I laugh while Alyssa shakes her head. "I can't believe he's the new rom-com guy."

"Me neither."

Deep down, part of me was happy for Griffin when I saw that he finally caught his big break. But the fact that I found out from my friends accidentally turning on a rom-com with him as the leading man last week wasn't ideal.

It would've been nice to find out by, oh, I don't know, him telling me if he'd ever had the decency to call me after our date. But I guess he got too big for his britches once he became famous to think about little old me ever again.

After I learned his last name, it was all too easy to type his name into an internet search engine. I discovered that he starred in a lesser-known rom-com movie two years ago—likely the one he auditioned for when he ghosted me. What that film lacked in success, it must've made up for him in auditions to have landed this big role that started the rise of his career.

The interviewer nudges Griffin. "Come on, your relationship has been pretty hush-hush in the media. Can't you give us a little bit more than that?"

"Maybe for you, Silas." Griffin chuckles, but his laugh sounds unfamiliar to me. Not at all like his real, unrestrained laughter that I can still hear playing in my mind like a favorite song. He hooks his arm around Brittany's waist. "What do you want to know?"

"There's so much chemistry between you in the movie. Does that chemistry extend *beyond* the screen?" Silas raises his eyebrow, a wry smirk on his lips.

"What movie do you want to watch, Mal? I think you should pick tonight," Kelsey says above the sound of the television, like she's trying to save me from hearing his answer.

I can't answer Kelsey's question. Apparently, I'm a masochist now because I can't tear my eyes away from the screen, holding my breath as I wait to hear if Griffin is dating Brittany.

Griffin cocks his lips in a crooked grin. "I'm gonna plead the fifth here and say no comment."

"Oh." Silas pouts. "You tease us all."

"He's good at that, isn't he?" Brittany giggles and places her perfectly manicured talons on Griffin's chest.

The interviewer turns his attention to her. "Britt, will *you* give the world the answers they're craving?"

She taps her plump bottom lip. "I'm not one to kiss and tell."

I wrap my arms around my middle. I think I'm going to be sick. "Okay, I've seen enough." My voice is barely above a whisper, but Shayna immediately switches to another streaming platform.

"Maybe they're not really together." Her words are full of optimism, but her wary smile tells me Shay doesn't fully believe what she's saying.

"Yeah," Alyssa agrees. "Don't actors pretend to date as a publicity stunt?"

"I heard it's a thing." Kelsey tucks her leg under her, avoiding my gaze. Maybe I'd believe her if I hadn't known her for more than half my life.

"Y'all don't have to cheer me up. It's fine. I'm over Griffin." The lie doesn't even sound convincing to me. "I just don't want to see him all cozy with his new girlfriend."

"Let's watch one of your faves." Shayna turns on *Jurassic World*. I know action movies give her nightmares, so I must look as distressed as I feel for her to put it on.

Shay leans her head on my shoulder, threading her arm through mine. Alyssa squeezes my hand. Kelsey holds half of a hand-heart toward me, and I mimic the motion.

These are my girls—my family—and I know I can make it through anything with their support.

———— ♡ ♡ ♡ ————

I flip onto my back in bed with a huff. Falling asleep tonight has proven more difficult than quieting a rowdy classroom after seeing Griffin on my TV screen. The flood of feelings that I'd rather forget about came rushing back, making me lie here, stewing over what could have been if he had felt the same way I did. Instead, now I'm just haunted by the memory of him.

With a weary sigh, I grab my phone off my nightstand and pull up the interview I found from one of my internet searches. Rewatching this interview is the perfect reminder of why I'm better off without him. With a shaky thumb, I press play, and talk show host Kelly Parker's voice comes through my phone's speaker.

"It's wonderful to have you here, Griffin."

He sits across from her, looking suave in a maroon suit. Griffin smiles and waves to the studio audience before turning back to Kelly. "It's an honor to be here."

She crosses her legs and angles her body toward him. "Congratulations on your first movie, *A Chance Romance*. Can you tell the audience a little bit about it if they haven't had the opportunity to see it yet?"

"Absolutely. I play the character of Peter. He's a bit of a serial dater, and takes every first date to the same restaurant. When a new waitress starts waiting on his table during his dates, she has him questioning everything he ever thought he wanted in life and love."

"It's a great movie," Kelly coos.

I snicker. The movie was a flop. Its Rotten Tomatoes rating was abysmal, so it went straight to streaming after only a week at the box office. Since I'm not on social media, I didn't even hear about the movie until last week, and it's already been out for a year and a half.

"I must say, I think we've only just seen the start of a long career ahead for you," she continues.

Well, I guess she wasn't wrong about that, seeing that his latest movie, *Accidentally in Matrimony*, was a box-office hit.

"Thank you." He dips his chin in humble appreciation.

"As a newcomer to the romance movie industry, I have to ask the question that all the ladies are wondering: Do you have any special women in your life?"

He nods. "My mother and grandmother."

The audience lets out a chorus of awws, and I roll my eyes. Can't all the women in the audience see that he's *acting*?

Griffin shoots his over-the-top smile at the studio audience, though it's not the lopsided one I remember from our date. "They've raised me into the man I am today. I truly wouldn't be who I am without them, let alone sitting in this seat across from you."

"That's sweet." Kelly nods along, but she doesn't look appeased by his answer. "But what about romance?"

He shakes his head. "I've had a few girlfriends in my life, but I haven't found the woman I have that forever kind of spark with."

I wince. His words are a direct stab to the heart and validation that he didn't feel the same spark I felt.

Kelly motions to the excited women in the audience. "I don't think that will be an issue for you for long." She glances at the notecard in her hand before looking back at Griffin. "Your character in the movie takes the love interest on multiple romantic dates. Can you tell us about the best date you've ever been on?"

Griffin's smile falters slightly. It's almost imperceptible, but I still catch it before his pearly whites are flashed at the camera again. "There's no contest. It was a Knoxville Fireflies game."

Even though I've already watched this interview multiple times, my stomach still drops like I'm on a roller coaster, careening down from the top of a hill. It was stupid of me to ever believe that someone as handsome as Griffin would ever be interested in me. Our hot chocolate date might've been the best date of my life, but it probably didn't even make his top five. Or *twenty*. Our little café outing will never compare to a date to an MLB game. That's like comparing fast food to fine dining—there's no dispute which is better quality.

"So, you're a baseball man?" Kelly asks.

I swipe out of the video with a huff, not needing to hear anymore. That was all the validation I needed. A painful reminder that our date didn't mean as much to him as it did to me. That I could never be what he needed beside him in Hollywood. Maybe he knew that before I did.

His acting skills are obviously top-notch, because he sure fooled me. I thought he had felt that our meeting was fate intertwining our paths together. But really, it was just me and my inability to read through his charm and acting skills.

I place my phone back on my nightstand and burrow under my comforter. "All of my feelings for him were one-sided," I whisper. "I will not waste another minute of my time thinking about Griffin Reynolds."

I know it's a lie the moment the words fall from my mouth. But maybe if I continue to tell myself not to waste another moment thinking about someone who obviously never gave me a second thought, the truth will sink in one day.

——————— ◦ ♡ ◦ ———————

Folding my arms across my chest, I take another small step forward in line at my favorite coffee shop.

I started going to Rise & Grind Café when Kelsey worked here. Even though she left to pursue her dream of opening a dog rescue, I still think they make the best coffee around. Well, aside from the homemade lattes Kelsey occasionally makes us, but I try not to ask her too often.

I rub my temples as the tension starts to build. It's ten on a Saturday morning, so I knew they'd be slammed, but my caffeine headache is hitting hard and fast after how little sleep I got last night.

When I finally reach the register, my head is throbbing.

"Good morning, what can I get for you today?" the barista asks.

"I'll have a large sugar cookie latte to go, please."

Seasonal drinks are my kryptonite. Even though I hate winter because of he-who-must-not-be-named, the sugar cookie latte comes close to making up for it. Plus, I have winter break—a glorious three weeks off from teaching—which is just the little reset I need to come back and finish out the school year strong.

I pay and move to stand by the pickup counter until my drink is ready. I grab a coffee cup sleeve and slide it onto my to-go cup. As I walk toward the door, I hold the cup under my nose. Sweet, heavenly notes of brown sugar and almond fill my senses.

Before I can reach the door, a towering figure walks toward me. He doesn't even bother to look my way as he walks dangerously close with the brim of his beanie pulled down low.

"Watch where you're going," I warn, but it's too late. He crashes into me.

My latte hits his rock-hard chest and goes flying, spilling hot coffee onto us and all over the floor. I hiss as drops of the latte hit my hand, reminding me of the day a few years ago when I was similarly burned with a hot drink. A day that I'd really like to *forget*.

I try to move away from the man, but my foot hits a puddle of the latte and sends me flying backward. I reach up, trying to grab anything I can to avoid falling on my butt in front of this crowded coffee shop. One of my hands wraps around his neck, and the other grabs his beanie, yanking it off his head.

Thankfully, he wraps his arms around my waist, catching me before I go tumbling to the floor. The hair on the back of my neck rises as a familiar tingling sensation courses through my body.

No. It can't be him.

My heart races as I move my gaze to his face, but all words are stuck in my throat as my eyes collide with none other than Griffin Reynolds.

His mouth falls open as he stares at me. "*Mallory?*" He whispers my name with a mixture of disbelief and excitement.

I scramble to stand on my own two feet again. When he notices, Griffin effortlessly rights me. Unfortunately, he's close. *Too* close.

One of my hands is still wrapped around his neck while the other falls to his chest. It reminds me of the moment before our first kiss, with the snow falling around us. I can smell the cinnamon scent of his gum, taking me back to how our first kiss tasted from my snickerdoodle hot chocolate. My stomach churns, and I grit my teeth, pushing all thoughts of my past with him away.

I try to step away, but his arm holds me against him like an immovable tree trunk. "*Mallory.*" He repeats my name as if he's incapable of saying anything else. His eyes light up, crinkling at the corners as a grin I would've once described as *heart-stopping* graces his lips.

"Do you have a concussion?" My first words to him in three years spew out full of pent-up bitterness.

His brows furrow. "No."

"Then why do you keep repeating my name?"

Griffin doesn't answer my question. Instead, he moves a hand to my face, brushing the back of his knuckles along my cheek as he tucks a rogue curl behind my ear.

I grit my teeth against all the feelings that threaten to rise to the surface at his touch.

"It's really you."

I swat his hand away. "We already established that. I seriously think you need to see a doctor."

He shakes his head, and a little bit of the stupor leaves his blue eyes. I avert my gaze, not wanting to be drawn in like I was when I first met him.

That's when I notice the entire coffee shop staring at us unashamedly. Multiple people have their phones aimed our way, likely recording the entire interaction. Great. This is definitely *not* how I expected the start of my winter break to go.

Griffin finally lets go of his hold on my waist, and I release a shaky breath as he steps toward the pickup counter. He smiles at the blushing barista. "Can you please remake this beautiful lady's drink?" He tosses a hundred-dollar bill across the counter as if it's nothing to him. I suppose it isn't now.

The woman stands taller at the sight of the tip. "Right away, Mr. Reynolds."

Under different circumstances, I'd be opposed to him paying for my replacement drink, but I have a raging headache, so I'm not going to turn down the caffeine. Especially after he just ruined my drink…*again*.

I grab a few napkins and pat the sleeve of my coat, soaking up the little bit of liquid there. I throw them away and turn. My jaw drops in shock at the sight in front of me—Mr. Hollywood *mopping*. I mean, he has no qualms about making women have feelings for him on a date and then ghosting them, so why would he care about cleaning up the mess he caused? Where did he even get the mop? And is he *humming*?

The nerve of this man, acting as if he's happy to see me—*acting* being the keyword here.

"Here you go." The barista hands me a large sugar cookie latte, good as new.

"Thanks." I take it and turn to leave, nearly running into Griffin again.

He places his hands on my arms, steadying me. "Whoa, there."

I scoff. "I'm not a horse."

Griffin smirks. "I forgot how funny you are."

"Just your everyday comedian," I deadpan. "Now, if you'll excuse me, I need to go."

His smile falls. "I thought we could sit and catch up."

Sit and catch up? Is this guy for real?

"Give me one good reason why I should talk to you."

The light in his eyes dims as if I've hurt him. "I've been looking for you for years."

CHAPTER EIGHT

GRIFFIN

MALLORY IS HERE.

In the flesh.

Right in front of me.

She's a vision in pink plucked straight out of my dreams.

I couldn't hold back my smile if I tried. I found her. I *finally* found her after three years of searching.

"Obviously not very hard." She snorts.

I press my lips into a firm line. If I'd known all I needed to do was show up at this coffee shop on a Saturday morning, I would've been here the week after I met her and saved myself a lot of trouble.

"You could've just called me. You know there are these devices called *phones* now." Mallory is as sassy as I remember, except her words feel more biting than playful.

"If I hadn't dropped the napkin with your phone number on it into a puddle of muddy, snowy slush, I would have."

She rolls her eyes. "Likely story. I'm sure it's what you say to all the girls."

"All the—" I cut my sentence off, shaking my head. "Can we please sit for a minute? I'll explain everything. Then if you never want to see me again, I'll leave you alone."

Mallory eyes me up and down. Her gaze slowly drags along my frame like she's trying to decide if I'm worthy of being in her presence. Honestly, I'm not even worthy to walk on the ground she walks on. But I'm trying to be. And I'd be a fool if I let her go now that I have an opportunity to explain what happened three years ago.

"Please," I say before she can tell me no.

With a long, exaggerated sigh, Mallory says, "Fine. You have five minutes."

That's all I need. I gesture to a more secluded table in the back of the coffee shop, wanting to be as far away from prying eyes as possible. I already saw multiple people with their phones out. I send up a prayer that this interaction doesn't go viral. That's not the kind of publicity I need when I'm supposed to be maintaining the façade of dating my costar. But this is the life I signed up for when I chose to be an actor. Any of my public interactions are subject to scrutiny for the rest of my life.

I love my fans—it still feels wild to say I have fans. They call themselves *Griffies*.

But the woman who captured my heart called me Griff.

I'm pretty sure my Granny is the one who started the Griffies with the ode to the nickname she's called me my whole life. Even though I love them, it can be hard to feel like I'm living my life under a microscope. Especially in this moment where I want the world around us to fade away.

Mallory presses her lips into a thin line as she walks to the back of the shop. She takes her pink beanie off, revealing her wavy, light-brown hair that's just as gorgeous as it was three years ago. I want to wrap my fingers around each strand and memorize their feel.

When I finally drag my eyes away from her hair, I find her glaring at me, arms crossed and lips pursed. "You have four and a half minutes now, so you'd better make this quick."

I sigh. "I know you have every reason to hate me. Heck, I would hate it if I went on as amazing a date as we had and never heard from that person again." It's hard not to hate *myself* for losing out on this amazing woman for three years. "But I promise you, it wasn't intentional. After your friend and her brothers picked you up from the restaurant, I drove to my parents' house. I grabbed the napkin with your phone number from my cupholder, but when I got out of the car, it fell number-side down into a slushy pile of snow. I tried to save it, but the numbers were too smeared." It was truly a scene from a rom-com, except I didn't end up with the girl.

Mallory doesn't say anything, but her expression softens the slightest bit.

"When you didn't hear from me, did you ever consider looking me up?" I ask.

Mallory crosses her arms. "I forgot that you existed."

I press a hand to my chest, prone to dramatic flair. But I'd be lying if I said her words didn't hurt. "Ouch, am I that forgettable?"

"Yes." But the way her eyes move down to my lips before slowly dragging back to my eyes says *no*. She takes a sip of her replacement drink before crossing her arms again.

"I tried to find you after my audition. But when all the information I had was your first name, your hometown, and the school you went to, it wasn't much to go off of."

She nods slowly. "You actually didn't even have my first name."

I raise an eyebrow. "You gave me a fake name?"

"Not exactly. Mallory is my middle name. It's what I've gone by since I was a kid."

It's better than her giving me a fake name, but it explains why my team was unable to find her.

"What's your first name?"

"Wouldn't you like to know."

"Yes, that's why I asked." I grin.

She rolls her eyes. "Fine, it's Veronica. Veronica Mallory Porter."

"Veronica…" I say the name slowly. "Doesn't quite roll off the tongue like Mallory."

"Yeah, I've never really felt like a Veronica. Even my parents have always called me Mallory."

"That explains why I couldn't find you. Well, that and I had no chance of finding you on social media without your last name."

"Oh, you never would've found me on social media." She takes a sip of her drink.

I blink. "Why's that?"

"I don't have it."

"Really?" I laugh.

She shrugs. "I always wanted to be a teacher, but I didn't want my students to find embarrassing pictures of me online, so I never created a social media account."

"You know that makes you really hard to find, right?"

Her eyes narrow. "That's kind of the point."

This conversation is not going how I'd envisioned. In my mind, I always thought that if I ever saw Mallory again, it would be this grand moment when we would see each other across the way and run to each other. She would jump into my arms, and we would ride off into the sunset together, kissing until we couldn't breathe.

"Why are you even here?" She sounds annoyed, bursting my dream bubble of our reunion.

"I wanted coffee."

Mallory sighs. "No. I mean, why are you *here*? In Louisville?"

"My granny had hip-replacement surgery. She's in a rehab facility now while she recovers."

She frowns. "She couldn't have gotten the surgery in your small town?"

"Not unless the town nurse suddenly became a surgeon overnight." I laugh. "One of her friends had the same procedure from a doctor in Louisville, so she felt comfortable getting it here."

"That still doesn't explain why *you're* here." She glances around the café, anywhere but at me.

I look at Mallory until she finally meets my gaze, and I'm taken aback when I see a hint of emotion in her eyes. It's obvious she's trying to hide it, but I can see there's something she's grappling with, even if she's trying to make herself look composed.

I know the feeling. I've been trying to rein in my emotions from the moment I caught her in my arms and realized who she was. If this were a movie, I would've lifted her off the ground and spun her around, shouting her name like a victory cry, knowing I'd finally found her. Then the cameras would cut to slow motion as our lips met.

Instead, I've got a cold front on my hands, and I don't mean the one outside.

"I wanted to make sure Granny had the best care. My parents are still working, and I'm on a break between movies, so it made sense for me to be the one to come."

Mallory's eyes seem to soften slightly at that. I hope she's seeing the same man from the café all those years ago under the new Hollywood shine. I may have a slightly better haircut and whiter teeth, but I'm still me.

Plus, part of me was holding onto hope that I would run into Mallory, that I'd find her again. It seemed unattainable, a fantasy. But here she is, sitting across from me in a coffee shop just like three years ago.

Although it's nothing like my fantasy.

Mallory doesn't say anything, so I continue. "Are you seeing anyone?"

"No." She lets out a dry laugh. "I don't think love is for me."

"Love is for everyone."

"Debatable." She tilts her head. "Although it appears you've found it." I furrow my brows. "Shouldn't you be in LA with your costar girlfriend?" She spits out the words like they're venom.

I look around, trying to make sure no one is listening in on our conversation. "I can't talk about Brittany here, but I'll tell you everything in a private setting, if you're willing to hear me out."

"I don't need to hear any more lies from you." Mallory glances at her phone. "Lucky you, I graced you with six minutes instead of five." She pulls her beanie back on and grabs her drink, raising it toward me. "Have a nice life, Griffin."

I open my mouth to say...anything. But I don't know what to say to the woman I've been waiting three years to find again, who seems glad to have lost me. My hand itches to reach out and stop her as she breezes past me. But I don't even get out so much as a goodbye before she's out the front door of the coffee shop and my life.

Yeah, this chance encounter is nothing like the movies. Because if it were, we'd be walking out of this shop hand in hand.

And I'd never let her go again.

———— ♡ ♡ ♡ ————

"I don't need you to fuss over me." Granny swats my hand away. "It was just a hip replacement. I can hold a fork."

I place the utensil on her napkin. "Sorry, go ahead."

"Your kind, caring heart is my favorite quality about you." She leans forward and pinches my cheeks. "That's why you'll always be my Griffie boy."

I take it like a champ, even though it hurts like the dickens. For such a small woman, her fingers sure have a mighty grip.

"Are you ready to fess up to naming my fandom the Griffies?" I ask as she takes a bite of salad.

She offers me a closed-lip smile, her eyes crinkling at the corners. Once she's finished chewing, Granny shakes her head. "Never."

I walk into the small kitchen in her room at the rehab facility, making two plates of tri-tip steaks and baked potatoes with all the fixings. I carry them to the table, placing one in front of her and the other in front of my chair.

"You're spoiling me." She looks from the steak to me with wide eyes.

I take the seat across from her. "You deserve to be spoiled."

"What would I do without you?" Granny pushes her salad aside and cuts into her steak. After she eats a bite, she dives right back in for more. "You outdid yourself."

"Steak is one of the few things I know how to cook."

"You won't hear me complaining."

I dig into my plate. This cut of meat is my favorite, and something I treat myself to often. Life is too short not to eat your favorite foods.

I'm diving into my baked potato when Granny clears her throat. "You know that I love having you here, but I feel like I'm keeping you from your life in LA."

She would scold me if she knew that I have an offer on the table for another rom-com right now that I planned to pass on to stay here while she recovers. An opportunity I'm for sure going to pass on now that I know Mallory is here, too.

Granny already put up a fight about me paying for her surgery and her stay in the rehab facility. If she knew how much I was paying for my rental house, she'd probably insist on paying me back. Money means nothing in comparison to her health. I don't want her to feel like I'm missing out on something from being here, even though I am.

Family is my priority. They always have been.

"I'm in between projects right now," I fib. "You know I always travel back and forth as my schedule allows."

"This center gives me everything I need and more." Granny tuts. "I'll be here for at least a few months. I don't want to be a bother."

I reach across the table and set my hand gently on hers. "You're never a bother or a burden." I want to sell the fact that I want to be here. An idea pops into my mind, and my mouth is already moving before I can even think about what I'm saying. "I'm here for another reason, too."

This lie has Granny raising her eyebrows. "Do I have to pry it out of you?"

"I wanted to visit my girlfriend."

"Your costar lives here?"

"No, that's a publicity stunt." I rub a hand along my chin. "It's Mallory."

Granny's eyes light up. "The Mallory who sang carols for us at your parents' house? The Mallory you haven't stopped talking about for three years? *That* Mallory?"

I nod.

"How long have you been together?" She pouts. "How could you hide this from me?"

"It's pretty new." I press my lips together, knowing this is a terrible idea, but there's no stopping it now. "I finally found her. I always told you that when I found her again, I wouldn't be dumb enough to let her go. I'd love to stay for a while if you're up for it, so I can also date Mallory." I smile, trying to look more confident than I feel.

What if Granny wants to meet Mallory again or invite her over for dinner? She's totally going to want to invite her over for dinner. What was I thinking? This is a terrible idea. Mallory wants nothing to do with me. I need to tell Granny the truth.

"I—" I start, but she cuts me off.

"I'm not one to stop young love."

Well, I'm in this now. For better or for worse.

"I'm not exactly young anymore, Granny." I rub the back of my neck.

"You're young as a spring chicken to me."

I laugh. She's always used the funniest expressions and sayings.

"But if you don't want me to call it *young* love, then I'm not one to stop *true* love."

I swallow. "Love is a big word."

"I know, but I thought you were smart enough for it to be in your vocabulary."

"Hilarious." I cover my mouth with a napkin to hide my smile.

"Don't you hide that million-watt smile from me, Griffie," she scolds.

I drop my napkin, feeling like a reprimanded child again. "Sorry, Granny."

"Now, tell me all about how you reconnected with Mallory."

I take a giant bite of my steak, hoping to buy myself some time to come up with a semblance of a story to tell her. Just as I finish chewing, my phone vibrates on the wooden table. I flip it over and see a picture of my agent. Karina knows I'm here visiting with Granny, so if she's calling, it must be important.

"Sorry, I should get this." I swipe my thumb across the screen to answer the call. "How's it going, Karina?"

She clucks her tongue. "You never stop making work for me, do you?"

"It's why I'm your favorite client," I answer, trying to sound lighthearted when I know this conversation is about to be anything but.

"No, it's why you pay me the big bucks."

"True." I laugh before sobering, remembering she has a reason for calling. "What's up?"

"Have you checked your phone recently?"

"No." My mouth tugs into a frown. "Am I missing something?"

"Oh, only about one hundred pictures, videos, and articles about you and a mystery woman."

I rub a hand over my face. "I was worried about that when I saw a bunch of phones pointed at us."

"What were you thinking, Griffin?" I can practically see her pacing in her office, shaking her head. Because she's the kind of person who works in the office, even on a Sunday. "No. You *weren't* thinking," she continues. "That's the problem. How am I supposed to spin this for your benefit? We need your romantic comedy to do well, if you want to keep the new rom-com movie offer on the table. And especially if you still want me to try to get you an audition for that fantasy script you loved, *The Heartless Prince.*" Her tone rises an octave. "How is your rom-com going to do well, you ask?" Karina sighs. "By being seen everywhere with Britt. Not some mystery woman."

My heart constricts at the thought of losing my dream role. I rub the back of my neck, thankful she can't see me as I deflect. "I don't think I've ever heard you talk for so long. You're usually so busy."

"My role as your agent is to save your career. That's what I'm doing."

"That's why you're the best, Karina."

"Who is she, Griffin?" She sounds tired. I bet she's squeezing the stress ball I bought her after our first meeting. It has my face on it, so hopefully it's somewhat cathartic for her to squeeze the crap out of my head while working overtime. "What happened in that coffee shop?"

"That's the question that's been running through my head since yesterday."

"You don't even know who she is?"

"Oh, no. I know who she is. I just have no idea where we stand."

She sighs. "What's her name?"

"Veronica Mallory Porter. She goes by Mallory, though."

This bit of information seems to shock Karina into silence. After I landed my first movie and hired Karina as my agent, I told her all about Mallory. She could tell how upset I was that she even had her team try to look for her, but

Mallory was like a ghost in a cemetery: she haunted me, but I could never find her.

A few beats later, Karina exhales loudly. "No kidding. After all these years of looking, you found her in a coffee shop?"

"Right where it all began. Well, not the actual coffee shop, but you get the picture."

Karina groans. "I'm going to take a wild guess that you're not going to change your mind about the latest rom-com? The offer's already on the table, and it's a good role."

But it's not the role I've dreamed of. There will always be another movie. There's only *one* Mallory.

"I'm not changing my mind," I say, resolute. "I'm going to stay in Louisville, but I'm still interested in an audition for *The Heartless Prince*."

"I'll try to work my magic, but this situation just got a whole lot stickier. I think we need to include her in the conversation."

My heart drops into my stomach. I've been thinking about how much work this will be for my agent, but I failed to consider how much this will impact Mallory. The girl who doesn't have social media because she didn't want her students to ever find anything online about her that could be embarrassing.

This is worse. *So* much worse. Like her life is being put on a billboard with spotlights shining on it for the entire city—the entire *world*—to see.

"Can you contact her and set up a call for the three of us tomorrow?" Karina asks. "That way, I don't have to go over everything twice."

I'll have to track down Mallory's phone number, but that shouldn't be hard considering I know her full name now. "Aye aye, captain."

"And try to stay in your rental until this blows over."

"Affirmative."

"You can't see it, but I'm rolling my eyes."

"You'd better go catch them."

Karina lets out a long breath. "You don't pay me enough for this."

"I'll have Granny make you her famous buttermilk pie once she's back on her feet and overnight it to you."

"Now you're talking." Her voice sounds softer, more concerned, as she says, "I know you're still getting used to the spotlight, Griffin. But just remember that the paparazzi won't stop until they get what they want. So be careful, and call that girl before this blows up even more."

With that, the line clicks. Karina never signs off phone calls. Usually, I don't mind it. But this time, it feels ominous, like the current predicament I'm in.

Looks like I need to find Mallory...

Again.

CHAPTER NINE
MALLORY

"I don't know about y'all, but I'm ready for some bonuts."

The biscuit shop that the four of us girls go to every Sunday morning, when we're free, makes the best biscuit donut holes. They're covered in cinnamon sugar and come with a delicious berry compote for dipping. We only order them for breakups, breakdowns, or on my breaks from school.

Now that winter break is here, I can't wait to dive into an order of them with my besties.

"Me too." Shayna smiles with her entire face, even though it's way too early in the morning to be that energetic without caffeine. "Let's go."

I slide into my Ugg dupes and open our front door. Immediately, I'm bombarded by a barrage of camera flashes and loud questions shouted in my direction.

"Veronica! Veronica, look over here!"

"Can you confirm the rumors that you're dating Griffin Reynolds?"

"Veronica, what's your statement regarding those claiming that you broke up Griffin and Brittany?"

I stand there stunned, unable to move or process what the heck is happening. Not only do the paparazzi know my name, but they found my address and are linking me with *Griffin*. I might've considered this lifestyle, living in the spotlight, after my first date with him. But that ship sailed long ago, yet I'm still being thrown overboard and dragged beneath the water's surface, drowning in a sea of questions I want nothing to do with.

Kelsey steps around me and pushes me back inside before shutting the door and locking it. She presses her full weight against the door, as if her body acts as an extra barricade. "What was that about?"

"Why are they calling you Veronica?" Shayna shakes her head. "I mean, obviously I know that's your legal first name, but how do the *paparazzi* know that?"

"Why are they here?" Alyssa purses her lips. "We know you went on that hot chocolate date with Griffin, but that was years ago. Why are they suddenly interested in that now?"

I'm still internally freaking out that there is a whole swarm of paparazzi in front of our house, but my friends' questions break me out of my stupor. "We should sit down. I have something to share." My heart races as I shut the curtains over our front windows and double-check that the front door is locked, even though I watched Kelsey do it.

My besties move to the living room, assuming their usual spots. It's uncommonly silent as they wait for me to talk.

"I wanted to tell y'all right away, but I needed time to process everything." I take a deep breath, then blurt out, "I ran into Griffin yesterday."

Shayna gasps. "Where?"

"Rise & Grind Café. And when I say 'ran into Griffin,' I mean that he *literally* ran into me."

"Oh, no." Kelsey grimaces. "Please tell me he didn't spill another hot drink on you."

I nod. "He sure did."

She narrows her eyes. "We ride at dawn."

"As much as I like to think the worst of him, it wasn't intentional. Plus, he bought me a replacement drink." I shake my head, still trying to wrap my mind around my interaction with him yesterday. "But what are the odds it would happen twice?"

"Little to none." Kelsey crosses her arms.

"Unless it's fate." Shayna tilts her head, always the optimist. A more naïve version of me thought the same thing before, but I know better now.

"Okay, so you ran into him yesterday." Shayna runs her hands along her floral-print joggers. "But that doesn't explain why the paparazzi are outside our house."

Alyssa stares wide-eyed at her phone. "I think I know why." She passes it to me, and I feel like I'm going to be sick. On the screen is a picture of me wrapped in Griffin's arms at the coffee shop.

No wonder people think we're dating. I'm not just wrapped in Griffin's arms in the photo...he's dipping me. It looks romantic and intimate, even though I know he was only catching me from falling on my butt. But from the angle the picture was taken, you can't see my anger. All that's visible is the lovestruck look on Griffin's face.

If I didn't know any better, I would say the two people in the photo were a couple in love.

But, obviously, I do know better.

There's no love between us. Griffin can say all he wants about how he searched for me. If Griffin wanted to find me that badly, he would have. Besides, his answers in the interview he did with Kelly Parker are just further evidence that our date didn't mean as much to him as it meant to me. So, no, this photo might tell one story, but I know the truth.

"This isn't at all how I remember it." I groan, passing the phone to Shayna. "How do they know my name? How did they find me?"

She looks at it with Kelsey, and they all send me pitying looks.

"It looks like they didn't know your name yesterday. They called you the mystery woman." Alyssa takes her phone back and continues scrolling. "But it sounds like more footage was sent to tabloids today. You must've said your name in it."

I think back to yesterday and grimace when I remember telling Griffin my full name during our conversation…while all the phones were around us. Shoot. It looks like I'm the one to blame for the paparazzi finding me.

No. Griffin is to blame for all of this. I wanted to leave right after I got my replacement drink, but he just *had* to convince me to stay and talk for a few minutes. Now look at what's happened.

Alyssa gasps. "No, she did *not*."

I groan, letting my face fall into my hands. "Do I even want to know?"

Kelsey grabs the phone from her, and her jaw drops. "She did *not* call our Mallory a homewrecker!"

"Do you think Griffin's dating his costar?" I wouldn't have even given him a five-minute conversation if he had a girlfriend.

"Some of the people in these comments seem to think so." Alyssa shoots me a sympathetic look.

My brows furrow as I try to get a grasp on what's happening right now. Yesterday, I was just an elementary school teacher who was excited for winter break to begin, but today, apparently, I'm Hollywood's newest homewrecker.

Why would Griffin ask me if I was seeing anyone if he's dating his costar? Why did I get pulled into all this? I spent three years trying to forget he existed, only for him to jump back in and upend my life again.

Kelsey stands and walks to our front windows, peeking out from around the curtains. "They're still there. This is ridiculous. I'm calling Tyler." She pulls out her phone.

Someone knocks on our back door.

We all gasp.

"Do you think it's the paparazzi?" Shayna whispers.

"They're not allowed onto private property, right?" Alyssa worries her bottom lip.

We all lock arms and take hesitant steps together into our kitchen, peering at the back door. I sigh in relief when I see Kelsey's boyfriend, Tyler Reed, standing there.

Kelsey steps forward and unlocks the door. Tyler opens it and pulls Kelsey in for a kiss. It's brief, but the look he shoots her afterward is filled with so much passion that I look away, feeling like I'm intruding on a private moment.

When he sees the rest of us staring at them, Tyler waves good-naturedly. "Good morning, ladies. I just got home from the store and came right over when I saw the zoo outside."

"You've got that right." Kelsey sighs and brings him up to speed.

Tyler looks at me. "Do I need to go kick some paparazzi butt for you?"

"Does this mean we're *friends* now, Reed?"

"I don't know." He crosses his arms. "I distinctly remember you telling me you didn't like me. But I suppose a truce could be in order."

Joke's on him, because I've liked him ever since he worked so hard to prove to Kelsey that romantic love can exist for her and that he was never going to let her go. But I'm not about to tell him that. "If you get rid of those paparazzi so I can get my bonuts, you'll be on my friends list forever. Unless you break Kelsey's heart."

"I would never," Tyler says in mock offense. He extends his fist toward me. "You have yourself a deal."

I knock mine against it. He walks through our house and out the front door.

We all peek through the curtains and watch as Tyler approaches the paparazzi. He stands to his full height; his broad shoulders and stature look intimidating even from behind. I don't know what he says to them, but within minutes, they're moving off our sidewalk, getting back in their cars, and driving off.

By the time I'm eating bonuts with my besties, I can't even enjoy them. There's not a paparazzo in sight, but I don't feel at peace. I can't with the niggling sensation that this is only the beginning.

———— ♡ ♥ ♡ ————

I've done everything I can to keep my mind off the articles since I read them. Yesterday, I caught up on all my laundry and cleaned the bathroom I share with Shayna. Now, I'm deep cleaning our kitchen.

"What are you doing?" Kelsey sounds cautious, like I'm a dog that will spook if she takes one wrong step.

I don't look up from my kneeling position on the tile floor. "I'm cleaning the grout. Do you know the last time we cleaned it?" I laugh hollowly. "Probably never." I dip the toothbrush into the soapy water and get back to scrubbing.

"Did you know your phone is blowing up?"

I still don't glance up, trying to focus on the task at hand. "It's probably just more news outlets calling me for a statement." I got multiple calls yesterday asking for a comment, so I assume today is more of the same.

Kelsey blows out a long breath. "They must really want to get in touch with you. It looks like you have a ton of notifications."

I haven't been on my phone all morning, trying to avoid reality and live in ignorant bliss, so maybe I should check it. Who knows, there could be a family emergency.

I push up from the ground and wash my hands before grabbing my phone off the kitchen table. There are a few missed calls and voicemails from different numbers that I ignore, but one of the unknown numbers also sent me eleven text messages. I open the thread and roll my eyes when I read the first texts.

UNKNOWN NUMBER

> Hi, you have every right to be mad at me for finding your number now that I know your full name. I'm sorry, but please hear me out.

> This is Griffin, by the way.

"Ugh, it's Griffin." I roll my eyes.

"What does *he* want?"

I look back at my phone and keep reading.

UNKNOWN NUMBER

I'm not sure if you've seen all the articles, but it seems we've suddenly become the subject of every news outlet's attention.

If you haven't, I'm sorry I'm the one break-ing the news.

If you have, then you know this narrative is already getting out of control.

I have a proposition for you that I think will be mutually beneficial for us.

Okay, that kinda sounds dirty.

I promise it's not dirty.

Anyway, my agent wants to speak with us together, so if you're able to come over today, I can send a car for you.

And by IF, I mean that my agent NEEDS to talk to both of us since this now concerns you, too. So, please agree to this, and we can get everything sorted out together.

Sorry for all the texts. I'll stop now.

I stare at my phone, a storm of anger brewing inside me. I'm infuriated that this even happened. That Griffin just waltzed back into my life like it was nothing. But in reality, he's the Mento dropped in my Coke bottle, making a giant explosion and a mess that I'm left to clean up when he inevitably ghosts me again. Because he will.

The problem now is that I'm also filled with dread. He's right. I could handle him walking in and out of my life the first time—okay, I could at least wallow in peace—but I'm out of my wheelhouse this time.

I have no clue what I'm supposed to do when my face is plastered on every tabloid. When lies are being spread about me to my face and behind my back, and comment sections are filled with unspeakable things that my friends won't even let me read.

I'm mature enough to admit that I need guidance from his agent. And, like it or not, maybe I even need help from Griffin.

I shudder at the thought.

But I'm also petty enough to save his name in my phone contacts as Mr. Too Late. Shoutout to my girl Taylor for such an iconic song bridge from "Mr. Perfectly Fine (Taylor's Version)." She's the real MVP.

"Well?" Kelsey nudges my elbow.

"His agent wants to talk to both of us together about everything going on."

Her demeanor softens. "That doesn't sound too bad." She eyes me warily as I take a deep breath. "So, why do you still look like you just sucked on a lemon?"

"Because that means I have to spend more time with *him*."

"Just until this all gets sorted. Then you can say sayonara."

I nod. "You're right. Better to get this over with now."

Ugh, I can't even imagine how much more awful this would be if I weren't on winter break. All my students would be grilling me as if I were a hot dog and it was the

Fourth of July. Look at me looking at the bright side of things; Shayna would be proud.

I take a deep breath, steeling myself as I type out a response.

ME

> I'll come, but only because I want this all to be over with. You don't need to send a car. I can drive myself if you send me your address.

Seconds after my message says it's been delivered, the three little dots of doom appear, letting me know he's typing.

MR. TOO LATE

> Thank you! I'd rather send a car for you. It has tinted windows and someone I trust to keep you safe in case any paparazzi try to find you.

ME

> They already found me.

MR. TOO LATE

> I'm sorry. I can send a bodyguard as well.

ME

> My friend's boyfriend already scared them off, but I guess you sending a car wouldn't hurt.

I hate admitting that Griffin's right, but I don't know what I'd do if paparazzi followed my car around. I send him my address, and he responds immediately.

MR. TOO LATE

> My driver will be there in ten minutes. His name is Ted.

I thumbs-up his message, not wanting to prolong any interactions with him any more than necessary.

Glancing down at my matching sweat set, I consider changing before adamantly telling myself *no*. There's no need to impress Hot Cocoa Man. He doesn't deserve my time, let alone my cute outfits.

I cuddle with Kelsey's dog, Winston, on the couch until I hear a car pull up outside. Kelsey hugs me after I slide my feet into my Ugg dupes for the second time today.

"You've got this, Mal," she says with such confidence that I almost believe her.

With one last deep breath, I step away from their embrace and out our front door.

"Don't let him charm you with empty words. You are Veronica Mallory Porter, and you don't need a man," Kelsey yells after me.

I laugh, shaking my head as I approach the waiting car.

The driver gets out and extends his hand. "I'm Ted. You must be Mallory."

After a quick handshake, I say, "That's me."

Ted opens the rear passenger door for me, and I offer him as much of a smile as I can muster. Before I know it, we're off, and my stomach is in knots.

I repeat my friend's words like a mantra.

I am Veronica Mallory Porter, and I don't need a man.

Griffin's flattery may have sucked me in before, but I know better now. I won't let him charm me this time, only to throw me out like last year's jeans.

I am a crisp new pair of denim.

I am valuable.

I am Veronica Mallory Porter, and I don't need a man.

CHAPTER TEN
GRIFFIN

I HAVE AN HOUR with Mallory. One hour until I need to be at Granny's first follow-up appointment. One hour to change Mallory's mind about me.

Yesterday was an epic fail. I hope she'll give me another chance if I keep showing up and being myself, but I know that I need to rebuild trust with her.

I've been staring out the front window for five minutes, waiting for Mallory to arrive. I don't want to miss a single second with her. The falling snow takes me back to our hot chocolate date and our first kiss. I can almost feel the sensation of her lips on mine mixed with the feeling of snowflakes landing in my hair.

When a familiar black car with tinted windows finally pulls into the driveway, I rush out the front door.

Ted is getting out of the car, but I wave him off, mouthing, "I've got this." He wears a knowing smile as he gets back into the driver's seat.

I open the rear passenger door. Mallory looks stunning in her pink sweats. Her wavy hair is pulled up in a messy bun today with a few strands down framing her face. I smile as I extend a hand to her.

She doesn't accept my offered hand, rising out of the car and stepping past me, all while looking entirely indifferent. I wish she'd show me…something. I'd even take anger over this. Any type of emotion seems better than indifference.

"What did one snowflake say to the other?" I try to lighten the mood as we walk inside.

She sighs. "I don't know."

"Let's stick together."

Mallory's expression remains neutral as I let her into the house. "You need to up your joke game."

I run a hand through my hair and lead her through the foyer into the living room. "Do you have a better one?"

She sits on the edge of the couch cushion, looking like she's ready to dart out of here at any moment. "Now isn't the time for jokes."

I sober. "You're right. I'm sorry."

Her expression is pinched as she looks around the space. "I thought you'd rent a giant mansion." Her words hold a bite, finally giving me some type of emotion. This isn't the Mallory I met before, though I suppose I shouldn't be surprised since I'm the reason she's in this predicament.

"It's been the perfect rental for me to stay in while Granny recovers."

Now doesn't seem like the right time to tell her that I don't own *any* houses. I do have an apartment in Los Angeles, but I've waited to buy a house because I'm holding out to buy my first one with my dream girl.

Except, it's becoming more obvious by the minute that she wants absolutely nothing to do with me.

"Can we get to the *real* reason I'm here?"

"Yeah, sure." I grab my laptop from the coffee table and open the video call app. Only I am visible on the screen, so I wave Mallory closer. "I promise I don't bite."

She rolls her eyes and sighs like sitting beside me is pure torture, but she concedes, scooting closer until she's in the video frame.

"You ready?"

"As I'll ever be," she mutters.

I pull up Karina's name and press the video chat button. The familiar call tone rings for a moment before my agent's face appears on the screen. Dark circles are present under her eyes, and her brown hair, which is usually curled, hangs flat and limp around her face. I feel responsible for making her work overtime to figure out how to resolve this issue I've caused.

"Hi, Griffin. And you must be Mallory. I'm Griffin's agent, Karina." Her smile looks tired and makes me feel even more guilty.

"It's nice to meet you." Mallory offers her a smile in return.

I wish it were aimed at me.

"Let's dive right in, shall we?" Karina adjusts a stack of paperwork on her desk. "Photos of you two are all over the tabloids, and a video was posted by CelebritiesNow this morning. Have the paparazzi found where you live?"

I shake my head. Mallory nods. I hate that she had to deal with the paparazzi on her own, but she won't have to moving forward if I have any say about it.

"I had someone take care of it, but they found me early Sunday morning," Mallory says.

"You didn't give them a statement or any comments?" Karina asks.

"No, I knew better than to respond to their ridiculous questions."

Karina's shoulders fall slightly, making her look a tad less stressed. "Good, that saves some work. If the paparazzi approach you, just continue to ignore them. I can have security set up around both of your houses if you'd like."

"How much would that cost?" Mallory asks. "I'm on a teacher's salary, but I might be able to—"

"I'd like security at both our houses," I insert. "I'll pay whatever it takes."

Karina nods. "Send me Mallory's address, and I'll have teams out to both locations by the end of the day."

Based on the tense set in Mallory's jaw, she looks like she wants to argue, but she doesn't say anything.

I place my hand on her knee, trying to reassure her. She scoots her leg away, making my hand fall off.

I don't get it. I explained how I lost her number and have been looking for her ever since. No word fully encompasses how happy I felt when I ran into her in that coffee shop, and it stings that she doesn't seem to feel the same way about seeing me again.

Karina clears her throat. "Now that that's settled, we have the business side of things to attend to. Please, hear me out." She pauses. It might seem like it's for dramatic effect, but I know her well enough to know that she doesn't have time for things as frivolous as *dramatic effect*. My agent only speaks slowly when choosing her next words wisely. "I think we should roll with this narrative."

My eyebrows shoot up my forehead. Is she saying what I think she's saying? Does she want me to date Mallory? I approve tenfold. Where do I sign on the dotted line?

Mallory frowns. "What do you mean *roll with this narrative?*"

"We'll put a positive spin on this," Karina explains. "Everyone thinks you're already dating, so if we share the story of two people brought together by fate not once, but twice..." Her eyes light up. "Your story sells itself. No one will be talking about Griffin and Brittany anymore; the whole world will talk about you two. There's no way you won't get the audition for *The Heartless Prince* when your own story is one of fated soulmates."

"I think we're getting ahead of ourselves here." Mallory gestures with her thumb between us. "Griffin and I aren't *dating*."

The way Mallory says the word makes it sound like dating me is equivalent to getting a tooth pulled without Novocain. As for me, the idea of dating her is a dream come true. An answered prayer. What I've been waiting for since the moment I met her.

Karina's gaze bounces between us. "I thought you both felt the same way?" Mallory shrugs, and my agent's gaze narrows in on me through the screen. "You're telling me that you couldn't land the girl that you've been sear—"

"Mallory's made it very apparent she's not interested in dating me," I interrupt, not wanting the beautiful woman next to me to hear about the Mallory-shaped hole she left in my heart.

Karina taps her dark-red lips. "I still think we need to roll with this narrative if you don't want to end up looking like Hollywood's newest bad boy."

"But she doesn't want anything to do with me." Each time I say these words, it's like another stab to an already gaping wound. My hope is slowly bleeding out, my optimism waning with each reminder of rejection.

My agent stares us down, looking like a parent explaining something for the umpteenth time. "We can still say you two are an item and share your story, without you having to date."

"You mean you want us to *fake* it?" Mallory scoffs.

Karina nods. "I mean, Griffin and Britt weren't even faking it."

Mallory shoots me a look like she caught me lying red-handed.

I hold up my hands. "We *were* faking it."

"No," Karina corrects. "You both just never shot down the narrative. But if we share the story of how you and Mallory first met and how you found your way back to each other..." She taps a pen on her desk. "People will eat that up."

Mallory shifts on the couch cushion and looks out the window. I'm surprised she doesn't immediately reject the idea, laugh in my face at the ridiculousness of it.

She finally turns to me. "If I did this—" A smile immediately pulls at my lips, and she holds her pointer finger up. "*If*," Mallory repeats, with emphasis. "What would be in it for me?"

"That's a fair question." Karina leans back in her chair. "I'm speaking to both of you about this for the first time, so I'm not sure if Griffin's had a chance to consider—"

"Whatever she wants." I clear my throat and face Mallory. "Whatever *you* want."

"I don't think there's a dollar sign big enough for you to convince me to date you." She waves a hand in front of her face. "*Fake* date you."

I pull my phone out and text my agent how much I'd be willing to pay Mallory to do this. I know how inconvenient it would be for her to get pulled into the spotlight, especially since she wants nothing to do with me. It would make a dent in the savings I've built up from my two movie earnings, but money is just something we need to pay the bills. Spending time with Mallory? That's priceless.

Karina's eyes go wide as she glances at her phone. I can see the question in her gaze as she looks back at the camera, and I give the barest of nods.

"How about this?" My agent reads the amount I texted her.

Now, Mallory's eyes are the ones bugging out. She whips her head to look at me, the enticing tropical scent in her hair wafting my way. "It would take me over five years to make that with my teaching salary."

"I think it's only fair. I understand it's a big ask, so I want to make it worth your while."

She raises an eyebrow. "You're serious."

"I've learned that Griffin doesn't say anything he doesn't mean," Karina adds.

"I'd beg to differ," Mallory mutters under her breath.

I suppose I can't blame her. I'd be hurt if I were in her shoes. It just gives me even more reason to remind her who I am. And who we could be—*together*.

"Shall I draw up a contract?" Karina asks.

I wait for Mallory to answer. If we're going to do this, it needs to be on her terms. Her decision. I'll deal with whatever happens to my career. But I wouldn't be able to live with myself if I made Mallory uncomfortable or did something that hurt her. Again.

With a sigh, Mallory shrugs. "I'll do it as long as there are clear boundaries in place."

I nod. "Like I said, whatever you want. Whatever you need to be happy and feel comfortable."

She scoffs. "How about a time machine for this to never have happened?"

"Unfortunately, I just sold my last DeLorean," I tease, and she rolls her eyes.

"Seriously, if we're going to do this, I need rules."

"That's a good starting point." Karina types away on her keyboard. "Okay, let's discuss how often you'll post on social media to make this look believable."

"That's going to be a problem," Mallory cuts in. "I don't have any social media."

"You don't have..." Karina trails off, shaking her head. "You'll need to make an account. Congratulations, your first post can be a collaborative one with Griffin announcing your relationship."

Mallory pales.

"To make this look real," Karina goes on, "you need to post a picture together on your pages at least once a week. Twice a week, preferably. You can alternate who posts or figure that out amongst yourselves."

"If it's fake, how are we supposed to post pictures together twice a week?" Mallory crosses her arms.

"It'll require more effort from both of you if you want to make it believable. I think posting together, being seen in public, and going to an event or two of his should be enough to pull it off."

The more Karina explains what this would entail, the more worry expands in the pit of my stomach. There's no way Mallory's going to buy this. How am I supposed to get her to like me again if she won't spend time with me?

Mallory smirks. "Let me get this straight. You're paying me to hang out with you?"

"If that's what it takes." I smile, trying to play it off like a joke when that's *exactly* what I'm doing. It's embarrassing, but I can't find it in myself to care. If it allows me to rewrite my story with Mallory, I'll do anything. Walk around downtown in a banana costume. Get a tattoo of her name on my lip. Paint the brick exterior of this house pink. Literally *anything*.

"What are you proposing we do to be seen and get pictures to post?"

"What if we participate in our favorite winter traditions together?"

"Like a snowball fight?" Her laugh is dry.

"You two can work on the details later," Karina cuts in. "For now, is there anything else you'd like included in the contract?"

"How long is this arrangement going to last? I'm only on winter break for three weeks."

"I'm not sure we can sell our story in that short of a time." I purse my lips.

Karina nods. "He's right. We could include that it'll last two months, but the timing is subject to negotiation by both parties."

"That sounds reasonable," Mallory agrees, nodding slow-ly.

"Anything else?" My agent sounds like she's ready to get on to her next task.

"One more thing. I'd like the contract to include a line that either party reserves the right to back out at any time." I want Mallory to do this because she wants to spend time with me, and okay, I guess for the money, too. I just…I don't want her to feel trapped. I look right into her surprised brown eyes as I say, "No questions asked."

Mallory dips her head. I'm not sure if it's to hide her shock or her acceptance of my terms. But it's better than her hating me.

"How does this all sound, Mallory?" Karina pauses her typing to look back at the camera.

"I'm in. I'll give Griffin my email for you to send the contract over."

"Wonderful." Karina spins in her office chair to face her computer again. "I need you both to have this signed and back to me by the morning. I know it's fast, but that's Hollywood for you. You can send me more questions if you think of them, but otherwise, I'm off to another meeting." Per usual, Karina hangs up without a goodbye.

"Did we lose her?" Mallory leans toward my computer like she's about to call her back.

I place my hand on her arm, stopping her. "She hasn't said goodbye to me once in the years I've worked with her."

"Huh. I guess when you're getting paid by some of Hollywood's hottest new actors, you don't have time for things as *frivolous* as sign-offs."

I don't attempt to hide my smile. "You think I'm hot?"

She rolls her eyes. "Ugh, you know what I mean."

"Nope." I lean back on the couch. "I'm going to sleep like a baby tonight knowing you think I'm hot."

Mallory picks up a white throw pillow and smacks my arm with it. "You're the worst."

"Whatever you say, *girlfriend*."

"That's *fake* girlfriend to you." She cocks her head.

I wave a hand. "Eh, I've never been one for semantics."

"You've never been one for humility, is more like it."

"Again, semantics." My cheeks hurt from how much I'm smiling, but I can't help myself around her.

"I think that's my cue to leave." Mallory stands and starts walking to the door.

"Wait." I grab her hand and move in front of her. "Don't you think we should take our couple announcement photo and figure out what we're going to do for our first da—"

She shoots me a look. "Err, outing?"

Mallory gestures to her outfit. "You couldn't pay me enough money to take a picture that will be all over the news in a sweat set."

"Why?" My brows furrow. "You look incredible."

She laughs. "I look frumpy. Plus, my hair is on day four, and my curls are struggling."

"I think you accidentally said frumpy instead of drop-dead gorgeous. And I don't know what the rest of that meant, but I love it when your curls are untamed. It fits your spirit."

"Messy?"

"I was thinking bold and free."

A blush spreads across her cheeks as she brushes her hands on her sweatpants. "Um, you can pick what you want us to do first since the winter traditions thing was your idea."

"I'll pick you up tomorrow afternoon, if that works for you."

She blinks. "Tomorrow? Don't you think that's a little soon?"

Not soon enough.

"We need to get our couple announcement out. Take over the narrative in the media." I hope the excuse sounds legit enough to hide my desperation to see her again. "I'll make sure a photographer is available so we can get professional pictures."

"You're not going to tell me what we're doing?"

"It's a surprise. Dress warm and make sure you're ready for our photo op."

"I'm just supposed to trust you?" she asks over her shoulder as we move outside.

I walk to the car and open the door for her. Ted tips his head and gets in the driver's seat. "That's usually how relationships work."

Mallory sighs. "Since we've made it clear that this isn't a relationship, how do I know I can trust you?"

"Would you have trusted the man from three years ago?" I ask, my voice softer as I struggle to hide the emotion I feel thinking back on all I've missed out on with her because of losing her phone number.

"What does that have to do with—"

"Just answer the question. No thinking. Just your gut response."

"Yes." Her voice is barely above a whisper, and her eyes don't meet my gaze.

"Hold on to that. I know I'm Hollywood's hottest new actor now." This finally pulls a laugh out of her, and I'm pleased that I was the one to cause it. "But I'm still the man who bought you entirely too much hot chocolate. Let me show you he's still here." I tap my chest and smile softly before shutting the car door.

Two months. I have about two months to show her that I'm still the same man I've always been.

Once I convince her of that, there's not a chance I'm ever letting her go again.

CHAPTER ELEVEN
MALLORY

ONE QUESTION fills my mind long after I leave Griffin's.

What the heck did I get myself into?

Middle school me would be lying on my magenta comforter, squealing and kicking my feet if she knew I was fake dating a celebrity. I'm literally living her dream. But nothing about this feels like a childhood dream, but more like a living nightmare.

So much for promising myself I wouldn't get charmed by Griffin. But, honestly, it was the giant dollar signs he offered that drew me in. It might make me sound like a gold digger, but if any sane person told me they'd pass up a big, fat check to fake date someone for a few months, they're not lying to me…they're lying to *themselves*. I would be an idiot not to take the kind of money that would allow me to live more comfortably and give back to my school and community.

It doesn't mean I'm forgetting what Griffin did. I'm just making him pay for it.

As he should.

Emotional damage is expensive. Honestly, I think he deserves prison, but he won't get time. No man who destroys a woman's confidence and view of love seems to have to pay for what they did. They're like tornadoes, just going along their jolly way, leaving a trail of devastation in their wake. And Griffin is a completely unaware EF5, at least in my book.

But now I get to make more money than I'd make in five years in just a few months, and he has to pay for it. So, who's the real winner here—the guy who broke my heart, or the girl who gets to break his bank account? Only time will tell.

"Mal." Kelsey knocks on my bedroom door. "Get your gorgeous booty to the living room. Everyone is home, and we're dying for an explanation."

"I'll be down in a sec." I wait until I hear her receding footsteps to take a deep breath.

I'd texted my besties in our Long Live Girlies group chat an SOS message on the car ride back from Griffin's. Thankfully, we always make time for a girl chat.

I push up on my memory-foam mattress and walk downstairs. The antique steps creak beneath my feet. It feels like I'm one wrong step from falling to my doom.

Their chatter quiets as I walk into the living room, taking my usual spot on the couch.

"I'm sure you're wondering why I sent the SOS." None of them says anything. I turn my focus to Kelsey. "Or Kels already told y'all who I met with this afternoon."

"Sorry." She winces. "I was worried about you."

"It's fine. It saves me having to explain why I went to his house."

"Was it massive?" Shayna looks at me like this is her reality TV fix for the week.

"Surprisingly, the house was modest."

"Okay, enough chit chat." Alyssa leans in. "What did his agent want to talk to you about?"

"Well, first things first. We're going to have a small security team outside our house for a while because things aren't going to settle down anytime soon."

"I thought Tyler fixed our paparazzi problem?" Kelsey quirks a brow.

"He did, but it's about to get a whole lot bigger when the world finds out we're dating." I brace myself for their responses, and they deliver.

"What?" My friends ask the same question, the word coming out like something between a squeal and a yell.

"Don't worry," I assure them. "It's fake."

"Hold up." Alyssa raises her hand. "We need an explanation, stat."

I dive right in, not sparing any details as I share about my conversation with Griffin and Karina. "Then his agent had me sign a contract and an NDA."

"NDA?" Shayna asks.

"Nondisclosure agreement," I explain.

"Meaning you *aren't* supposed to disclose that it's fake?" Shayna is a rule follower to a tee.

"For the most part, yes, but I had her write into the contract that I was allowed to tell you three. I can't keep a secret from my besties. You all know too much."

"Yeah, it would've been a hard sell to convince us you were dating Griffin Reynolds after knowing your feelings about him ghosting you." Kelsey purses her lips. "I'm honestly shocked you agreed to it."

"When you find out how much he's paying me to be his pretend girlfriend for a few months, you might feel differently." I type out the amount Griffin is paying me in the notes app on my phone and place it on our coffee table.

My besties lean in, and a collective gasp echoes throughout our living room. Kelsey's dog, Winston, runs between
them, checking on their well-being.

"Did you accidentally add some extra zeroes?" Shayna
chokes out, staring at me wide-eyed.

I shake my head and smile. "You'd think so, but no.
That's how much he's paying me."

"Does Griffin know of another celebrity in need of a
fake girlfriend?" Alyssa points at my phone screen. "If so,
I volunteer as tribute."

"You already have Austin." Kelsey tilts her head in jest.

Alyssa groans. "When are y'all going to cool it with the
whole me and Austin thing?"

"Once you convince us that it's *not* a thing," I respond.

"Et tu, Brute?"

"Ooh, me three!" Shayna raises her hand, smiling glee-
fully.

Alyssa lets out a slow breath. "Remind me why I'm
friends with y'all?"

"Because you love us." I wrap my arm around her, and
she reluctantly hugs me back.

"Enough about my best guy *friend*. Tell us how this
arrangement with Griffin is going to work."

All attention is back on me. I haven't had time to process
this situation with Griffin yet, but there's nobody better to
debrief with than my girls.

"I have to make a social media account where we'll post
together once or twice a week." I sigh. "Unfortunately, that
means we have to see each other multiple times a week."

"How do you feel about having to spend time with him?"
Shayna's eyes are riddled with concern for me.

"I'm terrified, if I'm being honest." I wrap my arms
around my middle, trying not to freak out as I think about

spending the coming months with Griffin. "I truly considered telling him no. But then I realized it's an opportunity for him to compensate me, in some way, for the damage he caused when he ghosted me, plus his ridiculous interview answers." I hug myself tighter. "It doesn't make up for what he did and said, but it's something. And I'd be lying if I said the money wasn't life-changing."

Don't even get me started on how teachers don't get enough compensation for helping raise and teach the next generation.

Kelsey moves to sit on the coffee table in front of me while Alyssa and Shayna wrap their arms around me.

"He deserves to pay for the way he hurt you, but *you* deserve to be happy." Alyssa's voice is soft and calming, like a gentle spring breeze. "*Are* you happy?"

The question catches me off guard. "I hadn't thought about much more than making him pay…" I trail off, trying to uncover how I feel, but I come up blank. "I don't have a real answer yet. I think I'm happy, but ask me again after I've spent more time with Hot Cocoa Man."

"We will." Alyssa nods.

"We're here for you." Kelsey pats my knee.

"For*evermore*," Shayna adds.

"For*evermore*," we all echo back.

"When are you seeing him next?" Kelsey asks.

"Tomorrow. I have to be ready for a photoshoot with a professional photographer. Y'all, these pictures are going to show up everywhere, so I need you to help me pick my outfit and figure out what I'm going to do with my crazy curls." I reach up and squeeze my messy bun for emphasis.

"Good thing you have a bestie who's a hairdresser and also loves fashion." Alyssa stands and places her hands on her hips like she's my fairy godmother or superhero for the day. "To the closets."

Today's the day the world will know my name. Even though I know I look ready, I don't feel ready. But does one ever *feel ready* to be thrust into the spotlight? Probably not.

Alyssa went through all four of our closets to curate a magazine-worthy outfit. I feel confident in Kelsey's cream-colored sweater, my favorite pair of jeans, a pair of Shayna's floral-patterned socks, and Alyssa's ankle-high boots. The look is finished off with my plaid pink peacoat. Plus, Alyssa tamed my natural waves to perfection. There isn't a strand of frizz in sight. She also gave me a natural glam makeup look that I hope will look perfect for pictures.

I'm wearing leggings underneath my jeans and set out black earmuffs and faux-leather gloves to bring with me since Griffin told me to dress warm. He still won't tell me what we're doing—aside from the photoshoot—even though I texted him again this morning to ask.

I glance at my phone, waiting for Griffin to let me know he's here. As if he knew I was looking, a text pops up on my home screen from him.

MR. TOO LATE

I'm one minute out.

I thumbs-up his message, pull on my coat, and slide into the ankle-high boots before grabbing my purse. All my friends are at work, so I say goodbye to Kelsey's dog, Winston.

"Wish me luck, boy."

He thumps his sandy tail in response, almost as if he knows I'm going to need it.

I step onto the front porch and lock the door behind me as Griffin pulls up in the same black car that picked me up yesterday. He jumps out of the driver's side and jogs over to me. Griffin Reynolds has no business looking this good. He's wearing dark jeans, a gray pullover, and casual oxford shoes. The outfit gives off a classic winter vibe that perfectly complements mine.

Then there are his aviator sunglasses. He takes them off, and it's like a slow video montage in my mind. Yep, I'm in trouble. I cannot be attracted to my fake boyfriend.

But then there's his five-o'clock shadow that's doing him all sorts of favors, accentuating his jawline and drawing my gaze to his lips—lips that I once found very kissable. But not anymore.

I avert my gaze.

"Hey, beautiful." Griffin smiles at me. "Did you do something different with your hair?" He reaches up, running his fingers along one of the curls.

"Yeah, Alyssa did it for me. They're more tame than usual."

"I love your curls, tamed or not." He looks at the ground. "Are you ready for our photoshoot?"

"What would you do if I said no?"

"Cancel this whole thing."

I raise a brow. "Really? You'd just let me back out just like that?"

"I would never pressure the force of nature that is Veronica Mallory Porter to do something she didn't want to. I couldn't even if I tried." He shoots me a crooked smile. One that I've never seen on the big screens or in his interview videos. The same tilted one I saw in a coffee shop years ago, when I believed he was a different man.

This is a smile he gives lots of women, I remind myself. *This is fake.*

"And don't you forget it." I gesture toward his car as we begin walking toward it. "Where's Ted?"

"I gave him the rest of the day off." Griffin opens the passenger door for me, and I get in.

"Really?" I set my purse by my feet as he closes my door.

He rounds the car and gets in the driver's seat. "I'm a simple man from Tennessee. I can drive myself around."

"Whatever you say, Griffie. Or, should I say, Mr. Razzle-Dazzle?"

A blush covers his cheeks. Seeing him embarrassed brings a smile to my lips. "You found it?"

"Of course, I did." I'm offended he didn't think I would. I found the video of his toothpaste commercial almost immediately after our hot chocolate date. They really should hire women to do online detective work for the FBI, CIA, or even dating shows. Goodness knows some of those contestants need better vetting.

"There wasn't a chance I would miss out on making fun of you forever." I clear my throat, ready to mimic his commercial from a few years back. "'You handle the razzle, we'll bring the dazzle. Dazzle the world with your smile when you use...'" I do jazz hands for emphasis. "'DazzlePaste.'"

"How many times did you watch that to have it memorized?"

"None of your business."

"Maybe they should've hired you instead." Griffin laughs.

"I would never want to take your star role from you."

"She has a sense of humor, folks." He claps.

I roll my eyes. "Always with the jokes."

"We only get one life to live. Why not focus on the humor and bright side of things?"

"You have a point."

He gasps, and I whip my head to the side to look at him, heart racing.

"What?" I squeal.

"I can't believe you think I'm right. I'm marking that win in my book forever."

I smack his arm. "You scared me. I thought you were about to hit an animal."

"That would've been less shocking than you agreeing with me."

"I'm not *that* stubborn," I mumble.

He wipes his mouth, failing to hide his grin. "I'd beg to differ." I whack his arm again. "Hey, it's a compliment." Griffin holds his hand up to block me from any future attacks. "It's one of the things that drew me to you."

"You don't really know me. It was only one date."

"It only took one date for me to learn that I love that you give it to me straight." He taps his fingers on the steering wheel and opens and shuts his mouth multiple times, like he's choosing his next words wisely. "I never have to question your thoughts or feelings because I know you'll tell me. You can definitely be stubborn, but I like it when a woman knows what she wants and isn't willing to compromise. It's admirable to be steadfast in who you are."

It suddenly feels like there's no air in the car. I suck in a breath. I can't deal with his flattering words or *acting* when he's always been fake with me. But what strikes me the most is that everything he just said is true. He described *me*—the deepest parts of who I am.

My skin flames. I feel like I'm on display, emotionally naked in front of an audience, showing all the most vulnerable parts of me.

"Uh, thanks." The short, generic response is all Griffin gets from me. He doesn't deserve my heart or vulnerability. Just the briefest of interactions and responses will do until I get my check and never have to see him again.

His shoulders and smile fall, making him look like a sad, deflated balloon. "Yeah, anytime."

We're quiet for the remainder of the ride to an area of Old Louisville I haven't been to since I was a kid. He slows the car near a lot across from an outdoor rink, and I gasp.

"Are we going ice skating?"

"Yeah, I rented out the rink for us. There are a lot of good photo ops in this area, too."

He rented out an entire ice rink. For me. I can't begin to imagine what he'd do for someone he was actually dating. Rent out a five-Michelin-star restaurant? Fly her to Paris just for dinner?

Griffin points to another car in the parking lot as we pull in. "I think that's our photographer. Are you ready to look like you like me?"

I sigh. "Let's just hope I'm a better actor than you."

CHAPTER TWELVE

GRIFFIN

MALLORY MUST HATE ME with the burning passion of a thousand suns if she has to act her butt off to pretend she *likes* me.

The average human likes a lot of things. A warm towel straight from the dryer. Free food samples at Costco. Baby animals. A cold drink on a hot summer day.

As for me, Mallory has topped my list from the moment I met her and she opened her sassy mouth. I know I may not beat a cute puppy or kitten, but it's hard to imagine not even being ranked on her list.

"All those times watching my commercial have prepared you for this moment," I say. "It's your time to shine."

Once I put the car in park, Mallory hops out and walks to my side. She places her hands on her hips, a challenge in her eyes. "Prepare to be dazzled, Mr. Razzle-Dazzle."

I lean closer, our faces a few inches apart. "I can't wait."

She takes a step back. "These photos won't take themselves."

"Then let's go find our photographer." I offer her my arm. She hesitates. "It's an arm," I muse. "You know, a common thing to hold as you walk while dating someone. Unless you want to hold my hand instead?"

That statement has her looping her hand through my arm faster than a hot knife through butter. I grit my teeth, wishing she had taken me up on the hand-holding, but at least she's touching me in some capacity. That's progress.

We head across the parking lot, and the photographer hops out of his car, approaching us with a lifted hand.

"It's an honor to meet you, Griffin." He shakes my hand and then smiles at Mallory. "You must be Mallory. It's a pleasure."

"The pleasure is all ours…" Mallory pauses, fishing for his name.

"Antonio."

"Antonio," Mallory echoes with a smile. I wish she would dish out her smiles to *me* that freely.

"Did you have any places in mind for the pictures?" I ask.

He nods. "There's a historic building the next block over that will make a wonderful backdrop."

"Lead the way."

Mallory's hand remains wrapped around my arm as we walk, but her attention is solely on Antonio. They're talking about something local that I don't understand. I'm completely out of the loop, feeling like a third wheel with my own girlfriend. I should put the word *fake* in there, but nothing about my feelings for Mallory is fabricated.

An emotion I can't name settles in my gut.

Mallory laughs at something Antonio said, and the sensation grows.

Jealousy—utter and complete jealousy that this man is the recipient of her smiles and laughs. Ones that I had to work hard for three years ago and would do anything to see aimed toward me again.

I take a deep breath, trying to stay quiet and not show my cards when I'm supposed to look the role of a doting boyfriend, not a jealous onlooker.

We reach the building not a moment too soon, and Mallory drops her hand. I instantly miss the feeling of her delicate fingers wrapped around my bicep.

"Give me just a minute, and I'll be ready to go." Antonio sets his bag on the ground and pulls out his camera. He points it around us, adjusting the settings.

Mallory wrings her hands together nervously. I reach over and wrap my hand around hers. "It's just you and me here taking some pictures. Nothing to worry about."

"Yeah, except for the fact that millions of people will see them," she mutters.

"Only the ones we *want* them to see," I remind her.

"That's supposed to make me feel better?" Her laugh rings hollow.

"I won't let Karina send any photos to the tabloids that you and I don't agree on together. We're a team in this, you and me." I move my pointer finger between us. She looks at it with skepticism.

"All right, I'm ready to get started if you are." Antonio's peppy voice makes me jump. Whenever I'm around Mallory, it's like I'm sucked into an alternate reality. One where only the two of us exist. One where nothing else matters.

Unfortunately, I'm stuck in this reality, where everything else matters. But it's also what brought me back to her, so I can't be too upset about it.

I look at Mallory for confirmation. She meets my gaze for a brief second before turning to Antonio. "We're ready."

"Wonderful, we'll start with typical poses first." He gestures behind us. "I'll have you move a little closer to the building."

We follow his instructions, and he smiles. "Perfect. Now, Griffin, I want you to hold her hand." I intertwine our fingers, and Antonio nods in approval. "Mallory, I want you to place your free hand on his arm."

I can see why he's good at his job. This feels like a natural position for a couple in love. But for me, it feels like the ultimate tease...something I can't have.

"I'll have both of you look at the camera and smile."

I do as Antonio says and hear the clicks of the camera.

"Great, now, Griffin, I'll have you smile while looking down at Mallory. And, Mallory, keep your eyes on the camera."

I'm sure I'm wearing a dopey grin while I look at her, but I can't help it. It's just the *Mallory Effect*.

"These are wonderful." Antonio rocks enthusiastically on his feet. "Griffin, could I talk to you privately for a second?"

Oh no. Is he about to tell me that he knows this is all fake? Did we already fail this ruse? I jog over to him. "What's up?"

"I need you to do something for the next shots, but the element of surprise is key." Antonio lowers his voice. "You're going to be behind Mallory, and I want you to come forward and wrap your arms around her middle and hug her. Make sure your head is visible beside hers in the shots. You can smile, laugh, or look at her. Whatever feels most natural."

He doesn't have to tell me twice. "You've got it."

"Great." Antonio turns to Mallory, whose brow is furrowed, while I walk back to my spot. "Mallory, Griffin will be standing behind you in this shot, so you'll be in the forefront of the images. Just keep your hands at your sides for me this time, okay?"

Mallory follows his instruction, and Antonio readies the shot. When he nods at me, I barrel forward, wrapping my arms around her middle.

Mallory gasps as I tighten my hold around her. As if out of instinct, she grabs onto my arms and laughs. Actual laughter bellows out of her. I can't hold back the goofy grin that pulls at my lips, a tilted one just for her, as I look at her. I'm amazed that I get to have this beautiful woman in my arms. That the world gets to think she's *mine*.

When she looks up at me, her laughter dies, but a small smile remains on her lips.

Don't read into it, Griffin, I remind myself. I know she's playing up her reaction for the cameras, but deep down, I can't help but wish she weren't. I wish I knew what was holding her back. What's changed for her.

"These are a masterpiece," Antonio breathes. "The whole world is going to fall in love with you two. You're going to be the next Brangelina. Well, minus the breaking up part. It's obvious that you are in this for the long haul."

"Oh, if he only knew," Mallory mutters.

I respond by squeezing her waist.

Antonio lowers his camera. "Next, I want you to talk like normal. Tell the other person an inside joke to make them laugh. Whatever feels most normal for you as a couple."

Mallory moves to my side, my arms still settled around her waist. "If we're going to do our version of normal, I don't think he's going to get much good footage since I'll be constantly rolling my eyes at your ridiculousness."

"Then let's lean into our fake normal. The one where you actually like me and can't help but look at me like I'm the center of your world."

"Do you *want* me to throw up?" Her eyes glitter with mirth. "I'm sure that will make an excellent cover photo for all the tabloids."

"I can see the headline now: *Lovesick.*"

She smirks and pats my chest. "Always full of yourself. I guess some things never change."

I laugh. "Only when I'm trying to draw out that beautiful smile of yours." I slide my hand up to cup her jaw. The edges of my fingertips graze her ear, and Mallory sucks in a breath. I run my thumb along her bottom lip, and she stiffens. Leaning down until my lips graze her other ear, I whisper, "This might be a crazy idea, but I think most girlfriends like being in their boyfriend's arms."

"I'm not the common girlfriend." She loosens up a little bit, wrapping her arms around my waist, bunching my coat in her fists.

"Then it's a good thing you've practiced my commercial so many times."

She laughs, and it sounds like hearing my old favorite song on the radio—unexpected, but an instant onslaught of joy.

"That's what I'm talking about." Antonio clicks away on the camera. "More of this. Pretend I'm not even here."

"That's going to be difficult." Mallory presses her lips together, and my eyes drop to them.

"What is?"

"I can pretend he's not here. But if we're doing our normal couple thing, I'd be glaring at you, and I'm pretty sure that wouldn't do much good selling our fated soulmates storyline."

"Then allow me to take the lead." I tighten my hold on her waist and move my other hand to the back of her head before I dip her, low and slow.

Mallory lets out a small gasp of surprise, and I smile, loving that I was the source of that sound.

"Yes, that's perfect. Feel free to kiss now."

My eyes find Mallory's, asking her with a look if this is okay. She gives me the barest of nods. It kills me knowing she's only saying yes for the charade when I want nothing more than for this to be real. But I have a fake relationship and believable chemistry to uphold, so I lean in and press a brief kiss to Mallory's lips. One that looks practiced and nice on the cameras—a movie kiss, if you will.

It's nothing like our first kiss, lacking the emotions I feel stirring inside me. As quickly as it began, it's over. I pull back, not wanting to scare Mallory away.

A rosy pink hue colors her cheeks, but the jury's still out if it's a blush or a physical manifestation of her anger. When I meet her gaze, there's a heat in her eyes that still doesn't explain whether she's feeling the chemistry or seething.

I pull Mallory out of the dip, setting her back on her feet. She doesn't immediately step away from me, so I'm taking that as a good sign.

"You good?"

She squeezes my jacket, so I take that as a yes.

"The sparks are flying between you. I see why your recent movie was such a hit, Griffin." Antonio wiggles his eyebrows before thumbing through the photos on his camera. "I was going to take you to another location, but you lovebirds made my job easy."

"Really? You don't need any more?" I ask, wanting an excuse to keep Mallory in my arms longer.

"Nope, I got everything I need." He smiles.

"Great." Mallory all but jumps out of my arms. "You're the best, Antonio."

"Yeah, the best ever," I mutter under my breath.

"What was that?" she asks.

"I was just agreeing with you." If I were hooked up to a lie detector, let's just say there would be a massive spike right now.

Antonio walks over and shakes my hand. "Thanks for trusting me to take your photos." He moves to Mallory, taking one of her hands and bowing before her. "Make sure he treats you like the princess you are."

"I will, Antonio. Thank you."

We wave goodbye to him, and Mallory sighs. "He was right about two things."

When she doesn't finish her thought, I run a hand along my scruff. "Care to elaborate?"

"I plan to be a royal pain for you to deal with over the next few months."

Laughter slips out of my mouth, uncontainable. "Thanks for the heads up."

She shrugs. "I'm nothing but honest."

Yet another trait I love about her.

"And the second thing?"

She folds her arms across her chest. "You're a great actor."

It almost sounds as if she means it, but I detect an underlying bitterness there. There's something she's not telling me—something more than the fact that I lost her number. I need to find a way to figure out what it is without scaring her away. For now, all I can do is keep reminding her who I really am.

"You flatter me." I smile before gesturing toward the heart of Old Louisville. "Ready for me to kick your butt out on the rink?"

"I didn't know it was a competition." Mallory smirks. "But if it is, I'm definitely winning."

She's right. Because I would let her win a hundred times over just to see a satisfied smile on her lips. To see her *happy*.

Once we reach the ice rink, the attendant gets us our skates. I take both sets from him, making a mental note of Mallory's shoe size, and carry them to the bench area.

"Thanks." Mallory accepts her skates from me and slides out of her boots.

After I get laced up, I glance over at her. She looks adorable with her black earmuffs and gloves paired with her pink plaid coat.

"What has made you happy the last three years?" I ask.

Her eyes dart up from her skates to meet mine. They hold both shock and fire in their depths. "Why do you even care?"

I try to ignore the sting from her words and push forward. "My highlights have all been public knowledge, but I want to hear how you've been."

She moves her attention back to lacing her skates.

Great, now she's ignoring me.

I look out at the rink, wondering where I went wrong to get this icy front from her.

"The past three years have been great," Mallory finally responds.

I turn to face her, not wanting to miss a single word.

"I graduated from college, moved in with my three best friends, and started my first teaching job." She stands up, looking ready for the ice.

"I feel like you're living every girl's dream, getting to have your best friends as roommates."

"Sure am." Mallory places her gloved hands on her hips. "Did we come here to talk or skate?"

There's still time to break down her walls, I remind myself.

I gesture toward the rink, trying to be a gentleman and let her go first.

"No, after you."

I should've expected that response. She always has to challenge me.

Cautiously, I step onto the ice and instantly feel like a baby who's learning how to walk. I'm sure this is getting me major brownie points with Mallory. Super attractive to have my arms flailing around when I should be making sure she feels safe and comfortable.

Looks like I'm zero-for-one on my date planning scale.

I grimace. "I promise that I wasn't this bad before."

Mallory leans her arms on the railing of the rink. "Let me guess. Last time you were on the ice, you were a kid pushing a traffic cone, and you thought your skills had improved over time enough to impress me."

"No."

Yes.

But I'm not telling her that.

Mallory steps onto the ice. I'm about to say that this was a terrible idea and suggest we get out of here when she starts skating *backward* while talking to me at the same time, like some expert-level multitasker.

"You beautiful little liar."

"What are you talking about?" She plays the nonchalant game well.

"You said you haven't been skating since you were a kid." I gesture to the rink around us. "But you look like an ice princess out here."

"I was good back in the day." She does another spin, stopping with a toe pick to the ice. "Guess I've still got it."

I skate over and wrap my arms around her middle, more for the sake of not wanting to fall on my face than wanting to be close to her—though that's a valid reason, too. "I'd say you've *more* than got it."

Mallory untangles herself from my hold. "There are no cameras around. You don't have to do that."

"Rule number one of being a celebrity." I gently take her hand. "There are almost always cameras around when you're in public. Whether you see them or not."

She scoffs. "There are rules to being a celebrity?"

I shake my head. "Just generally understood rules of thumb so stars don't ruin their career by being careless in public."

"Sounds more like common sense if you ask me."

"You're the one who just said there were no cameras around." I tuck one of her curls behind her ear.

Her eyes narrow. "Touché."

"Is Mallory Porter admitting she makes *mistakes*?" I gasp, my tone playful.

"It's not often, so don't get used to it."

"Don't worry, your secret's safe with me." I smile. When she doesn't say anything else, I let go of her and carefully maneuver my way over to the rink wall one little waddle-shimmy at a time. I grab hold of the railing and turn to shoot her an encouraging grin. "Show me what you can do, Ice Princess."

This brings a hint of a smile to her lips. "Gladly."

I watch her glide across the ice, making each movement look effortless. She does a series of small midair jumps and ends with a spin so quick that I don't know how she stays on her feet once she comes to a stop. "Did you ever think about going pro? Like the Olympics or something?" I ask when she nears me.

Mallory stops with the sides of her skates, spraying me with a dusting of ice while looking pleased with herself. I brush off my coat, secretly happy she's showing me some kind of emotion.

"I considered it, but we would've had to leave Kentucky to live near a state-of-the-art Olympic training ice arena." She shrugs. "I never would have asked that of my family. I'm sure they would've done it, but they're not my only family here."

"Your friends," I say with understanding.

She nods. "I couldn't leave them. I always wanted to help kids, so studying to be a teacher became my new passion."

I lean my elbow on the railing, attempting to look casual rather than like I'm gripping it like it's my lifeline. "What about teaching little kids ice skating lessons on the side?"

She purses her lips. "I've never thought about that."

"You're already an amazing teacher. Hopefully, it wouldn't be hard to combine two things you love."

"We'll see." Mallory surprises me by offering a gloved hand my way. "Come on, Reynolds. Let's get you out on the ice."

I grip the railing, not wanting to embarrass myself in front of her. "I'm fine here watching you."

She raises a brow. "Aren't you the one who said there are always cameras around?"

"You're going to use my own words against me?"

"Maybe I just want to see you fall on your face."

"Fine, you're asking for it." I wrap my fingers around her glove, close my eyes, and push off the wall.

"Bend your knees to help you balance, and start with small movements."

My left arm goes flailing as I try to regain my balance.

"You look like a flightless bird."

"If I'm a bird, you're a bird," I tease, finally gaining my balance as we move at a snail's pace around the rink.

"Is that supposed to be a play on the quote from *The Notebook?*"

"I'm in the film industry, beautiful. My life is a series of movie quotes."

"Good to know." Mallory gestures to our skates. "Look, you're doing it. Apparently, you just needed a distraction."

"Or maybe I needed a good teacher."

She blushes under my praise. I smile down at her but quickly realize my mistake. Looking at her made my body angle slightly, causing my skate to collide with hers. We both fall to the ice, and I pull Mallory into my arms instinctively, trying to take the brunt of the fall.

I hit the ice and immediately feel shooting pain in my back and tailbone. Mallory falls on top of me with a whoosh that knocks the breath right out of me.

"Are you okay?" I ask through rasped breaths.

"Yeah, are you?"

She blows out a puff of air. Our breaths meld together into a small cloud between us in the cold. I'm jealous of the air leaving my lungs that gets to mingle with hers when all I get is forced touches.

"You hit the ice pretty hard." Mallory looks more amused than concerned, but at least it's something.

I wrap my arms tighter around her as she lies on top of me, and I become extremely aware of everywhere her body is pressed to mine. It's like something out of a dream, except if this were really a dream, we'd be kissing right now.

She can probably smell my cinnamon gum—the flavor I've chewed since I learned the snickerdoodle hot chocolate was her favorite, so my breath could smell like her favorite flavor if I ever found her again. I wonder if the scent makes her think about kissing me, too.

I gaze into her brown eyes and suddenly feel breathless for an entirely different reason. "I've never been better."

Even though my tailbone—and my ego—might be a little bruised, I'll never pass up a single second of holding Mallory Porter in my arms.

CHAPTER THIRTEEN
GRIFFIN

I STARE AT MY phone screen, my thumb hovering over the share button. If the post were just about me, I wouldn't second-guess pressing it, but this involves someone else. A woman I want to protect at all costs.

After Karina sent over the photos she received from Antonio, I wanted Mallory to make the final call on which photos were seen publicly, so I texted all of them to her.

Well, *almost* all of them.

There was one photo in particular I saved on my phone just for me. The picture where I'm hugging her from behind and looking at her with the kind of adoration and chemistry you can't write into a movie script—the *real* kind. Mallory is laughing in it, and she seems truly happy.

The world doesn't deserve to see that photo. And, quite honestly, if Mallory saw it, the depth of my feelings for her would be obvious, and I'm not ready for that yet. She might believe I'm only a good actor. But I'm sure if she knew how I truly feel, she'd back out of our agreement and never look back. Mallory made it abundantly clear that she had no interest in dating me when we discussed the terms of our contract. I need to give her time to believe my intentions are pure before I lay everything on the table.

After Mallory selected her five favorite photos, I sent those to Karina this morning to send to the tabloids, along with the story we came up with.

Now, I'm staring at the picture of us that Mallory and I agreed to post as our couple announcement on social media. It's one of the first ones we took where we're holding hands, and her free hand is wrapped around my arm. While she's looking at the camera, I'm looking at her with a tilted grin and a warm look in my eyes that translates even through the photo.

The caption I wrote is simple.

My leading lady [red heart emoji].

Hopefully, it won't leave any room for speculation about who I'm dating. Once the story of how we met and fate brought us together, not once but *twice*, is shared in the media, the narrative will be abundantly clear: Mallory is my girl.

With a shaky breath, knowing Mallory's life is about to change, I press share and text Mallory.

ME

Hey, just wanted to let you know the post is live. You'll need to accept the collaborator position in your direct messages.

MALLORY

I accepted it.

I pause and bite my lip. The need to check on her is there, but I'm not sure if she'll appreciate it.

I shake my head. She should know that I care enough to make sure she's okay.

ME

How are you feeling about this?

MALLORY

I'm a little terrified, but seeing as I have an entire security team out front, I think I'll be okay.

ME

But how are YOU feeling?

MALLORY

You mean about the fact that my life is about to change forever?

I can imagine her scoffing and rolling her eyes as clearly as if she were right in front of me.

MALLORY

I don't fully know what to expect, but I can deal with anything for a while.

Especially knowing there's an end in sight.

Her words are a slap to the face. I wish that even an ounce of her was doing this because she felt the pull of attraction or feelings toward me still. I'd even take something smaller than an ounce. An atom. A dust particle. Just some tiny semblance of hope to hold onto.

But, as of now, the outlook is grim, a dark cloud hovering and threatening a downpour at any moment.

I click on the notifications icon—it's already flooded with thousands of likes and hundreds of comments. They range from people saying they knew it and offering congratulations to those saying hateful things about Mallory wrecking my "relationship" with Brittany.

I want to respond to those comments, letting them know that was all smoke, that the only girl who has ever had any kind of grasp on my heart is the one in the photo, but my agent taught me early on that replying to comments was a slippery slope that would only lead to more hate. Ones that would *not* paint me in a positive light and could be a reason I don't get auditions.

I've just exited the app when a familiar face—a man with messily styled dark-blond hair and a cheesy smile—pops up on my screen with an incoming call.

Most of the world knows him as country music sensation, Rhett Hayes.

As for me, I just call him my best friend.

I slide my thumb across the screen, answering the call. "Hey, man."

"*Hey, man?* That's all you have to say?" Rhett scoffs. "No explanation for the fact that I just discovered you're finally dating your dream girl after all these years, from a social media post rather than from you?"

"Sorry, dude. Let's just say a lot has happened in the last week."

"I'd say so."

"I ran into Mallory over the weekend, and some locals took pictures that ended up in the tabloids." I sigh. "Now, I'm paying her to be my fake girlfriend."

"Whoa, whoa, whoa." Rhett sounds like a true Southern man, his accent thick and pronounced over the phone. "It's not real?"

"It is for *me*."

"Oh, no. You've got it bad, don't you?"

"You have no idea, bro." I run a hand over my chin and dive in, explaining everything that's happened over the past four days.

Once I've finished, Rhett blows out a low whistle. "You're in big trouble."

I let out a mirthless laugh. "Yeah, you're telling me."

"Why do you think it's only real for you?"

"That's what I'm trying to figure out." I sigh. "I apologized and explained how I lost her number, but she still acts like she wants nothing to do with me."

Rhett clucks his tongue. "Man, it sucks that she hates you after you've been pining over her for three years."

"Way to kick a man when he's down."

"Hey, I'm just trying to empathize with you."

"Try harder," I joke, trying to ignore the sting of his words. Words that are true but burn like salt on an open wound.

"Do I need to play you a sad song? I've been working on one—"

"I don't need one of your tragic country songs. I need Mallory to fall hopelessly in love with me."

"Or at least like you," Rhett says.

"What's wrong with you, man?"

"You're the one who said you love how honest Mallory is. I'm shooting it straight."

"It's okay when Mallory does it because she challenges me. And, well, because she's gorgeous."

"You don't think I'm pretty?" Rhett pouts.

"Go get compliments from all your female fans. I'm sure they'd love to boost your ego."

"You know that I hate all the attention from fans."

"I *do* know. It's why we're best friends."

"Aww," Rhett gushes. "Bro, I'm your best friend?"

"Maybe not anymore." I smile, rolling my eyes.

"You love me. We're going to be best friends forever. So, don't let me find out about your engagement on social media next time, okay? I wanna meet her first, too."

"Maybe you can meet her sometime. And we won't be getting engaged anytime soon, trust me. It's fake, remember?"

"I have a good feeling about this," Rhett says, sounding optimistic. "I'll write you a love song you can play and say it was commissioned just for her. Girls love that."

"I'm not sure if that's Mallory's thing."

"Well, just know that the offer's on the table."

"Thanks, man." I glance at the time on my phone, and my eyes widen. "Shoot, I have to go pick Granny up from her physical therapy appointment."

"I'll catch you later, bro. Tell Granny and Mallory hi for me."

"Will do. Later."

Driving to Granny's doctor's office, I run through ideas for fun winter activities I can do with Mallory. If there's one thing that's become clear, it's this: I need to up my game.

———— ♡ ♡ ♡ ————

MALLORY

I'm freaking out!!

ME

What's wrong?

MALLORY

My family wants to have you over for dinner tonight. We don't have to go.

And by "we don't have to go," I mean that we shouldn't go.

ME

I'm so there, it's insane.

MALLORY

She's the Man? I didn't think that was your kind of movie.

ME

It's highly underrated.

I'm surprised you know it.

MALLORY

My friend, Shayna, is obsessed with all things romance. So, I think I've seen every rom-com known to man at least twice.

ME

Even *A Chance Romance* and *Accidentally in Matrimony*?

MALLORY

Shay wouldn't dare make me watch those.

We're solidarity sisters.

ME

So, my only acting you've seen is my commercial? *face with peeking eye emoji*

MALLORY

Yep, your true claim to fame.

ME

Wonderful.

Also, nice try.

MALLORY

???

ME

Trying to distract me from the fact that we're going to have dinner with your family.

MALLORY

I have no idea what you're talking about.

ME

Let me know what time!

MALLORY

Fine. I'll pick you up at five.

ME

Can't wait!

———— ♡ ♡ ♡ ————

"Are you ready?" Mallory puts her car in park.

I glance over at her trembling hands. "I think the real question is, are *you* ready?"

She sighs. "I have to be."

"But you aren't." That much is obvious. I wish I could reach over and take her shaking fingers in mine to steady her.

"No, but they'd be suspicious if I declined a dinner invite."

"What has you worried? I thought you were close with your family."

"That's *why* I'm anxious." She frowns. "It feels awful lying to them."

I nod in understanding. "I hate lying to my parents and Granny, too. I can check with Karina to see if we can amend the NDA, if that would make things easier for you."

Mallory turns sideways in the seat to look at me. "You'd do that?"

"For you? *Anything.*" I'm not sure if she catches the true meaning behind my words, but it's there, nonetheless.

She taps her fingers on the center console. "That's kind of you to offer, but I feel like we're too far in for me to change our story now. Telling them this is all fake would only confuse them."

"As long as you're sure. You can still back out at any time," I offer, hoping she won't take me up on it.

Mallory shakes her head. "No, I can do this." She starts to open her door.

"Hold on, I'll get that for you." I hop out of the car and jog over to the driver's side, opening it for her.

"I can open my own door."

"Not when I'm around."

She steps onto the driveway and mumbles, "Thanks."

"You're welcome." I open the back door and grab the bouquet I bought for her mother. "Let's do this."

Before we reach the front door, a middle-aged woman with brown hair and a bright smile walks out of it, clutching her hands to her chest. "You were amazing in *Accidentally in Matrimony*. I can't believe a movie star is dating my daughter."

Mallory gestures to her. "This is my mom, Angela."

"Please, call me Angie." She extends her hand, shaking mine before pulling me in for a tight hug. "I'm just so happy Mallory is finally bringing a boy home."

"Mom, what did we talk about?" A blush covers Mallory's cheeks.

"Sorry." Angie swipes under her eyes. "I can't help it."

Mallory's father joins us outside and rubs gentle circles on Angie's back. "You can tell how excited she is by what she cooks for dinner." He extends a hand toward me. "I'm Todd."

I give his hand a firm shake. "Griffin. Nice to meet you."

"Did you make my favorite meal?" Mallory perks up, looking expectantly at her mom.

Angie's smile falls. "No. Sorry, sweetie. I'll make chicken and dumplings next time you come for dinner."

"She made a meal fit for royalty." Todd laughs, giving Angie's shoulder a squeeze.

I wrap my arm around Mallory's waist. "You didn't have to make anything special for me."

"Well, I hope you like filet mignon and lobster mac and cheese." Todd claps me on the shoulder before leading me inside.

Mallory groans. "I told you not to go all out."

"I wasn't about to serve a *celebrity* food like chicken. A rich person on a reality show I watch called it 'peasant food.'"

"Chicken wings are actually his favorite."

My eyes fly to Mallory, surprised that she remembers. She blushes and looks at the ground, avoiding my gaze. But even that can't stifle the glimmer of hope rising in me.

"Oh, no." Angie grimaces. "I guess I shouldn't trust those reality shows. I can run to the store and grab some wings." She moves toward the front door.

I place my hand on her arm. "What you made sounds wonderful. Please never feel like you need to go out of your way for me, though. I'm just a boy from Tennessee."

She smiles warmly at me before turning to her daughter. "You found yourself a keeper."

"I know." Mallory's words come out strained. It's a lie, but her parents don't know that.

Even if nothing about our relationship is fake to me, I know it still is to Mallory. So, partaking in being dishonest to her family makes me feel awful.

"The filets should be done resting now." Angie walks into the kitchen. "Let's eat before dinner gets cold."

Despite our protests, she sends us to the table and makes our plates. Angie brings them to the table, setting a plate in front of each of us. The cheesy notes mixed with the perfectly seared scent of the meat hit my nose.

"This smells delicious," I say. "Thank you."

"Anytime, dear." She shoots me a thankful smile as she takes her seat.

Todd says a quick blessing, and we all dive in. The meat is seasoned to perfection and melts in my mouth.

"I cook a lot of meat, but this is the best filet I've ever had."

"You don't have to say that." Angie flourishes her napkin.

"It's the truth." I take a bite of macaroni and cheese. It's decadent with the lobster, and the combination of all the cheeses is delicious. "Mmm, I'll eat your food any day, Angie."

Angie blushes. "You're always welcome here." She wipes her mouth with her napkin. "Speaking of, do you have plans for Christmas?"

Mallory sputters mid-chew. She coughs, and I reach over, patting her back. "You good?"

She nods and takes a sip of her Dr. Pepper.

I clear my throat. "My parents are going on a cruise for Christmas, so I'll just be here with my granny since she can't travel far right now. I'm not sure if Mallory told you, but she had a hip replacement. That's why I'm here, and how I got back in touch with your daughter." I smile at Mallory, who looks like she'd like the earth to open up and swallow her whole.

"I want to hear your story in a minute, but as for Christmas…" Angie pouts. "That won't do. You and your grandmother will come spend Christmas Eve and Christmas Day with us."

I study Mallory, trying to gauge her reaction. From her deer-in-the-headlights look, I'd say she doesn't want me at her family's holiday. "I don't want to impose."

Angie shakes her head with a tone of finality. "It's a huge ordeal with all the extended cousins, and there's always room for more."

"Griffin, let me teach you something." Todd sets down his utensils and steeples his hands. "Once my wife has her mind set on something, *no one* can change it."

"Heard, sir." I turn to Angie. "My granny and I would be honored to join your family for Christmas."

"Wonderful." She smiles and digs into her food.

I place my hand on Mallory's knee and tap it, wondering how she feels about all of this. Her knee twitches against my touch, but she doesn't have time to respond before her mother asks another question.

"I've been dying to hear the story of how you two met. I read about it in the tabloids, but they never get things right. And since Mallory hasn't told me anything"—Angie shoots her daughter a look—"I was hoping you'd tell me the full story."

"Gladly." I finish my steak and lean back, clasping my hands in my lap. "It all started on a snowy winter night…"

CHAPTER FOURTEEN

MALLORY

THERE'S NOT ENOUGH PATIENCE in the world to help me suppress my eye roll as Griffin starts our story the way one would a fairy tale.

"I was enjoying the evening with my granny while my parents were out on their weekly date night, when there was a knock at the front door. Carolers. That's when I walked onto the porch and saw this beautiful woman"—he reaches over, intertwining our fingers—"and everything else faded away."

I take a sip of Dr. Pepper, trying to hide my annoyed look behind my cup—it doesn't exactly say *romance*.

"I couldn't look at anyone but her while she sang 'Deck the Halls' with a choreographed routine. It truly felt like fate had brought her to my doorstep." He rubs the stubble on his chin. "Anyway, I saw that they were all holding cups and stupidly thought they were collecting money for charity. I pulled a handful of change out of my pocket and proceeded to drop it into Mallory's half-full cup of hot chocolate."

"Oh no." My mom laughs. "I can picture that scene playing out perfectly."

"It was a meet-cute straight out of a rom-com." Griffin squeezes my hand. "Until I dropped the change in her cup, and the hot liquid sloshed over and burned her fingers. I held some snow to it, trying to help the best I could."

"What a gentleman." Mom looks between us, doe-eyed.

"I try my best, ma'am." He smiles at her. "To make up for my terrible mistake, I offered to buy her a hot chocolate at a local place the next day."

"Mallory never meets up with strangers." My dad raises a skeptical brow.

"I wasn't sure she'd agree to it, sir. But when she countered with me buying her two cups, we had a deal."

"That's my girl." Dad nods at me like he's proud I got an extra hot chocolate out of the encounter.

Griffin glances at me, looking the picture of calm, cool, and collected. A complete contrast to my current anxious, sweaty, and frazzled state.

Why did I ever agree to this?

It feels wrong lying to my family. But I suppose Griffin's only told the truth thus far.

"The next afternoon, I met her at my favorite local coffee shop, and we enjoyed hot chocolates and talked for hours until we were both starving. Plus, I was looking for any excuse to spend more time with her." He shoots me a grin.

I hate when he fake flirts with me. It's been clear to me since watching his interview that our date didn't mean as much to him as it did to me. So, I don't understand why he's making it out to be as wonderful as I thought it was when he doesn't believe the words he's saying. I guess he's a better actor than I gave him credit for.

"That's when we decided to grab wings before Daisy picked her up," Griffin adds. Conveniently, he left out a crucial element: our earth-shattering first kiss with the snow slowly falling around us. Though I'm glad he didn't mention it. I'd be mortified talking to my parents about our kiss.

"Then what?" my mom asks, leaning forward expectantly.

Griffin's expression falls. "Unfortunately, our story paused there for a few years, courtesy of two dead phones, a phone number on a napkin, and a slushy puddle of snow."

I meet my mom's unexpectedly emotional gaze. "Is that why you never told me about him?"

I nod solemnly. "I thought he wasn't interested when he never called."

"Oh, sweetie." She frowns before turning back to Griffin, waiting for more of the story.

"But that couldn't have been further from the truth." He places his hand on my thigh, giving it a gentle squeeze. "I left for an audition right after our date, and that was what landed me my first leading role in *A Chance Romance*. I hired an agent shortly after and worked with her to try to find Mallory. Unfortunately, our searches always came up empty-handed."

He should win an award for his Oscar-worthy sigh and look of dejection. It's pure torture having to sit here and listen to Griffin share our story. Because, while my parents think it ends in a happily-ever-after...I know that it ends in a tragedy with a fairytale façade.

Griffin leans toward me and tucks a strand of hair behind my ear. The back of his fingers brushes along my jaw, sending my thoughts tumbling back to when he did the same thing before our first kiss in the snow. My eyes dart to his, and I can see the same memory reflected in his eyes. His gaze drops to my mouth, and the desire to feel his lips on mine builds.

I shove those feelings away into a deep abyss where they belong. I've always thought that the chemistry I felt was one-sided, but the way Griffin's talking and the heated way he's looking at me makes it seem like it wasn't one-sided at all. So, what's the truth? This story he's selling now, or what he said on the interview a few months after he met me?

He shoots me a small smile before turning back to my parents. "I didn't even have a last name to go off. And now I know that I was searching using her middle name rather than her first name, so it makes sense why I always came up empty-handed. I tried her school, but the university wouldn't give out any information, and a lot of Mallorys popped up with a search for Louisville, but none of them were her."

"How did you find our Mallory again, then?" My mom has never sounded so invested.

"Granny recently got a hip replacement. Some of her friends recommended a doctor here. I was between projects, so I rented a house to be nearby while she recovers from the surgery at a rehab facility." He rubs the pad of his thumb along mine. "This past Saturday, I was checking out one of the local coffee shops when I ran into Mallory."

"And he means that he *literally* ran into me," I chime in, realizing I've been pretty quiet this entire conversation. I haven't been able to keep my eyes off Griffin as he's shared our story. Not because I believe he really was interested in me after our first date, but because he really is captivating as an actor. He's literally been trained for a moment like this, so I guess all his hard work has paid off.

"Yeah, it wasn't my best moment." He laughs good-naturedly. "I caused a hot drink to spill on her for the second time. But I couldn't get over how fate brought us together not once but twice in the same way, almost exactly three years apart."

"And that's the first picture the media got ahold of? The one in the coffee shop?" My mom nods like she's putting the whole picture together.

"Exactly." A blush climbs his neck as he looks between my parents. "I always told myself that if I found Mallory again, I'd never let her go. So I did just that. And, well, here we are."

I should give him a standing ovation or a trophy for his performance. Maybe I still have a soccer participation one somewhere up in my childhood bedroom. I'm sure Griffin knows how to play the field, so it's fitting. "I'm sorry we couldn't tell you before it went public. It all happened in the blink of an eye." Guilt still swirls inside, knowing that my parents found out the same way the rest of the world did.

"I was a little sad," my mom admits. "But I can understand how the tabloids pick something up and run with it before you've had a chance to talk to loved ones first."

"Thanks for being so understanding." Griffin's expression oozes gratitude. He grabs my hand and kisses the back of it before placing our joined hands on the table.

I don't know what to believe. The lines between what's an act and what's real feel blurry. They're lines that *I* don't want to cross. But I'm unsure what Griffin's stance is. It probably should've been something we talked about before all of this. Made some ground rules and set boundaries.

I mean, he kissed me during our photoshoot. I never planned on our lips meeting ever again, but when it seemed necessary to keep up this charade, I caved. And although the kiss was gentle and ended before it even started, it still affected me.

It brought me back to the flurries of snow hitting my face, the taste of snickerdoodle hot chocolate, and the warmth and safety I felt in his arms.

Those are things I cannot be feeling right now. Memories I'd rather stay in the long-term reserve, never to pop up again. But it seems that's what Griffin does. He just pops into my life and reels me in like a fish on a rod with no chance of escape.

Griffin squeezes my hand hard, like he's trying to get my attention. "I'll check with Granny as long as it's okay with you, beautiful?"

My eyes widen as they dart to him. "Hmm?"

He smiles, and I wonder if he knows that he's the source of my distraction. I wouldn't put mind reading past him at this point.

"Your mom said Granny and I better be at Christmas next week."

"Right. You both should come." I hate how breathless I sound.

Griffin's brows dart up in surprise. I blame it on this stupid trance he put me in with all the touching and thoughts of kissing.

"Wonderful. Mallory's brother will be thrilled to meet you." Mom looks like she's about to burst with joy. Probably at the idea of having the whole family here, but also at the fact that her only daughter just brought a man home for the first time...ever.

I snort. My older brother, Connor, is one of the most reserved people I know. He has a grumpy exterior that no one has ever been able to break. I glance over at our family photos hanging on the living room wall and find him smiling in only a handful—one handful of smiles in photos across a lifetime. Yeah, I'm sure he's going to be *thrilled* to meet my celebrity fake boyfriend.

My parents pepper Griffin with more questions while I lean back and enjoy the focus not being on me. Well, as much as I can enjoy myself when Griffin's fingers are laced through mine. He rubs his thumb along the palm of my hand, sending goosebumps trailing up my arm. It doesn't seem to bother him in the slightest, like it's instinctual to touch me like this.

I tighten my grip on his hand, forcing him to stop moving. I can't think straight with him doing that, and I need to keep a clear mind around him to avoid falling back into his arms.

Griffin shoots a worried glance my way before turning back to my parents. "I had a wonderful time tonight. But Mallory picked me up, and I want her to be able to get home before it's too late. I heard it's supposed to get icy tonight."

"So thoughtful." My mother flings her hand to her chest, looking at us like we're a couple from a romance movie come to life in her dining room.

Griffin insists on carrying all the dishes to the kitchen while I say goodbye to my parents.

"You found yourself a real keeper, sweetie," my mother whispers in my ear as she hugs me tightly.

"I know." The words taste bitter coming out of my mouth. I hate that the first man I brought home to meet my parents is all a sham. I want a relationship like my parents have someday, and I know they want the same for me. I feel awful giving them hope for a famous future son-in-law when it's all a lie. But I think it would be even worse to tell them the truth now.

My dad pulls me in for a hug next, cracking my back with the force of his squeeze. "I love you. And I like Griffin, but you let me know if he ever wrongs you, and I'll take care of it."

"Um, thanks, Dad," I manage to say without laughing.

Griffin walks back into the dining room and shakes Dad's hand before giving Mom a hug. She holds onto him for longer than I expect, patting his back as she says something too quiet for me to hear.

When he finally pulls back, he says, "Yes, ma'am. Thank you again for dinner." Griffin returns to my side, wrapping his arm around my waist. "You ready, beautiful?"

I nod, and he leads me outside and opens the car door for me. I slide into the driver's seat and turn it on, blasting the heat. Cold air blows out of the vents, and I slide my hands under my thighs, trying to stay warm as Linda heats up.

"You've got this, girl," I encourage her.

Griffin hops into the passenger seat and rubs his hands together. "Man, it got cold out."

I don't respond, and the silence starts to feel deafening as I watch two minutes pass on the dashboard clock.

"So." I draw out the word. "That was rough."

His throat bobs as he swallows. "Really? I thought it went well. Do you think they hated me?"

"No, they loved you." I roll my eyes. "I just hated being dishonest with them."

He holds his hands around his mouth, blowing hot air into his palms as we wait for the car to heat up. "I don't know about you, but I wasn't lying about anything."

There he goes again, making me question what's real. Desperately needing a change in conversation, I say, "How does it make you feel that my mother has seen one of your movies but I haven't?"

He laughs, his breath forming a small cloud in the car. "Honestly, I'm glad you haven't seen it."

"Really?" My eyes widen in surprise.

"My girlfriend doesn't need to see me kiss another woman, even if it's only on-screen."

"*Fake* girlfriend," I correct him.

"Po-tay-to, po-tah-to."

"You really just woke up today and chose violence, didn't you?" I deadpan.

Griffin's laughter rings throughout the car as I move the gear shift into reverse. "If calling you my girlfriend is violence, then I'll happily be the villain in your story. But can I at least be the morally gray one that you fall in love with at the end?"

Nothing about this man is morally gray. "You're more of the golden retriever type." I back out onto the road and begin the drive to Griffin's rental.

"Then why is it so hard for you to like me?"

"Can't you accept that not everyone is going to like you?"

"Not you." He leans his head back and sighs. "*Never* you."

My body has a visceral reaction to his words. Butterflies flutter in my stomach. My heart does a little pitter-patter. "You can't go around saying things like that."

"Like what, the *truth*?"

I shake my head. "I think I like it better when you don't talk."

Griffin reaches over and brushes a curl back from my face.

"Or touch me," I add.

He doesn't pull back, leaving his hand cupping my chin. "You can't tell me you don't feel this spark between us."

My pesky heart that doesn't seem to have a grasp on reality pounds in my chest. "Sparks aren't enough. All it takes is a little water to put it out."

"I'd much rather fan the flame." His lips pull up into a tilted grin.

I lean back, making his hand fall away and breaking the spell of his touch.

"What can I do if I can't talk or touch you?"

"Sit there and look pretty."

"At least she thinks I'm pretty," Griffin mutters under his breath.

Maybe miracles do exist because the car remains blessedly silent for the remainder of the drive to his house, granting me the peace I've been craving.

Once I park in his driveway, Griffin gets out of the car and leans on the frame, poking his head back in. "Do you have any plans Friday night?"

"I have girls' night with my best friends every Friday. It's tradition."

He smiles. "I'd love to meet them."

"I wasn't offering—"

"There's a Winter Market downtown that night. It would be a great photo op, and I feel like I should meet your friends since they're my friends by proxy. You know, the whole 'what's yours is mine' part of a relationship?"

I roll my eyes. "You're not going to take no for an answer, are you?"

"I mean, I would…but there would be a lot of begging involved first that you probably don't want to deal with." He shoots me a crooked smile—the one that I've never seen on-screen. "You may as well avoid all the begging and say yes now."

"Fine," I groan. "We'll be there."

His grin widens. "I'm looking forward to it." He starts to stand before his annoying face reappears in my car. "Text me when you get home, please?"

"Seriously?" I huff. "You already are infiltrating all areas of my life, and now you want me to text you all the time?"

His eyes drop to the driveway, and his smile falters. "To let me know that you made it home safe."

Well, now I feel like the world's biggest jerk.

"Oh." My voice sounds as small as I feel. "Yeah, I'll let you know."

He nods, still averting his gaze. "Good night, Mallory." Griffin shuts the door and walks inside.

It shouldn't bother me that he said my name rather than a playful *good night, beautiful.*

I don't like him. He's my fake boyfriend, and I intend for us to stay like that until we part ways at the end of this contract, never to see each other again.

But then why is my heart twinging with something that feels awfully close to sadness for the duration of my drive home?

CHAPTER FIFTEEN
GRIFFIN

I walk through the Christmas Market with a pep in my step after I spot Mallory standing encircled by a full entourage of people. It's a cold night with the bitter chill of winter in the air, but I don't notice. Just spotting Mallory across the crowd sends heat rushing to my cheeks, warding off the cold.

She's in her signature pink plaid coat—the same one she wore on our first date. Memories fill my mind of her wearing it, of *kissing* her in it. She's also wearing black pants tucked into the same ankle boots she wore for our photoshoot. But it's the smile on her face that has me blushing—a genuine one that I haven't seen since our first date all those years ago. This one is aimed at her friends, but my romantic heart doesn't seem to know the difference.

I hold two fingers up in a small wave as I approach them, and her smile falls. Her reactions have me feeling more whiplash than a wooden rollercoaster. I mean, sometimes it looks like she wants to kiss me, and other times it looks like she's plotting my demise. Okay, not really, but I can feel her apprehension. I still need to get to the bottom of *why*.

"These are my besties." Mallory gestures to the women beside her.

"I think I know them from your descriptions."

"From three years ago?" The look on her face says she doesn't believe me. "By all means."

The first woman is a tall blonde. She's wearing one of the fancy coats I've seen some actresses in, and her hair is curled and up in little buns with some type of silk wrapped around them. "You're Alyssa, the hairdresser."

She taps her nose. "Spot on, movie star."

I turn to the second woman, who is glaring at me with her arms crossed. She looks small but mighty, just like Mallory. Her caramel-brown hair is pulled back in a ponytail. "You're definitely Kelsey." I nod to the tall, muscular man standing behind her. "Which makes you Tyler."

"And you must be Shayna." I smile at the woman with dark hair and a knotted headband covered in pearls. She's wearing a coat covered in a floral pattern in vibrant shades of pink, green, and blue. It doesn't read winter, but I think that's the point. Mallory always described her as the bright, positive friend. If my memory serves correctly, she works at a flower shop, so it's fitting.

"What about her?" Kelsey points to the girl next to Shayna. She's about as tall as Alyssa, but she has dark hair and facial features similar to Tyler's.

"I'd guess she has some relation to Tyler, but unfortunately, I don't know your name."

"Tess." She steps forward, extending her hand.

I give it a firm shake. "Nice to meet you, Tess."

A little girl jumps out from behind her. "I'm Evie! I *love* Christmas."

"It's lovely to meet you, Evie." I shake her hand too, making her giggle. "I love Christmas too."

"My mom needs a new husband. Are you single?"

I choke on nothing but air.

"He's dating Ms. Mallory." Tess kneels to be on her daughter's level. "And honey, you can't just walk around telling people I need a new husband and asking if they're single."

"Why not?" Her little nose scrunches. "How else will you find me a new daddy?"

Tess blows out a breath and stands to her full height. "Okay, on that note, we're going to go find a snack. Nice to meet you, Griffin." She shoots me a hurried smile before leading her away from the group.

Mallory tugs my arm, pulling me down to whisper in my ear. "Maybe she's a better bet for your fake girlfriend. I mean, a girlfriend and an adorable daughter who loves Christmas? Everyone would adore y'all."

"There's just one glaring issue with that idea." I pull back to look into her brown eyes, pools of silky chocolate that I could bask in forever. "She's not you."

Her shoulders rise and fall like she's letting out a heavy sigh, although I don't hear one. Is there such a thing as an internal sigh? If so, then she's probably internally rolling her eyes too.

When will she understand that there's *no one* I want but her?

"Who's up for a round of hot chocolates?" I ask, addressing her friend group. "It's on me."

All the girls' eyes move to Mallory, then back to me.

"You know Mallory doesn't drink hot chocolate anymore, right?" Kelsey steps closer, looping her arm through Mallory's.

I look at my fake girlfriend as she elbows Kelsey in the side, and I wonder what else could have changed in the last few years. "I thought you loved it."

"I used to." Mallory won't meet my gaze. It looks like she's having a silent conversation with her friend, one I wish I were privy to.

I lower my voice, not wanting to draw attention to her discomfort. "Is it because of me?"

Kelsey answers on Mallory's behalf. "What do you think?"

She walks back to her friend group, and Mallory shifts on her feet. I feel awful. I never meant to be the reason she stopped drinking hot chocolate. Or the cause of her pain when she never got my call.

I wish I could go back in time and zip the napkin with her phone number up in my pocket, safe from harm. But this is the hand we were dealt.

On a more positive note, if Mallory felt strongly enough about me to forgo one of her favorite things, then that means she may have felt as strongly for me as I did for her. And if she felt it once, then maybe she'll get that feeling back. Because a once-in-a-lifetime love doesn't just disappear.

"There's always a first step to falling in love all over again," I whisper.

Mallory finally looks at me. Her eyes are riddled with confusion and a dose of hurt rather than the fire I expect. Hurt, I can work with, even though it kills me to see her wounded.

"Are you still talking about the hot chocolate?"

"I'm talking about whatever you want me to be talking about." My voice is husky, a mix of sadness and desire.

She rolls her eyes. "Is that a line from one of your movies?"

"That was a Griffin original."

Mallory glances around me at her friends. "You should buy everyone hot chocolate. I can get something else."

"Or you can take a chance again." I wrap my gloved hands around hers. "You don't know what you could be missing out on until you try."

She pulls her hands back and shoves them in her pockets. "I don't think I'm ready for that quite yet."

"I'm here whenever you are." I hope she catches my double entendre.

"Drinks are on Griffin," Mallory calls to her friends. They smile but eye her warily. I'm glad Mallory has such caring and fierce friends, even if their apprehension is because of me at the moment.

I let everyone order their drinks ahead of me and Mallory. Once we finally reach the register, Mallory fidgets on her feet. "I'll take a vanilla cappuccino."

"Make it two, please," I say before lowering my voice and adding, "And two additional hot chocolates." After passing over my card to pay for the group, I move to the pickup area beside Mallory.

"You're not going to have hot chocolate?"

"I'm waiting."

"For what?" She laughs.

If she's going to ask, I'm going to give her the truth. "Whatever day you decide to drink it again."

Mallory raises a brow. "Why?"

"Because you…you are—" I look at the ground, shuffling my feet along the pavement. I can't tell her she's everything to me. Not yet. I force myself to meet her gaze. "I'd never want to do anything that might cause you pain."

"It's just hot chocolate."

"If it's just hot chocolate, then why don't you take a sip?"

Her eyes soften as she shrugs. "You didn't buy me one."

I shake my head. "I'll get you to drink it again one day."

"Griffin," the woman behind the counter of the drink cart calls.

I pass out the cups of hot chocolate to her friends before handing one cappuccino to Mallory and taking the other for myself.

"Who are the extra drinks for?" Mallory gestures to the drink carrier in my other hand.

Tess and Evie rejoin us with sugar cookies in hand.

"We couldn't leave out Tess and Evie."

I hand the carrier over to Tess, who shoots me a grateful smile. "That was thoughtful. Thank you."

"Are you trying to *buy* my friends?" Mallory takes a sip of her cappuccino.

"It's not about the money spent, but investing my time with the people you love most." She may not let me in, but maybe the people she loves will know of a secret door and be willing to help once they see my true intentions.

She huffs. "Well, that's sweet. How am I supposed to be sassy now?"

"You could just talk about how amazing I am."

"There's that confidence again." Mallory taps my chest.

"You never seemed to have an issue with my confidence before." I step closer, placing my mouth beside her ear. "If I'm remembering correctly, you also told me my face was pretty."

She flushes a deep pink that matches her coat. "Really? I think I meant insufferable."

I wrap my arm around her lower back and pull back enough to look at her. "Good thing I have time to change your mind."

"Don't you remember that I'm stubborn?"

I smile. "It's one of the things I like most about you."

Mallory shakes her head. "What am I going to do with you, Griff?"

Hearing her use my preferred nickname has me feeling a thrill of hope. "Oh, I don't know. Keep me forever?"

She shoves me away with a light push to my stomach, and I'm not ashamed to admit I flex my ab muscles. A man's gotta do what a man's gotta do.

Mallory pulls her hand back, her blush more prominent.

We move closer to her friends when I spot a group of carolers in front of the giant Christmas tree in the middle of the square. "We should join them." I point toward the tree.

"Is that even allowed?"

"I don't think there are any caroling laws." I shrug. "It would be like Christmas Cheer Police."

Shayna laughs. "Can you imagine if there were Christmas Cheer Police? Talk about *un*holiday spirit."

"Right?" I point at Shayna. "See, she gets it."

"You're not helping," Mallory grumbles at her friend.

"Sorry." Shayna grimaces and mimes locking her lips and throwing away the key.

"Come on." I nudge Mallory's arm. "This is supposed to be a photo op for our next social media post. What better photo is there than one in front of the tree?"

"An invisible one," she deadpans.

I tilt my head back and forth like I'm mulling over the idea. "I was thinking more like a kiss on the cheek with the glittering lights on the tree behind us."

"If you insist. But do we have to sing?"

Mallory wraps her hand around my arm as we walk toward the tree. The feel of it, even though she's wearing gloves and I'm in a thick coat, causes goosebumps to trail across my skin. I clear my throat. When I speak, my breath fogs in front of me. "I thought you'd love it, having seen your caroling abilities."

"I was coerced into that performance by Daisy's family, who take their caroling tradition way too seriously."

"You looked really into it."

"Yeah, because they told me I needed to sing and dance with more gusto after every house." She sighs. "I'm thankful her family let me stay with them when I was snowed in, and I really love Daisy. But even you couldn't pay me enough to carol with them again."

I laugh. "I know no one is ever convincing you to do something you don't want to."

"You've got that right."

If she doesn't do anything she doesn't want to, does that mean she *wants* to be my fake girlfriend? Beyond the money, that is. I glance over at her, mesmerized by the silhouette of her face. Her long eyelashes are gorgeous and draw more attention to the adorable freckles covering her cheeks and forehead. Then there's her hair that my fingers crave combing through again.

I shake my head. It's too soon to be having these thoughts when the jury's still out on whether she *wants* to spend time with me. But I can't help but wish on every star tonight that Mallory is starting to enjoy being around me just as much as I like being around her.

After taking a sip of my cappuccino for a little liquid luck, I motion to the tree. "You ready for our next social media picture?"

"I have to be." She slides her purse off, handing it to Alyssa, who reaches her hand out for it automatically.

Is this a normal girl thing? Holding your friend's purse while they take pictures?

Shayna comes out of nowhere, taking both our cappuccinos.

Seriously, is there some kind of friend assembly line I don't know about?

Kelsey holds a phone up as Mallory drags me in front of the tree.

"What pose do you want this time?" she asks. "You mentioned a kiss on the cheek, but our height difference may be a hindrance. We don't want you looking like the Hunchback of Louisville."

"I can fix that." I bend down, wrapping my arms around her legs, under her butt, and lifting her into the air with ease.

"What are you doing?" Her voice is breathless.

"Getting rid of the height difference." I smile as she scowls at me. "Now, maybe keep one of your legs straight and pop the other foot up. And I'll kiss you on the cheek if you want to look at the camera." Leaning my face toward hers, my nose brushes her cheek. "Remember to look like you like me, beautiful."

I close my eyes and press my lips to her cheek in a featherlight kiss. Her skin is cold beneath my lips. I'd spend all night warming it up with a thousand kisses if she were really mine.

"Okay, I got some good shots." Kelsey's voice breaks me out of the moment.

I blink, opening my eyes to find Mallory looking at me like I'm a puzzle she's trying to put together without the picture on the box—not impossible to solve, but harder to do without the full picture.

I don't realize I'm just standing there staring at her until she presses her lips into a firm line. "Can you put me down?"

"Right." I carefully set her back on her feet. "Sorry."

Kelsey sends us the pictures, and I immediately select my favorite.

"Mind if I post this one?" I show it to Mallory, and she nods.

"That's fine."

I do a few small edits to lighten the photo and type up a quick caption: *The only present I want under the tree this year.*

I tag Mallory as a collaborator on the post and press the share button, which she quickly accepts. "You might need to be the one to post the next picture. You could even do a story tonight, holding your drink with me in the background or something. We don't want the relationship to look too one-sided."

"You're probably right." She slides her purse back on while I grab our drinks from Shayna. I hand Mallory hers and take a long drag of mine.

She pulls her phone back out, holding her drink out in front of her. "Say cappuccino."

"Cappuccino." I smile.

"What kind of words do people put on their stories?" She blushes. "Does that make me sound like a total social media newbie?"

"It's refreshing." I step behind her, looking at the photo over her shoulder. Even though the focus is on the cup in the photo, the way I feel about her is written all over my face. My stupid, lopsided, dopey grin that only she seems to pull out of me is plastered on my face, and my eyes are squinty but bright, filled with adoration for this woman.

I clear my throat. "People handle stories a lot of different ways, but you can tag my username in it, if you'd like, and put emojis or a few words on it."

She bites her bottom lip while typing for a minute. "How's this?" Mallory hands me her phone while she sips on her drink.

In the bottom right corner of the screen, she added the words *I only have ice for you*, followed by the eyes emoji.

My hopeless romantic heart pounds in my chest. The little traitor. "That's perfect. Very punny."

"I thought you'd like it. Seemed like it matched the lovesick expression you were going for."

I'm not sure whether to celebrate or feel devastated by the fact that she thinks I'm acting. Is that why she's seemed so confused since I ran into her again?

"Posted." She looks up at me with a small smile. "My first story."

"Congratulations, you've officially graduated from social media school." I glance over at the carolers as they begin to sing "Joy to the World." I cock my head. "That's my favorite carol."

Mallory's eyes light up as she takes on a nostalgic look. "Mine, too." With a sigh, she grabs my hand and pulls me toward them. "Come on before I change my mind, Mr. Razzle-Dazzle."

Under the glow of the Christmas tree lights, singing my favorite carol with the woman I'm head over heels for right beside me, I've never felt happier.

I can't think about the idea that she may never come around without feeling a deep pain in my chest. Plus, I'm sure the media would have a field day if a leading man in Hollywood couldn't even land his dream girl. But I'd rather every tabloid talk about me being forever alone than be with anyone else. Because no one would ever match up to Mallory.

CHAPTER SIXTEEN

MALLORY

"Mama, I want to look like Elsa!" Evie declares, pointing at a face-painting booth.

"I can take her," Griffin volunteers, then looks between me and Tess. "That is, if it's all right with both of you. You can have some girl time since Tyler's off getting more snacks."

"If you don't mind, that would be great," Tess says.

I gesture toward the booth. "Be my guest."

"That's the wrong Disney movie," he teases.

I roll my eyes. "You'd better go before she starts singing 'Let It Go.'"

He picks up a squealing Evie and heads toward the booth, leaving me alone with my girls.

"Okay, he's perfect for you." Shayna grins ear to ear while everyone else nods in agreement.

My mouth falls open, aghast at what I'm hearing from my so-called best friends. "You can't seriously like him."

"He looks at you like you're the only girl he sees, Mal. I'd give anything for a man to look at *me* like that." Shayna's demeanor softens as she takes in my frown. "I know he hurt you, but don't you think people can change? Or that we mistook them in the first place?"

I shut my gaping mouth. That may be a valid point. I've never asked Griffin about his answers in that interview. Maybe there's a reason he responded the way he did.

Kelsey gets that dreamy look she always has when thinking of Tyler. "Take it from me that first impressions aren't always everything."

"He explained the whole ghosting thing and said he's been looking for you ever since," Alyssa says.

"And he's been looking at you like a lovesick teenager all night," Tess adds.

"Yes, but—"

Kelsey shrugs. "It sounds to me like you have a man who's been looking for you for years because he still wants you. You're just scared to let him in again and potentially get hurt."

Shayna pulls me in for a side hug. "We're always on your side, Mal. We're your best friends, your ride or dies…which is why we're telling you the truth."

Alyssa points at Griffin across the way. I follow her finger to find him already looking at me with a smile.

"See." Alyssa slaps her hand on her hip. "He might be an actor, Mal. But you can't fake the way he's constantly searching for you in the crowd or the way he smiles when he sees you."

"Yeah, he doesn't have that lopsided, infatuated smile when he looks at Brittany Clearwater's character in the movie," Tess agrees.

"Trust me when I say that I was firmly on the *mad at Griffin* train." Kelsey grabs my arms. "Heck, I was the one driving it for you. But after seeing him here with you tonight, I see why you liked him so much after meeting him. And I liked seeing the old Mallory again."

I blink. "What old Mallory?"

"The one who wasn't hardened to love," Alyssa answers while Kelsey, Tess, and Shayna nod in agreement.

"I'm not hardened to love," I argue. "It's just that no guy has ever liked me enough to choose me."

"Because you've never let them in." Alyssa's voice is quiet, like she's trying not to spook or hurt me.

"Not since Griffin broke your heart." Kelsey squeezes my upper arms, and I'm glad for it because I feel otherwise numb.

Have I really closed myself off from relationships? Once I graduated and accepted my teaching job, I always told myself that trying to date would add too much to my plate. Well, that and the guys on the apps were *not* it. I'm glad they work out for some people, but I don't fall into that category.

And I'm always so tired after I get home from school that I never dive into any other activities that I used to love, like ice skating. So, I never had any opportunities to meet a man the old-fashioned way. And I'd *never* date another teacher from my school. That would be way too much of an HR nightmare when things eventually fizzled out.

But what if my friends are right? Could all of Griffin's flirting, heated looks, and lingering touches be real? What if *I'm* the reason that I never date? My mind roams back to a memory from just a few months ago, when a man let me go ahead of him in the check-out line at the grocery store when I had way more things in my cart than he did. Then there was the guy at the coffee shop I kept making eye contact with over my laptop when I worked on my lesson plans.

They're right. I've been blind all along.

Well, all along post-Griffin.

"Did a good old dose of reality just smack you in the face?" Kelsey teases.

"Yeah, I guess you could say that," I croak. Feeling parched, I take a sip of my cappuccino. I think coffee actually dehydrates you, but it's the best I've got at the moment.

I thought I was over Griffin, but when I saw his face on our television screen a few months ago, I was hit with a Mack truck of feelings. I told myself that it was feelings of loathing, but if I'm being honest, it was feelings of attraction. Desire.

All the things I wanted with him, but never thought I'd have.

Would he hurt me again if I let him back in? All the signs in my brain are still screaming yes as his interview answers play in my mind on repeat.

"Okay, let's pretend for a minute that he's not acting," I say. All my friends nod like this is already obvious. "Then how do you explain this?" I pull my phone out of my purse and select the interview from my recently viewed videos before handing it to them.

They lean their heads in close, listening intently. Once the video is done, they hand back my phone.

"Well?" I ask.

Shayna's eyes are full of sympathy. "Are you upset he didn't mention your first date as the best one he's ever been on?"

"Yeah. How can you tell me he's not acting when he obviously wasn't thinking of me then?"

"Have you asked Griffin why he didn't mention you?" Kelsey squeezes my arm.

"Nope." I purse my lips. "Honestly, I think it made me too angry to think rationally when I saw him again."

"You should talk to him about it," Tess encourages. "Maybe his answer will surprise you."

Deep down, a part of me hopes that there's an explanation for what Griffin said, but if that's the case, then I'm even more terrified to let myself feel for this man a second time.

I lean into Kelsey's hold on my arm, feeling weak in the knees. She leads me over to a wooden bench. I sit, and my friends plop down on either side of me while Kelsey squats in front of me, rubbing my arms.

I'm about to tell them how right they are and thank them for their tough love when Griffin jogs over, sliding to a stop in front of us. Kelsey quickly steps out of the way, and Griffin kneels on one knee before me. I know he's not proposing. But my stupid heart doesn't. It pounds in my chest, and everything feels hazy as I look into Griffin's worried gaze.

"I saw your friends practically carry you over here." His words come out breathless and worried. He gently frames my face, then runs his hands down my neck, arms, and legs before settling them on my knees. The graze of his fingers along my body leaves a trail of raised hairs. I bite my bottom lip to keep from gasping.

"Are you okay? Do I need to take you to the doctor?"

"Just a little dehydrated, I think." I push to stand, but my legs give out.

Griffin wraps his arms around me. "I've got you."

Not only does he have me…he sweeps me off my feet, effectively sucking all the air from my lungs.

"Let's get you home, beautiful," he murmurs in my ear. Turning to my friends, he says, "Would you ladies please lead me to whatever car you drove here?"

I glance at them, seeing excitement written all over their faces from their wide eyes to gleaming smiles.

"Of course," Shayna squeaks, stepping in front of him. "I drove."

As she leads him to the parking lot, I look back at my other friends over Griffin's shoulder. Alyssa, Kelsey, and Tess are whispering behind us, looking thrilled. When they see me looking, they pump their fists in the air and mime a mixture of gestures from fireworks and giant muscles to making out. I roll my eyes and try to calm my racing heart. He's carrying me to the car. Nothing else.

While I might be ready to admit that I'm still attracted to Griffin, I'm not sure that I'm open to a future with him in it. Not when the whole purpose of this fake-dating contract is for him to get his dream movie role—one that will have him leaving for LA before we'd ever have the opportunity to explore *whatever this is* between us.

He sets me in the backseat of Shayna's car, Daisy Mae—affectionately named after one of her favorite Taylor Swift songs. "I can find you a water bottle before you drive home."

"I'll be okay. Thanks, though." I don't meet his gaze, knowing that if I look at him right now and see concern written all over his face—concern for *me*—that I might very well give in and kiss him. I can't let that happen, not when I still have questions I need him to answer.

He's quiet for so long that I finally glance up at him. Griffin is staring at me, his blue eyes soft but searching, as if he can feel the shift. As if he can see my attraction to him building and my walls slowly falling. That I finally believe this may not have been an act.

The hope, excitement, and uncertainty I feel are all reflected in his gaze. It makes me feel seen and known without sharing any words, reminding me of how I felt on our first date. Like there's a connection between us that supersedes anything I've ever known. I don't know how long we sit there like that, lost in each other's gazes, before Shayna clears her throat.

"We should probably get Mal home so she can rest," she says.

Reluctantly, his eyes leave mine, and he smiles softly at my friends. "Right." Griffin leans back in the car and presses a kiss to my forehead. "Please don't hesitate to call if you need anything tonight."

"She won't." Tess wiggles her eyebrows.

Once he's a few paces away, my friends bounce excitedly.

"He's in love with you," Alyssa squeals.

"Totally," Kelsey and Tess say at the same time.

"Did you see the way he went all broody, scooping her up in his arms like he was in an action movie and saving the woman he loves from all the falling buildings around them?" Shayna lets out a dreamy sigh, leaning against her car.

"What are you going to do, Mal?" Tess asks, looking at me knowingly. Since Kelsey started dating Tess's brother, she's become the perfect addition to our friend group, fitting in seamlessly like the puzzle piece we didn't know we were missing.

"You looked like you were about to kiss each other like the world was ending." Alyssa fans herself with her hand.

"I felt like I was watching a romance movie play out right in front of me." Shayna giggles.

I'd be lying if I didn't feel the same way. I felt more flutters in my stomach from Griffin's eye contact alone than I've ever felt kissing another man. The only thing that beat that feeling was my first kiss with Griffin.

"I should go save my brother before Evie starts asking him where babies come from." Tess blows us a kiss goodbye.

The rest of my friends pile into Daisy Mae.

"When are you going to see him next?" Alyssa shakes her shoulders and makes a kissy face.

I shove her arm. "Probably not until Christmas Eve at my parents' house."

"He's coming to your house for Christmas?" They squeal again like a horde of schoolgirls at a boy band concert.

"Did I not tell y'all that?" I hum.

"You certainly did *not*." Shayna frowns—as much as the epitome of sunshine can frown—at me in the rearview mirror.

"Oh, this is about to be good." Kelsey turns in the passenger seat, grinning at me.

Once I've talked to Griffin about the interview, I think it might be time to see if the sparks are still there because they were definitely buzzing between us tonight.

If I still feel them, then I think it'll be just like Kelsey said: the story of us is about to get good.

———— ♡ ♡ ♡ ————

If the snow falling outside is any indication of how today will go, I'm hopeful for a peaceful day. A fresh start.

But I agreed to spend today with Griffin, so my anxious anticipation to see him doesn't leave me feeling very peaceful.

I had told myself I wouldn't see him again until the Christmas celebrations at my parents' house. However, Griffin made it impossible to deny his request to see me today. He wants to find his granny a small tree from the local lot for her to have in her facility. Once my mom learned what we were doing, she gave me all her extra Christmas decorations so we could jazz up the space.

I'd be lying if I said I wasn't scared to see his granny again—to *lie* to her. But Griffin said he couldn't put her off any longer. Turns out, she's been asking to see me again since the day our faces appeared in the tabloids. And I may be stubborn about many things, but I'd never deny her wishes to see her grandson happy, even if she doesn't know that it's not entirely real.

At least, not yet.

I glance outside just as Griffin's driver, Ted, drops him off. He offered to have Ted chauffeur us, but I told him that wasn't necessary.

Looking around, I let out a relieved sigh. It doesn't look like there are any paparazzi here today, thanks to the security team that has been coming by our property around the clock.

I walk outside to greet Griffin. He opens his arms like he's about to go in for a hug. As I'm about to step into his embrace, he must think better of the idea and extends his hand my way.

This results in an awkward embrace where I have my arms around him, and his hand is poking my stomach.

He jumps back. "Ah, sorry. I don't know what I just did."

"Don't mention it." I shove my hands in my pockets, realizing I forgot my gloves. "Shoot, I need to run back inside. Will you get her warming up?" I pull my car key from my key fob and toss it to him.

"Aye aye, Captain." He salutes me before slowly shutting his eyes and shaking his head.

I hear him muttering to himself as I head into the house and grab my gloves and earmuffs off the coffee table where I left them. Winston runs over to me, excited that I've already returned.

"Sorry, boy." I grimace. "I'll give you a big treat later when Kelsey isn't looking."

I walk outside, locking the door behind me. I notice Griffin is in the driver's seat, so I head to the passenger side. I've barely opened the door when I hear Griffin talking to my car.

"You've got this, Linda, girl." He rubs his hand across the dashboard. "It's just a little drive across the city. Don't let the snow bother you."

"What are you doing?" I sputter, sliding into the passenger seat, shocked to find him sweet-talking my vehicle.

He blushes, leaning back in his seat. "You said Linda hates the snow, so I was giving her a pep talk."

"You remember that?" I can't believe that he remembers something I casually mentioned in passing years ago.

Griffin's eyes never leave mine as he says, "I remember everything about you, Mallory."

I decide to test my friends' observations from the Winter Market. "No one is around, Griffin. You don't have to act."

"What if I said that I wasn't acting?"

I take a deep breath, mustering all my courage. "Then I think there's a bigger conversation we need to have soon."

He smiles, reaching across the center console and squeezing my hand. "I'd love that."

Not ready to have that conversation yet, I say, "You don't mind driving Linda?"

"Nope, you get to be my passenger princess today." He leans over, his mouth a breath away from mine.

My whole body buzzes with awareness.

He's about to kiss me. My head leans forward of its own accord, like my lips can't help but be drawn to him. Except Griffin *doesn't* kiss me. He reaches around me and grabs my seatbelt, pulling it ever so slowly across my body. I never knew buckling up could be so sexy.

Once he's clicked my seatbelt in place, Griffin smiles at me, looking pleased with himself. "Safety first."

As Kelsey would say, for the love of biscuits. Now this man has my own body betraying me.

If he keeps doing things like this, I've got no chance of surviving this 'fake' relationship without falling for him.

CHAPTER SEVENTEEN
GRIFFIN

"WE HAVE QUITE THE pick of the litter." Mirth dances in Mallory's eyes.

I look from her to the three trees remaining on the lot. They've seen better days. Two are probably around six feet tall with patches of missing branches. The third is barely half my height, with only five branches total. I'm pretty sure I just watched multiple pine needles fall off it.

"I should've known this is all that would be left two days before Christmas Eve." I rub my chin. I've failed my granny. None of these will do much to spruce up her room. They might even make it worse. A blue Christmas, indeed.

"Did you end up checking with her facility to make sure we can bring a live tree?"

"Yeah, it just has to be under seven feet, but I don't think we'll have an issue there." I gesture to the meager selection.

Mallory moves forward, walking between the trees as if assessing the value. She finally stops beside the little one. "I think this one will be perfect for your granny's facility."

"Right." My laugh is dry. I step closer, examining the other two trees, trying to decide which one is the least damaged.

"I'm serious." Mallory grabs my arm, pulling me to her side. The small motion doesn't go unnoticed. Something changed in Mallory after I carried her to Shayna's car at the Winter Market. It might have been my eyes playing a cruel trick on me, but it looked like she wanted me to kiss her in the car before we came here. And when she said she wanted to talk soon, after I said that I wasn't acting…well, let's just say I hope we can have that conversation *very* soon.

"It's a little Charlie Brown tree, neglected by everyone else. It deserves a good home for Christmas, too." She shrugs. "Plus, it's small, so it should fit well in her room."

She's not wrong. A large tree would take up the majority of Granny's living space.

"As long as you think we can make it look full of cheer." I look at her and she nods, so I raise my hand to draw the attention of the lot attendant. I didn't think that would be hard to do when we're the only people here…with three trees. But I could've had all of them loaded and strapped down atop Mallory's car in the time it takes him to walk over to us. This teenager likely hates his job, but I can't blame him. I wouldn't want to be working here while on winter break either.

When he reaches us, the boy sounds bored as he asks, "How can I help you?"

"We'll take this one." I gesture to the small tree.

"That one?" The boy's mouth falls open. "You sure?" When I nod, he laughs. "Just take it. My parents would kill me if I made you pay for it."

"What do you normally charge per tree?"

"Usually ten dollars per foot, but it'd feel wrong taking thirty for that."

I reach into my pocket, grab my wallet, and pull out three hundred dollars. "I think this should more than cover all three trees so you can go home and spend time with your family."

The boy's entire demeanor changes. He lights up brighter than the star atop the tree downtown. "Really?"

"Absolutely." I give him the bills. "On one condition."

"Anything." He bounces on the balls of his feet.

"You drop the other two trees off somewhere they can bring joy to someone. A homeless shelter. A nursing home. Anywhere you can think of."

The boy salutes me. "Yes, sir. Thank you." He shoves the bills in his pocket and moves with purpose, strapping down the little tree to the top of Mallory's car. It looks ridiculous—such a small tree atop a big car—when it could've easily fit in her trunk, but I'm not going to deny the kid his job.

Mallory sidles up next to me, fisting her hands on her hips. "You don't have to give money away to impress me."

"When I've been blessed, it only seems right to give to others." I kick the gravel in the lot. Realizing what she said earlier, I smile at her. "Did you say that you're *impressed* with me?"

"Did I?" A winter breeze hits, and she smooths back her curls.

I wrap my arms around her, surprised when she returns the embrace. "I like it when you talk sweet to me."

She pats my chest. "Don't get used to it."

Can she feel the rapid racing of my heart beneath her fingertips? I wonder what her reaction would be if she knew it beat that way for *her*.

Always her.

Only her.

"I wouldn't dare." My lips tilt into a smile.

Mallory's eyes dart to my lips before dragging back up to mine. She's looking at me like she did at the Winter Market and in the car. I almost kissed her both times, but I promised myself I'd let her make the first move. I'm not going to scare her away again, but keeping that promise is extremely difficult when she's looking at my lips like *that*.

I lower my head closer to hers. Our noses brush, and I—

The boy clears his throat, and we jump apart like two teenagers caught dancing too close together at homecoming. "Sorry to interrupt, but you're all loaded up."

"Thanks." I give him a forced smile. It's not his fault that I completely messed up the best thing that ever happened to me three years ago, and now that I'm finally getting the opportunity to make up for it, he interrupted a potential kiss.

"You ready?" I look at Mallory.

Her cheeks match the pink of her coat. "Yeah, let's go."

We walk to the car, and I open the passenger door for her.

"Thanks again," the boy calls after us, waving the bills I gave him in the air. "Merry Christmas!"

I give him a two-finger wave back before getting in the driver's seat.

"Are you ready to deck the halls?" I wiggle my eyebrows, a smirk plastered on my face, thinking I'm hilarious for bringing up the carol she was singing when I first laid eyes on her.

The sound of her laughter floating through the car is an instant serotonin boost.

When we arrive at the rehabilitation facility, I still haven't been able to wipe the smile from my face.

I walk into the building, one hand intertwined with Mallory's, the other carrying the tree.

"Hi, Stella." I wave to the receptionist in the lobby with my tree-filled hand.

She raises a brow, but waves back. "Good to see you, Mr. Reynolds."

We continue down the hall a ways until I gesture with our joined hands to a door. "That's it, Room 1104."

Mallory knocks on it for us.

"Come in," Granny yells from the other side.

Mallory opens the door, allowing me to enter the room first.

"Hi, Granny." She's wearing her Sunday best, a deep-purple dress with a pearl necklace. I help her out of the recliner, pulling her into a hug.

"Griffie, I told you that you didn't need to decorate my room. I'm happy just to have you here." She looks past me and smiles at Mallory, reaching out to her. "And I'm *very* happy to see you again."

"Since you were never formally introduced, Granny, this is Mallory," I say.

Mallory immediately steps forward, embracing my granny. Seeing the two of them together, and especially seeing Granny so happy, has tears threatening to rise to the surface. I swallow, emotion thick in my throat. Trying to lighten the mood, I say, "We wanted to go for a less sterile look, more holiday spirit."

While the rehab facility I have her in does a wonderful job of decorating their common areas for the holidays, Granny's room is whites and grays. I've been too preoccupied this past week to decorate it for her. Even though Christmas is only a few days away, it's never too late to liven up the space. Plus, Granny usually insists on leaving Christmas decor up until mid-January, so she'll have a few weeks to enjoy it.

"I have to go grab the box of decorations from the car." I look between them. "Will you two be okay here by yourself for a minute?"

"Of course." Granny sits back down with Mallory's assistance.

"We're going to be two peas in a pod by the time you return." Mallory smiles up at me, tossing me her car keys.

"Be right back." I make my way back to the car, grabbing the box Mallory brought. I can't get over how thoughtful it was of her to bring decorations for Granny's room. It will look a lot better with all this stuff rather than just the bare tree.

Mallory and Granny are laughing like old friends when I make it back to the room.

"What are you two talking about?" I ask.

"Oh, nothing," Mallory says. "Just girl stuff."

Granny grins. "I love this one, Griffie."

"So do I." I look right at Mallory as the words spill out of my mouth, like they can't be contained any longer. When I realize I practically just told Mallory I love her, the box of decorations slips from my hands, dropping to the floor with a loud thunk. Some jingle bells shake with the movement. I turn awkwardly in a half circle, moving my arms in strange motions that feel completely disconnected from my body.

What. Is. Wrong. With. Me?

Oh, right. I just accidentally told Mallory that I love her.

I glance at her and find her shoulders shaking lightly in laughter. Of course, she finds this funny. But I do spot a hint of pink in her cheeks, which gives me hope for the conversation she wants to have soon.

Granny watches us with a knowing smile. I'm pretty sure spotting love matches is her superpower. Maybe she missed her calling as a matchmaker, or maybe it's just the magic of

Lover's Grove running in her veins. But even if Granny didn't think we were dating, I know she would see my feelings for Mallory written all over my face.

"If I could walk on my own, I'd give you two the room." She winks at Mallory, whose blush deepens.

"Granny," I chide.

"What?" She holds her hand to her chest, feigning nonchalance. "I might be old, but I still remember what it's like to be in that honeymoon phase of a relationship. I bet you can't keep your hands off one another."

I shake my head, ignoring her remarks. You can always count on kids and the elderly to be honest. "Let's decorate, shall we?" I open the box, pull out the tree base, and get that set up with water. Mallory pulls out the garland and strings it around the room.

"Where did you get all this?" Granny wrings her hands in her lap. "I'd hate for you to have spent all this money on decorations."

"Her mom, Angie, was kind enough to let you borrow them," I say, shooting Mallory a smile across the room.

Granny places her hands on her cheeks. "I can't wait to thank her properly at Christmas. For this, and for having us join in your family's festivities."

"The more the merrier." Mallory finishes hanging the garland and moves back to the box, grabbing small holiday trinkets. "Would you like these to go anywhere specific?"

"Hmm," Granny muses. "Maybe a few on the table here and the others on my nightstand?"

"You've got it." She places a snowman and reindeer on the table before moving to the other room.

"I love her."

"You already said that." I laugh.

"It's worth saying twice." Granny sighs. "It does my heart a world of good seeing you this happy."

Mallory walks back into the living room, humming "Deck the Halls."

It's been torture knowing that our relationship has been fake to Mallory so far, but these recent changes in her have me hoping that won't be the case much longer.

CHAPTER EIGHTEEN

MALLORY

A MICHAEL BUBLÉ SONG plays over a speaker as I walk through my parents' front door, my arm linked through Granny's. I hold it open for Griffin as he carries in our luggage. His sweater is rolled up to his elbows, giving me a front-row view of the bulging muscles and veins in his forearms.

There must be some scientific reason behind why this man makes everything he does look so attractive. Maybe there's a law of attraction from carrying heavy items that I haven't heard of yet.

"They're here." My mom rounds the corner, heading into the foyer. She pulls Griffin's granny into a hug first. "I'm Angie. We're beyond happy to have you."

"I'm tickled pink to be here and meet Mallory's family." She pulls back, patting my mom's hand. "You can call me Granny. Everyone does."

Introductions are made between her and my dad before he helps her into the living room to sit. On the ride here, Griffin said she's been getting up a little more for her physical therapy, but still needs to be careful not to overdo it.

"Where should I put these?" Griffin lifts the luggage slightly.

"We have your granny staying in our guest room here on the main floor with an attached bathroom." Mom motions down the hallway to the left. "I thought that would be easiest for her after her surgery."

Griffin heads that way to drop off her things, and I'm pulled into my mom's warm embrace.

"Happy Christmas Eve, sweetie."

I return the sentiments, then ask, "What room is Griffin staying in?"

"Yours, of course."

I bite back a groan at the thought of Griffin in my childhood bedroom. "Am I in Connor's room?"

Her brows furrow. "No, Connor's in his room."

"Well, then, where am I staying?

"Your room."

My eyes widen. A big warning alarm in my brain flashes a red alert.

She squeezes my arm. "You don't have to pretend with me, Mal. I know Griffin's not in Louisville for long, so I'm sure you want to spend as much time with him as possible."

I force a smile as Griffin returns, carrying my small suitcase and his duffel bag.

Mom smiles at him. "Mallory can show you to her bedroom, where you can put those down." She winks at me. "Don't take too long up there."

I think I might be sick. Griffin and I haven't been alone in private long enough for me to have a conversation with him about the interview yet...and now I'm being forced to share a room—no, a *bed*—with him? I don't know how I'm going to keep my growing feelings at bay, let alone remain a safe distance away from him, when we're sharing a bed.

I climb the stairs, Griffin trailing behind me.

"What is she talking about?" he asks when we reach the landing.

"I'll tell you in a second," I say shakily, slightly out of breath from both the ascent and the bed-sharing news. Griffin, on the other hand, doesn't seem bothered in the slightest, even though he's the one carrying extra weight.

As I step into my bedroom, I'm transported back to my middle and high school years. Nothing has been touched. Posters of Taylor Swift, One Direction, the Jonas Brothers, Louisville Mustangs players, and the cast of *High School Musical* cover every inch of my walls. The gaps are filled in with taped-up photos of me with my besties or family members.

It's truly like stepping into a frozen moment in time. One where I dreamed of meeting a JoBro, and they would instantly sweep me off my feet and beg for my hand in marriage. Now, I'm living that life in a way—dating a celebrity. Well, fake dating. For now.

I can't bring myself to look at Griffin as he sets down our things and walks around the room, taking it all in. He runs his fingers across the trophy I won for ice skating in middle school, right before I quit at the top of my game. It feels intimate. Like I'm being forced to bare part of my soul to him.

When the silence becomes unbearable, I spit out the words I've been holding in. "We're sleeping in here tonight."

Griffin immediately turns my way. "We, as in you and me? *Together?*" I nod. "Are you okay with that?" He looks around the room. "I can sleep on the floor."

There's no way I'm letting him sleep on the scuffed hardwood floors. "You can't sleep on the floor." I look at the queen-sized bed. "We'll make a pillow wall." I nod my head slowly. "That should work. It'll be fine," I say, more for my benefit than his, as if uttering the words aloud will make them true.

"Yeah." Griffin runs a hand along his stubble. "We'll figure it out."

I take a step toward the door. "We should get downstairs before my mom thinks we're up to no good."

"Why would she think we're up to no good?" Griffin smirks.

"Because she thinks we're a real couple." I pick a piece of fuzz from my coat off my plum sweater, unable to meet his eyes as I add, "Madly in love."

"Well, we wouldn't want them thinking a couple has real feelings for each other," Griffin teases. He joins me by the door, intertwining our fingers.

I roll my eyes, tugging him into the hall. We walk downstairs, passing multiple extended family members, whom we say quick greetings to, until I spot the man I'm looking for in the living room.

"Con Con," I squeal, running over and throwing my arms around my older brother's neck.

He lets out a grunt, and I press my lips together to keep from laughing. He always hates it when I call him that, which is exactly why I still do it.

His blond hair is wild and longer than normal. "You need a haircut." I pull back, taking in his unkempt beard. "And a beard-care kit."

"My hair's fine," he grunts, gruff as ever.

"If by fine, you mean you look like a caveman before mirrors were discovered, then sure, your hair's *fine*."

Griffin snorts behind me.

Connor looks over my shoulder, eyeing him warily. "Who's this?"

I sigh. "Do you ever read the family group chat?"

"Not if I can help it."

"I see bluntness runs in the family," Griffin teases, wrapping one arm around my lower back and extending his right hand to my brother. "I'm Mallory's boyfriend, Griffin Reynolds. Nice to meet you, Connor."

My brother shakes Griffin's hand without an ounce of emotion crossing his face. He releases it immediately and turns to me. "You landed a guy?"

I cross my arms, shooting him a glare.

"It's a Christmas miracle," Connor deadpans.

"I'm the one who was lucky enough to land her." Griffin presses a kiss to my cheek.

The way he says it is so honest that I truly believe him.

My brother frowns as Griffin turns back to him and asks, "Do you live around here?"

"Washington, currently."

"Currently?" I raise my eyebrow.

"Yeah, it's where I live."

"But you wouldn't have felt the need to add the word *currently* if you weren't thinking about moving somewhere else. Isn't that right?"

"You ask a lot of questions."

"Excuse me for caring about my brother's life."

I know Connor cares about our family deep down, but he's always been quieter and more reserved than the rest of us. His grumpiness makes me look like a ray of sunshine, and that's saying something.

"What do you do for work?" Griffin asks, trying to lighten the mood, and I'm grateful for his effort.

"Firefighter."

Yep, there's my brother. Never using more words than necessary.

"That's some hard work right there." Griffin pulls me closer, but I'm not sure he even realizes he's doing it. "I have real respect for anyone in public service."

"Thanks." Connor looks around the room and sighs. "What do you do? Graham, was it?"

"Griffin." He smiles, looking relieved that there's someone in the world who *doesn't* know who he is. "I'm, uh, actually an actor." He rubs the back of his neck, surprisingly bashful. But I guess he doesn't often have to tell people what he does. He probably just takes pictures with people and thanks them when they say that they loved his latest movie.

"Huh." My brother doesn't say anything else.

I'm surprised he even seemed interested enough to ask Griffin a question. Although when he looked around the room, he was probably trying to find somewhere he could escape and avoid all conversations, but my parents' house is filled to the brim with family members.

"You seriously haven't seen any of the news articles about us?" I scoff. "I even made a social media account. I followed you."

Connor shakes his head. "I haven't logged into my account in years. And I don't get out much."

"What do you do with all your free time out there by yourself?"

"Sleep. Take a walk. Enjoy the peace and quiet."

"Have you done any good fishing out in Washington?" Griffin, bless his heart, attempts to carry on the very one-sided conversation.

"A bit."

"I fish as often as I can with my friend Rhett. He lives on a lake near Nashville. You're welcome anytime."

"Rhett?" My eyes fly to him. "As in the famous country singer Rhett Hayes?"

"Yeah, I didn't tell you that he's my best friend? He's dying to meet you."

"Rhett Hayes knows who *I* am?"

"Why do you keep referring to him by his full name?"

"Because he's *Rhett Hayes*."

Griffin cocks a brow. "I guess you're a fan?"

"We listen to his music a lot in our house. I mean, not as much as Taylor, but his songs are great."

"I bet you know all of Taylor's lyrics by heart, too." Griffin claps my brother on the shoulder.

"All the dances she and her friends made me watch are seared into my brain."

"Rude," I scoff. "Our routines were *amazing*."

Connor's mouth presses into a firm line as arms wrap around my middle from behind. They're little, and decidedly not Griffin's.

I turn, causing Griffin to release his hold on me, and smile when I see my cousin, Emmy. Her long curly red hair bounces as she envelops me in a tight hug. The curls run on my mother's side of the family, but while mine are more like uncontrollable waves that take on a different look every day, Emmy's are perfect ringlets. While she's only two years younger than me, she still has that youthful look and spirit about her—the spitting image of a Disney princess.

Even if we weren't family by blood, I'd choose her as mine, along with my besties.

Emmy pulls back, looking at me wide-eyed, gesturing her head to the side at Griffin. "Are you going to introduce me to your totally famous *boyfriend*?"

Connor must take our cousin's arrival as his exit cue, walking away without a glance back.

"Emmy," I say dramatically. "This is my…" She already called him my boyfriend, so it feels redundant to repeat it. But it's not like I'm about to call him the love of my life, so I change course. "Griffin."

"Hello, *her* Griffin," Emmy jests.

Griffin smiles the lopsided grin I'm coming to know like the back of my hand and pulls my cousin in for a hug. "It's a pleasure to meet you, Emmy."

A blush covers her cheeks. She looks at me and fans her face, mouthing *he's so cute.*

I know, I mouth back. My attraction to Griffin has never been the issue.

They pull back, and he turns his smile on me like he knows what we're talking about, even though there was no way for him to see with his back to me. Unless he grew another pair of eyes on the back of his head that I don't know about.

I narrow my eyes slightly, but I can't help the smile that tugs at my lips. "What?"

"I'm happy to be here with you." He smiles at me, then Emmy. "And meeting all your family. Everyone's been so welcoming." Shaking his head, he adds, "Well, maybe not your brother, but we'll work on it."

"Oh, don't be offended." Emmy waves him off. "That's how he is to everyone. I don't even need one hand to count the number of times I've seen him smile."

"She's not wrong."

Connor's always been stoic and reserved, even since he was a child.

"Emmy." My aunt waves my cousin over. "Come tell Griffin's grandmother about your time in Italy. She says it's her favorite place she's ever visited."

"Sounds like I'm being summoned." She tilts her head. "It was nice meeting you, Griffin." Looking at me pointedly, she says, "We'll talk more about *this* later."

"What was that about?" Griffin asks once she walks away.

"Hmm?"

"You know your thoughts are written all over your face, right?" He grabs my waist, tugging me closer.

My eyes move to his lips like they have their own brain that can only think about kissing Griffin Reynolds. I drag them back up to meet his. "No, they're not," I argue and take a deep breath, attempting to school my features.

"You think I'm insanely handsome." Griffin leans in, pressing a kiss to my cheek. The note of cinnamon on his breath is intoxicating. "Just admit it, beautiful."

I use every bit of willpower not to melt at the press of his lips to my skin, even though it stokes the fire burning inside me. Attraction. It's just attraction. I need to wait until I talk things through with him before I consider kissing him again.

My voice is somehow steady as I say, "And why would I do that?"

"We've always been honest with each other. There's no use lying now."

"And what makes you think I'm lying?" I stare up at him, trying to look more confident than I feel. If he's saying we've always been honest with each other, there might really be an explanation for everything. He may be a good actor, but this feels different.

"I could call it a hunch." He takes a step toward me. "But since we're honest, your dilated pupils and the way your eyes keep darting to my mouth tell me otherwise." Griffin's eyes drop to my lips. Although our mouths are inches apart,

I can feel the ghost of his touch run across my lips with the heated way he's looking at me.

"Fine." I press onto my tiptoes, my mouth by his ear so my words won't be overheard. "I think you're handsome, but we still need to talk before I can think about trusting you."

Griffin's eyes fill with hope. "I can work with that."

"Just be patient with me."

He presses a kiss to my forehead, lingering there for longer than necessary, as if he can't pull himself away. "Patient is my middle name."

I take a step back and clear my throat uncomfortably as I notice multiple family members around the room staring at us intently. "What's your *actual* middle name?"

"Whoa, you're crossing the line." He holds up his hands. "That's way too personal a question."

I roll my eyes. "You know my middle name. It's only fair."

"Okay, but you can't make fun of me." He eyes me until I agree.

"Yes, I won't make fun of you."

"It's...Bartholomew." The way he says it makes it sound as if his middle name is something super out there, like Broccoli.

"Griffin Bartholomew Razzle-Dazzle Reynolds," I repeat.

He shakes his head, smiling. "It's a family name. Although I don't plan on continuing the tradition if I ever have a son."

"Maybe you could continue the Razzle-Dazzle name instead," I suggest, trying to maintain a neutral expression.

"Mm-hmm." Griffin grabs the dips of my waist and squeezes.

A giggle slips past my lips. "You don't play fair," I gasp.

"Who says I'm playing at all?" His voice is husky as his eyes seek mine. They look soft and inviting, but they're an invitation I can't accept. Not yet. And especially not in a crowded room full of my family members.

I glance away, searching for an out. When I make eye contact with my mom, she waves me over. "Mallory, can you help get out the appetizers?"

"Be right there." I take a step back from Griffin.

His hands fall to his sides, hanging loose and lifeless, like they have no purpose if they're not touching me. "I can help."

I shake my head adamantly. "You should check on your granny."

"Is that what you want?" He meets my gaze again, asking—no, begging—me to change my mind.

Is being apart from him what I want? No. I want to be in his arms again. I want his hands in my hair, tugging me closer until my mouth meets his. But I can't. Distance is good. Distance is *safe* until we're able to talk things through.

CHAPTER NINETEEN
GRIFFIN

THE CHRISTMAS EVE CELEBRATION with Mallory's family feels natural. They don't just make me feel included—they make me feel like I'm one of them. Aside from a few of the women in her family blushing or making a comment about how they loved my movie, I feel like a normal person here. Just like I do at my family gatherings.

It's refreshing to have little bubbles of space where I'm not Griffin Reynolds the movie star, but just Griffin Reynolds the boy from Lover's Grove, Tennessee.

A smile forms on my lips as I look at Granny sitting in a recliner, reading 'Twas the Night Before Christmas. All the young children in Mallory's family sit around her on the floor, listening to the story with wide-eyed wonder.

"Merry Christmas to all, and to all a good night." Granny finishes the last line and closes the book. All the kids groan as their parents pull them into their arms.

"It's time to go to bed so Santa can come," Mallory's cousin says to his crying child.

Once all of her extended family has said their goodbyes and left, I walk over to the recliner, helping Granny up.

"Thank you for the honor of allowing me to read it." Granny smiles at Mallory's mom.

"We're so happy to have y'all here and partaking in our family traditions." Angie squeezes Granny's hand.

"I'm going to make sure she gets situated in her room, then I'll meet you upstairs," I say to Mallory, hoping she understands I'm giving her time to get ready for bed without me in there.

"Sounds good. Good night, Granny." She gives her a quick kiss on the cheek before heading upstairs.

"Night, man," I say to Connor, who lifts a hand in return before trudging up the stairs.

"Don't mind him." Angie shakes her head. "I hope you sleep well."

"You too." I smile at her and Todd. "Thank you both for having us. Your hospitality doesn't go unnoticed."

Angie blushes at my words while Todd ushers her upstairs. "Come on, darling. We have an early morning ahead of us."

I help Granny into her room, get her flannel nightgown and toiletries bag out of her suitcase, and hand them to her.

"Thanks, Griffie." She pats my arm.

"Do you need help, uh—" How does one ask their grandmother if they need help undressing and putting on their pajamas without sounding weird?

"I can take off and put on clothes by myself, thank you very much."

"Thank you, rehab," I tease.

Granny wags her finger at me. "Get out of here before you see something you can't unsee."

She doesn't need to tell me twice. I take a step back, running into the door and making her giggle. "Good night." I leave the room and shut the door behind me before jogging up the stairs. When I reach Mallory's room, I knock quietly, hoping her parents or brother won't hear. "You good, Mal?"

"Yeah, you can come in."

I gently open the door, letting myself inside. When I turn around, Mallory is standing on the opposite side of the room beside the bed, staring at me.

I take a tentative step toward her. "You okay, beautiful?"

She sucks in a deep breath, slowly releasing it through her mouth. "Since we're being honest, I'm terrified."

"Of what?" I look around, walking over to her wall of posters. "Me learning about your obsession with the Louisville Mustangs? I'm a die-hard fan of the Knoxville Fireflies, so I guess that makes us rivals."

"I know." The sadness in her tone has me questioning my playfulness.

"Hey, I'm sorry." I cross the room and place my hands on her arms. "I didn't mean to make light of things. What are you scared of, beautiful?"

"Talking about baseball."

That's not what I expected her to say. "We can talk about something else."

Mallory shakes her head. "Can we sit down?"

Oh. This is *that* conversation. The one she mentioned wanting to have with me. I nod, and she leads me over to the bed. Once we're sitting, she lets out a weary sigh. "I need to ask you about an interview you did after your first movie."

I try to think back to that time in my life. I participated in countless interviews, but none that stand out. "You're going to have to be a little more specific."

"Does one with Kelly Parker jog your memory?"

I close my eyes for a moment, digging through the interviews of my past until the right one pops up. "Yeah, that was one of the first ones I ever did. She was nice, but asked too many personal questions."

Mallory looks down at her joined hands. Her eyes glitter with unshed tears as she meets my gaze. "Like asking you what the best date you've ever been on was?"

My heart races. "I said something that hurt you, didn't I?" She nods.

I think back, my mind racing as I replay that interview in my head until the answer hits me. I feel like a complete jerk. No wonder Mallory wanted nothing to do with me when she saw me again in that coffee shop.

I take her hands in mine. "Mal, the baseball game wasn't the best date of my life. Ours was."

A single tear drops onto her cheek, and I wipe it away with my thumb. "Then why didn't you say that?"

I move my hands to my lap, clenching them into fists, hating myself that I made her feel this way when she's never second best. "I had just landed my agent and gone through media training. She told me to never get too personal in interviews if I didn't want the entire world knowing everything about me. Especially the private details of my love life." The words tumble out of my mouth like they can't come out fast enough. I want her to believe me more than I've ever wanted anything in my life. "The baseball game I was referring to wasn't even a date, unless you consider going to a game with Rhett a bro-date." I take her hand in mine. "The only date that has ever mattered to me is the one I had with you. You're the only girl that matters to me. Although I couldn't really say that in the interview either without the media having a field day looking for you. That wasn't how I wanted to find you again. I didn't want to pull you into my world unless you chose to be in it." I press my lips into a firm line. "But I guess that ended up happening anyway."

Mallory squeezes my hands as a few more tears drip down her cheeks. "After I thought you'd ghosted me, I saw that interview. To me, it was always the validation I needed that I never meant anything to you. That our date was you just acting, preparing for your audition."

Emotion stings my eyes. "I'm sorry I ever made you question that." With a shaky breath, I say, "I still don't know how you feel about my world and what that could look like. But I'd proudly walk any red carpet with you, if you decide you could see a future with me." I move my hands to cup her face. Looking directly into her hot chocolate-colored eyes, I say, "You are *everything* to me. Ever since I dropped that change into your drink, I didn't stand a chance."

She smiles softly. "I believe you."

I pull her into my arms, pressing a kiss to her temple before holding on tightly because I never plan on letting her go again. "Thank you for asking and hearing me out. And for agreeing to fake date me when you must've thought I was a real jerk."

Mallory pulls back, wiping the tears from her cheeks. "I did, but that's in the past now."

"Now that we've cleared up the fact that all of my feelings for you are—and have always been—real, does this mean I can take you on a date?"

"I'd like that." She smiles. "But maybe an at-home date? One where we can talk and not be bombarded by fans or paparazzi?"

"Sold." I glance at the old alarm clock on her dresser. "As much as I'd love to stay up and talk, I know we need to be downstairs early for breakfast with your family."

Mallory nods. "The bathroom is down the hall on the right, if you want to get ready for bed." She looks at the bed we're sitting on, her cheeks turning the blush pink of her pajamas.

"I promise to be a complete gentleman and stay on my side of the bed." I mimic the Boy Scout hand sign but feel more like Katniss, volunteering myself as tribute to sleep beside this beautiful woman. "Scout's honor."

Mirth fills her eyes. "Were you actually a Boy Scout?"

"No, but I mean what I say, especially when it comes to you."

She kisses me on the cheek, sending a shiver throughout my body. "I think I finally believe that."

Okay, I need to get up right now if I'm going to follow through on my promise to be a gentleman. I practically jump off the bed, heading over to my duffel. My sleep attire usually consists of *only* a pair of underwear, but that won't work for tonight.

I dig through my bag and grab a T-shirt and a pair of basketball shorts I luckily had the foresight to pack, along with the bag holding my toothbrush and toothpaste, and head to the bathroom.

Once my teeth are brushed and I'm in my makeshift pajamas, I head back to Mallory's room. My pulse skitters as I settle onto the bed beside her. One of my legs hangs off the bed as I try to find a comfortable position that doesn't involve me touching her.

When I finally stop moving, I let a long breath out through my nose. The whole room smells like a tropical dessert, enveloping me in Mallory's signature scent like a warm hug. The intoxicating aroma mixed with the knowledge that she's beside me begins to lull me to sleep when there's a shift on the bed beside me.

"Are you still awake?" she whispers.

"Yeah," I answer groggily, slowly blinking my eyes.

Mallory adjusts her position to look at me. "Do you think the world believes us?"

"You mean that we're dating?"

She nods.

"I don't usually read the comments section on my posts. I learned to stop doing that a long time ago."

"Why?" Mallory laughs.

"Let's just say that some overzealous fans have said things I wish I could forget." I grimace, thinking of the…*colorful* things some of the women said. "But I've read some of the comments on our posts lately, and people seem to have positive things to say. Plus, Karina would call me if there were concerns about the legitimacy of our relationship that I hadn't heard about."

"I'm glad it's working." She places her hand on my arm. Her fingers are cold, but warmth is the only thing coursing through me at her touch. Her willingly touching me while in the comfort of her childhood bedroom has joy coursing through my veins. Because here I know it's not for an audience or to make our relationship look believable…it's because she wants it, too. "Hopefully, it will help you get that audition for your dream role."

Those words put an instant stop to my joy. I spent one day with Mallory before, and spent years searching for her. *Waiting* for her. Now, the thought of leaving after I finally found her and we're taking positive steps forward seems unfathomable.

I swallow down the lump in my throat. "Thanks, but I'm happy just to be here with you."

She's quiet long enough that I think she's fallen asleep. I move to face the other direction because if I keep looking at her, I might not be able to keep the promise I made to stay on my side of the bed.

I feel her shiver beside me. "Griff?" Her tired voice calls to me in the darkness like the North Star guiding me home.

"Mmm?" I turn back to her.

"I'm cold, and there aren't any extra blankets." Mallory fidgets with the sheets. "Will you hold me?"

I rub my eyes, not positive that I'm awake because this feels like a sweet dream. "You're sure?"

She meets my gaze, nodding. So, I scoot closer, wrapping an arm around her. Mallory leans into my hold, resting her head on my chest and placing her hand beside it. Surely she can hear and feel how hard my heart is pounding, how it races for her. She snuggles against me, one of her legs intertwining with mine.

It takes only a few minutes for her breathing to even out as she falls asleep. I don't know when I'll get another moment like this, so I breathe it in, taking a mental snapshot of her in my arms. The rhythmic way her chest rises and falls against my side. The smell of her tropical shampoo under my chin.

I lean down, pressing a kiss to her mess of waves. "I'm falling for you, beautiful. I don't think I ever stopped." The whispered words don't feel as scary in the night, where no one else can hear them. But it doesn't make them any less true.

———— ♡ ♡ ♡ ————

Waking up with Mallory in my arms is an indescribable feeling. No words can accurately express what it feels like to hold her. How she fits against me as if we were molded for each other.

How can I ever leave her now that I know the small sounds she makes while she sleeps? And the adorable doe-eyed look she has when she stirs awake in the morning.

Everything about her is perfect to me. I wouldn't change a single thing.

I smile. "Good morning."

She blushes and sheepishly dips her head against my chest. "Morning."

"Are you ready to head downstairs? You know, before they think we're up to no good," I tease, repeating her words from yesterday.

She rolls her eyes, pushing up off me and scooting out of the foot of the bed. "I'm always ready for monkey bread and presents."

"What's monkey bread?" I hop out of bed and rifle through my bag, grabbing an emerald-green sweater and a pair of jeans, along with my deodorant.

Mallory stops rifling through her suitcase to turn and look at me. "You don't know what monkey bread is?"

I shake my head.

"You've been missing out," she tuts.

"You're not going to tell me what it is?" I laugh.

She shakes her head. "I'll let you experience it for yourself."

I let Mallory get ready in the bathroom first while I call my parents and wish them a Merry Christmas. As I set my phone down to get dressed, a series of texts from Rhett comes through.

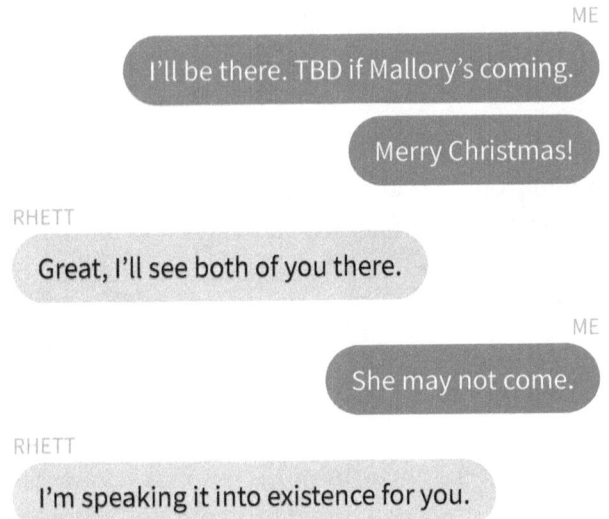

Merry Christmas, man.

Are you going to be at the showing of your movie in LA at the beginning of January?

I'd love to finally meet Mallory.

My agent had called me two days ago, letting me know that the movie was doing so well that the director wanted me and Brittany to do a surprise appearance at a movie event with influencers in LA. She wants me to bring Mallory with me, but I haven't worked up the courage to ask her yet.

ME

I'll be there. TBD if Mallory's coming.

Merry Christmas!

RHETT

Great, I'll see both of you there.

ME

She may not come.

RHETT

I'm speaking it into existence for you.

I wasn't optimistic before, but after last night, I definitely am. I throw my phone on the bed and get changed right before Mallory pops her head back in the room.

"You can have the bathroom now," she says. "I'll be downstairs."

I finish getting ready for the day and head down. When I walk into the kitchen, I'm hit with the sound of Mallory's laughter as she talks to Granny. Todd has his arms wrapped around Angie's middle and bends down to kiss her temple. Connor is quiet, sipping on a cup of coffee. I step farther into the room and am hit with a chorus of merry hellos.

I hug Granny. "It looks like you're having a good morning."

"The best."

"Can I get you any coffee?" Angie asks me.

"I can pour myself a cup if you point me in the direction of your mugs."

She shoots Mallory a wide-eyed look around my shoulder before pointing at the cabinet over the coffee maker. "There's creamer in the fridge unless you drink it black like Connor."

"I drink my coffee like it's dessert." I grab the largest mug I can find from the cabinet. It's covered in little red trucks carrying Christmas trees, which feels fitting for today.

"You and Mallory both." Angie laughs, grabbing two bottles of creamer from the fridge and setting them next to me. The oven timer goes off, and she perks up. "That'll be the monkey bread."

I choose the peppermint-mocha creamer and pour it into my mug until the coffee turns a light, milky color. "I've been hearing about this breakfast all morning." I turn and watch as Angie pulls a bundt cake pan out of the oven before carefully flipping it over onto a large circular tray.

It looks like some sort of cake, broken into pieces and slathered with gooey caramel. The room smells of cinnamon sugar and all things Christmas. My mouth instantly waters as I point at the food. "That smells delicious."

"It tastes even better." Todd claps me on the back before moving around me to grab a stack of plates.

Angie dishes us all out a serving, and we carry them over to the dining room table. I walk back into the kitchen, ready to help Granny into a seat. She's already clutching Connor's arm while walking over. Granny winks at me, squeezing his muscles. I take my seat beside Mallory, shaking my head.

When I take my first bite of monkey bread, I close my eyes, savoring the sweet dough. "I think this is what heaven tastes like," I say, once I finish chewing.

"Now you see why it's a family tradition to make every year," Mallory says before shoveling a bite into her mouth.

I grab a piece of bacon from a plate in the middle of the table. "Everything has been delicious. Thank you again." I smile at her parents.

"The pleasure is truly ours." Angie places a hand over her heart.

We dive into opening presents immediately after breakfast, at Mallory's insistence. Her parents even bought me my own flight of sauces to use when I make wings at home.

When there aren't any more presents under the tree, I grab the bag I stowed in Granny's room and pass out the gifts we brought.

"What's this?" Angie attempts to lift her gift onto her lap, but struggles with how heavy it is.

"Granny and I wanted to get each of you something for hosting us."

"You didn't have to do that." But she's already ripping the wrapping paper off her present. Angie gasps as she pulls out the wood stove cover I bought her, engraved with *The*

Porters. "I've been thinking about getting one of these."
She grabs Todd's shoulder and shakes him. "Wasn't I just
talking about this?"

Todd nods with a smirk. "She was."

"I love it." She gets up from the couch and gives Granny
and me a hug before returning to her husband's side. "Go
ahead and open yours, honey."

He pulls the tissue paper out of his gift bag until he finds
the piece of paper inside. Todd reads it carefully, then looks
at me, slack-jawed. "I can't believe it."

"What is it?" Angie looks over his shoulder, and her eyes
go wide. "You bought him an outdoor pizza oven?"

"It should be here next week." I gesture to Mallory. "She
said y'all love making pizza, so I thought you might enjoy
using that."

"We'll use it all the time." Angie smiles.

I turn to Mallory's brother. "I wasn't sure what to get you
since we hadn't met yet, but I hope you like it."

Connor opens his gift bag, pulling out the beard-care kit.
Mallory laughs so hard that she snorts. He looks up at me,
completely stone-faced.

I grimace. "Mallory said you had a beard before we met.
I swear I bought that before she said anything yesterday."

He sets it in his pile of gifts and turns to Mallory like he's
waiting for her to go.

"There's something else in there."

Connor reaches back into the bag, pulling out the concert tickets I got him. He examines them closely, his brows
raising slightly. "VIP Rhett Hayes tickets?"

"Mallory said you were a big country music fan, so I took
a gamble."

I see a flicker of happiness in Connor's expression before
it returns to neutral. "Thanks."

"You're welcome." I fix my gaze on Mallory. "I know we agreed no gifts this year," I say for the sake of her parents, who might be surprised if we didn't exchange something. I grab the wrapped box from behind the couch. "But I couldn't help myself."

Her eyes are the softest I've ever seen them as she accepts my present. "I didn't get you anything."

"Being with you is the greatest gift I could ask for." I lean forward and kiss her cheek.

"You two are the sweetest." Angie leans forward on the couch cushion, wrapping her arms around Connor's shoulders. "Aren't they the sweetest?"

"The sappiest," he mutters. I'll win him over one day. But all my attention right now is on my girl.

I nudge Mallory's arm. "Go ahead. Open it."

She tears the paper I not-so-expertly wrapped myself, but she doesn't seem to notice. Her eyes are glued to what's inside the box. She presses her fingers to her slightly parted lips, letting out a small gasp. Mallory slowly pulls out one of the light-pink ice skates. When her gaze meets mine, tears brim, though a soft smile settles on her lips.

"My own ice skates?" Her voice is higher than normal. Hearing her this happy because of something I did for her fills me with a joy like none other.

"Ones just as beautiful as you."

"This is too much." Mallory sets the skate back in the box, shaking her head.

"Nothing is ever too much for you." My words are earnest. There's truly nothing I wouldn't do for this girl. "I'd have bought you an entire ice rink with it if I thought you'd let me."

"*That* would've been too much," she says with a shaky laugh.

"I didn't know you still enjoyed skating." Angie moves to the floor to look at the skates.

"My love for it was recently reignited." She looks at me with a wide grin.

I would give her anything she wanted just to see her smile like that again. And to know that *I* was the reason behind it.

CHAPTER TWENTY

GRIFFIN

"Let's go for a walk." I look out the window in awe as snow flurries fall to the earth. It's so serene that it almost looks fake.

"Are you crazy?" Mallory steps up beside me, wrapping her arms around her middle. "It's freezing out."

She came over to my rental for a quick video call with my agent. According to Karina, everything is going smoothly. People believe our relationship is real, and she's confident that she'll hear back with confirmation of an audition for the fantasy movie I've been dreaming about in the next week or so.

I run a hand through my hair, trying to come up with a reason we should go outside. "It's barely below freezing. Don't you think a walk through a winter wonderland sounds romantic? You could stay, and we can have our first official date."

"I'm not dressed for a date."

"You're gorgeous." I drag my eyes over her sweatpants and sweatshirt. With how cozy she looks, I'm considering throwing my snowy walk idea out the window and asking her to cuddle on the couch.

She stares at the winter landscape for a few long moments before sighing. "Fine, but only because I brought my heavy winter coat."

I head to the coat closet and grab her dark-pink puffer jacket, holding it open as she slips her arms in. Grabbing my own coat from the closet, I pull it on over my navy long-sleeved tee. When I turn back to her, she has a bubblegum-pink beanie on with a hot-pink pom-pom on top. Her wavy brown hair is wild underneath it, shooting out like it has no desire to be contained.

I step forward, running my finger along a rogue curl. "I'm never going to get over your hair."

"You still love my curls?" She laughs, sounding amused.

I reluctantly let go of the strand and reach into my pocket, grabbing the light-gray hat that matches my coat and pulling it on. "They're incredible."

"They drive me nuts, so I'm glad you like them."

"It's part of the Mallory starter pack."

We both slip on our boots and walk out the front door. I lock it behind us and offer her my arm as we walk down the driveway. She takes it and, with the weight of her hand on my arm, I feel like I can conquer anything. Like I can be anyone. But right now, all I want to be is her boyfriend. A real one. One that gets to hold her anytime I want. *Kiss* her anytime I want.

The scene from *Sweet Home Alabama* with that quote plays on a loop in my head, forcing me to shove all my feelings down. I promised myself that I'd let Mallory make the first move. I'm in this for the long haul, not a short minute of satisfaction.

I focus on our surroundings, trying to calm my racing mind. There's something about walking beside Mallory in the snowy landscape that settles my soul and makes me feel like all is right in the world. It takes me back to the night we met and our hot chocolate date. The sense of déjà vu that hits feels like sweet serendipity or a fortunate stroke of luck that we're here together now on this cold winter day.

The snowy ground is slushy, but luckily, it doesn't seem to have left a layer of ice behind yet. Knowing that she's holding onto my arm because she wants to and not because she needs to in order to avoid slipping brings a smile to my lips.

"Let's see how well you know me." Mallory squeezes my arm, and I totally flex. No shame here. "What else do you think is in the Mallory starter pack?"

"Clothes in all shades of pink." I smile at the obvious answer. "Seasonally flavored coffee. Your mom's chicken and dumplings. Pink ice skates. All of Taylor Swift's music. Friday nights with your friends. McDonald's Dr. Pepper because you think it tastes better from their machine than from anywhere else."

"You've got me pegged," Mallory says when we reach a stop sign. She looks both ways before crossing the road.

"Oh, I'm not done yet." I dive a little deeper. "The way you light up whenever you're around your friends and family. The beautiful laugh you get when something someone says or does really gets you." I place my hand over hers, which rests on my arm. "The best part of the Mallory starter pack is that you're always undeniably you. You never hide how you feel. There's an honesty in your words and actions that's admirable." I let my hand fall back to my side as we continue walking. "Am I missing anything?"

She glances up at me, her eyes bright. "That's really how you see me?"

My lips pull up in a tilted grin. "That's only me scratching the surface, beautiful."

"I wasn't sure any man would ever love my bluntness."

"That might make some people push you away, but not me. I love that I never know what you're going to say next. That you challenge me in a way no one else ever has."

Mallory dabs her gloved hands under her eyes. "You have no idea how much I needed to hear that. Thank you."

"Anytime." I slide my free hand into my jacket pocket. "I can keep going if you want."

She squeezes my arm. "I think if you keep going, my head might start getting as inflated as yours."

"Okay, Ms. Confident, let's see if you know me well enough to say what's in *my* starter pack." I narrow my eyes while smiling at her, a challenge.

Mallory raises an eyebrow as if to say *game on*. "Chicken wings, for sure. Aviator sunglasses. Speaking in movie quotes. And I can't forget your million-watt smile, according to Granny."

"I prefer my Mallory-induced smile," I say before I can think any better of it.

She reaches up and touches the tilted corner of my mouth. "This one?" I nod. "I always wondered why your smile around me looked different than the one I see you use everywhere else."

"Do you like that it's only for you?" I tease.

She blushes, but mirth twinkles in her gaze. "I didn't say that."

"But your flushed cheeks did."

They flame a deeper shade of pink. "It's from the cold."

"If that's what you have to tell yourself to sleep at night." This back and forth with her is what I live for. It makes me feel alive in a way no one else can.

"I'm probably just getting frostbite since you dragged me out here in the freezing tundra."

"I think you'd have to be outside for hours to get frostbite with this temperature. It's barely cold enough for it to even be snowing." I watch as a flurry lands on the road and immediately melts.

"Can't you let a girl blush in peace? Or is confidence your main setting?"

I can't hold back the grin now that we've finally reached the truth. "I want to hear you say it. Out loud."

"I'm a vampire," she whispers. Her face remains neutral for a moment before she breaks into laughter. I can't help but chuckle with her at the *Twilight* reference.

Once we've both calmed down, I swipe at the tears under my eyes before they have a chance to freeze to my face. "That was hilarious."

"You set it up; I just knocked it out of the park."

"Are you a professional baseball player now?"

"No, but I could get you tickets to a Mustangs game. Make you finally cheer for the *right* team for once."

I don't say that I think I could easily get my own tickets. I don't want to sound conceited, and I try not to use my level of fame for things like that anyway. "Do you have a connection to the team? You know, other than the old posters over your bedroom wall?"

She knocks her hip into my leg. "Alyssa is friends with Austin Bradford."

"The shortstop?"

Mallory looks up at me, impressed. "I'm surprised you know anything about your team's rival."

"I like following baseball. Tennessee fans go hard for their teams in all sports, and I like knowing what I'm talking about."

"Wasn't it at a Fireflies game last year where all the fans threw so much food on the field after they thought the ump made a bad call that they had to postpone the game?"

Yes, yes, it was. There's no way I'm telling her I was at that game, even if I didn't participate in littering on the field. "I said we go hard, not that we're perfect."

She laughs. "Why are they even called the Fireflies, anyway? Because they're easy to squash?"

"Now you're just trying to pick a fight." I reach over and squeeze her side. "They named them the Knoxville Fireflies because of a synchronous firefly event that happens in Great Smoky Mountains National Park every year. It's legit. There's even a lottery to get a ticket to see it. I've only been once, but it was one of the coolest things I've ever seen. I'll have to take you sometime."

"I'd like that." She leans her head on my arm. "How did we even get on this topic?"

I don't care what we're talking about. We could be talking about why the sky is blue, or she could be telling me all her Taylor Swift Easter egg theories, and I'd be happy just to be talking to her.

I hear the sound of an approaching car and turn my head to the left, spotting one coming quickly and driving too close to the curb for comfort. Out of pure instinct, I gently push Mallory to the side, closer to the snow-covered grass of people's front yards.

I was more concerned about how close the car was to the curb—that if they hit any ice, they might jump the curb and hit us. But it seems I should've been more worried about the slush lining the road. Because while Mallory is out of the way, I'm directly in the splash zone.

The car drives past, spraying the muddy snow along the side of the road directly at me. I don't have enough time to react and jump out of the way myself, so I spread my arms wide, welcoming the gross spray of slush and doing my best to block any of it from hitting Mallory.

My coat and shirt are instantly soaked. A full-body shiver wracks through my body. The temperature didn't feel that cold before, but it's freezing now.

I turn to check on Mallory. Her eyes widen as they move up and down my body. Thankfully, she seems unscathed from the slushy spray. She steps toward me, her mouth agape and hands out in front of her like she wants to help me but doesn't know what to do. "We should get you home so you can put on some dry clothes."

I nod, unable to speak through my chattering teeth.

"Does it feel like it's getting colder to you?" She shoves her hands in her pockets.

I swallow hard, trying to stop my shivering long enough to speak clearly. "Maybe, but I'm also freezing for obvious reasons."

Mallory pulls her phone out and grimaces. "It's only twenty degrees now."

Snow begins to fall more steadily around us as we walk the remaining distance back to my rental. The short walk feels like miles in my state.

When we're finally walking up the driveway, Mallory turns to me. "Where are your keys? I can get the door."

I gesture to my coat pocket with a shaking finger. She uses her fingertips to pinch the edge of it, pull it open, and grab my key ring.

Mallory opens the door for me, and I immediately feel better stepping into the heated house. "Thanks," I murmur, shedding the soaked coat and hat and wrinkling my nose. It needs serious dry-cleaning. I'd take off my wet shirt, too, but I'll wait until I'm alone for that. I drop the jacket by the front door; I can worry about mopping later, but I don't want to drip the dirty water through the rental.

"I think a hot shower should help." I don't want Mallory to feel kicked out, but I'm not sure she wants to stay while I shower either. Leaving it up to her seems like the best option.

When she doesn't answer, I glance over and find her eyes focused on my chest. I can feel my shirt clinging to every contour of my muscles, showing them off to her. I'd like to thank my personal trainer for pushing me so hard in our sessions.

The way her eyes devour my torso warms me right up. When she sees that I noticed her staring, her cheeks warm. "Shower. Right. I'll let you get to that, then." She laughs awkwardly. "You're sure you're okay?"

I nod. "The only casualty was that I looked like a wet rat in front of you."

She steps closer, looking earnest. "I don't think you looked like a wet rat."

"A sad puppy?"

"More like a hot protector."

My jaw drops at her calling me *hot*. My gaze lowers to her lips. I want to kiss her so badly. Just not when I smell like the muddy street. *And not until she makes the first move,* I remind myself. But it's getting more difficult to keep that promise when she is looking at me like *that*.

"I'll remember that for later, beautiful." I smile, and her cheeks turn light pink. "Do you want me to walk you out?" I gesture toward my couch. "Or we could eat some food and watch a movie once I no longer smell like dirt?"

"With the way the snow is picking up, I should probably head home."

My hope deflates like a helium-deprived balloon. Of course, I want her to make it home safely, but I'll always want to spend more time with Mallory.

"Text me when you make it home?" I open the door for her.

"Yeah, I'll text you." She steps outside and wiggles her fingers. "See ya."

After I close the door behind her, I rip my long-sleeved tee off over my head, adding it to the pile on the floor. It already feels infinitely better not having the sopping material clinging to my body.

I haven't even made it to my bedroom to take a shower when there's a knock at the door. My heart pounds in my chest. Maybe Mallory changed her mind and wants to spend more time with me. But that's probably wishful thinking.

I walk back and open the front door to find Mallory standing there as if I willed it. She stares at my bare chest like it's God's personal gift to her. I don't mind one bit.

"Everything okay?" I ask, trying to keep satisfaction out of my tone.

Her eyes drop to the porch. "Uh, Linda won't start."

I've never been more grateful that her car hates the cold. "I can call Ted and see if he can come take you home," I offer, really hoping she doesn't take me up on it.

She shakes her head. "The snow is starting to stick. I don't want him to have to drive in this."

I gesture inside. "You're welcome to stay here until the snow lets up."

Or however long you want. The rest of forever would be fine too.

"If you're sure." Mallory finally looks at me. Her eyes drag across my stomach, making me glad I did an ab workout this morning. Her eyes are still stuck on my stomach when she gasps.

"What's wrong?"

She closes the distance between us and lifts my right arm, brushing her cold fingers along my rib cage. I suck in a breath, both because it feels like an ice cube running along my already cold skin, but also because of the flood of attraction that fills me as Mallory's fingers trace my abdomen.

"What's this?"

I look down to see where she tapped, spotting the little secret I've kept hidden from everyone since I got it over two years ago.

"A tattoo?" There's no way out of this. She was bound to find out sooner or later, but I was hoping for much, *much* later.

She rolls her eyes. "I mean, what is it supposed to be?"

My voice is husky, barely above a whisper as I respond, "A to-go cup of hot chocolate."

CHAPTER TWENTY-ONE

MALLORY

I can't talk. Can't think. Can't *breathe*.

All I can do is stare at the black outline of a to-go cup tattooed on his skin. One that looks nearly identical to the one from our first date.

After a few seconds of trailing my finger along it, I force myself to look away from his ribs, finding his heated gaze fixed on me.

There's only one word my lips can form. "When?"

His throat bobs as he swallows hard. I don't think he planned on me seeing this today. Heck, I wouldn't have seen it if my car had started. I suppose I should be thanking Linda for hating the cold.

"Around two and a half years ago."

I can't believe he chose this symbol to be forever inked on his skin. "Is this your only tattoo?" He nods. My brain is running a million miles a minute as it tries to process everything, but only one word comes out. "Why?" Apparently, I can only speak in single syllables now.

"Why, what?" Griffin reaches up, wrapping his fingers around mine.

I suck in a shaky breath. Words. I can form words. Clearing my throat, I slowly get them out. "Why did you choose a to-go cup of hot chocolate?"

"I thought it was obvious." He pulls my hand to his lips, pressing a kiss to the inside of my wrist. Then my palm. "Because of you." His blue eyes are crystal clear as they look into mine. Sincerity is all I find there. No humor. No teasing. No games.

"But, *why*?" There's something he's not saying. An explanation behind why he'd get a tattoo related to me after one date.

He's quiet for so long that I'm convinced he's not going to answer. I'm forever going to live in the land of unknowing, wondering why he got a tattoo…for *me*.

"I thought I'd lost you forever." Griffin drops his hand from mine, running his fingers over the tattoo absentmindedly. "I got it as a reminder that sparks and all the things I thought were only in the movies truly do exist." His gaze settles on mine, searching.

And I feel *everything*. Everything for him that I had shoved down and tried to forget after I never heard from him again. The fire I used to feel inside for him stoked back to life from the embers that remained, holding onto hope that he was exactly who I thought after we first met. A man worth holding onto. A man worth the risk, worth burning for.

I see many of the same emotions mirrored in his eyes before they glint with boldness as he says, "To never settle for less than what I feel for you."

I wrap my arms around my middle, trying to hold in all the feelings bubbling up inside me. "You think our date was better than the movies?"

"I think everything about you is better than any fictional character in all of existence." He brushes his knuckles along my cheekbone. "No one could ever write the perfection that is Veronica Mallory Porter." Griffin tips my chin up, forcing me to look into his eyes. "There's only you."

I lean forward, running my fingers along his scruff. "As scary as it is for me to admit, there's only you, too." If I don't pull back right now, something is going to happen between us—something I'm not sure I'm ready for yet. The tattoo was enough revelation for one day. Trying to cut the tension between us, I smirk. "Which is good because I don't think the world could handle two Griffin Bartholomew Razzle-Dazzle Reynolds."

He pulls back, laughing. "I should go shower. We can order dinner when I'm done, but feel free to raid my fridge or pantry if you need anything. I'll be quick." He starts walking away, but stops when he reaches a hallway. He turns back to face me. "I want to continue this conversation later, though."

With that, he leaves to shower, and I plop down on the couch. I'm scrolling through the comments on the most recent photo I posted with Griffin and am immediately reminded why I never had social media.

Most of the comments are nice, but then there are the ones that I know are delusional or petty, but they hurt nonetheless.

@xogriffinsgirlxo: Can someone tell me what he sees in her? I mean, look at her hair. Does she own a mirror?

@futuremrsgriffinreynolds01: At least I know I have a chance with Griffin since he obviously doesn't mind dating 6s when he's a 10 *face with hand over mouth emoji*

@griffieforlifeee: Me waiting for the day he dumps her so I can shoot my shot: *stopwatch emoji*

"That was a terrible idea." I exit the app with no plans to open it again for the foreseeable future. The best thing for my sanity moving forward is to post and ghost. No more reading comments from people who know nothing about me.

The only opinions I care about are from the people I love, and my girls are on the Team Griffin train.

Speaking of my friends, if I don't tell them that I'm likely not coming home tonight, they're going to worry. Or send a search party out for me. Probably both. I pull up the "Long Live Girlies" group text thread and start the conversation.

ME

Y'all can't freak out, okay?

SHAYNA

Whenever someone says that, I immediately start freaking out *grinning face with sweat emoji*

ALYSSA

Same.

KELSEY

What happened?

Or should I say, what did Griffin do?

ALYSSA

eyes emoji

ME

Well, unless he caused the snowstorm that trapped me at his house for the night, I'm not sure I can blame him this time…

SHAYNA

Is that your way of telling us you're having ANOTHER sleepover with him?!?!

ME

Maybe *woman shrugging emoji*

Did I mention he also has a secret tattoo of a to-go cup of hot chocolate?

Like the one from our first date.

ALYSSA

SHUT THE FRONT DOOR!

SHAYNA

I'M NOT SCREAMING, YOU ARE!!!

KELSEY

FOR THE LOVE OF BISCUITS (you're welcome for not swearing for you, Shay).

SHAYNA

Thank you *sparkling heart emoji*

But seriously, that's the most romantic thing I've ever heard *melting face emoji*

ALYSSA

He's SO in love with you.

SHAYNA

A certified down bad man!

I hear the shower water turn off, and the last thing I want is for Griffin to accidentally see any of this conversation, so I shoot off another quick text.

ME

Okay, I gotta go. Wish me luck.

ALYSSA

Your lips should fall onto his tonight. Just saying!

KELSEY

Have fun!

SHAYNA

Imagine me as Sebastian screaming KISS THE GIRL at him. Love you!

ME

I asked for luck, not a kiss...

KELSEY

Yeah, because we want you to get lucky tonight!

ALYSSA

AYYYY!

SHAYNA

Whoop! There it is.

While I'm in the messages app, I click on my thread with Griffin. Before I can second-guess myself, I change his contact name from 'Mr. Too Late' to 'Griff.' If we're going to move forward together, I may as well start here.

"How's it going?" I jump as Griffin walks into the room wearing a Knoxville Fireflies sweatshirt. I can forgive his choice of baseball team because of how deliciously good he looks in his light-gray joggers.

Everyone always talks about the attractiveness level of baseball pants, but I think joggers are severely underrated—especially when Griffin is wearing them.

I lock my phone screen and toss it on the couch like it will burn me if I hold it too long. "Great."

He smiles before settling on the couch beside me. The fresh scent of soap and eucalyptus wafts my way and has me thinking about my friends' texts. My gaze drops to his lips. When I meet his eyes again, I find mirth mixed with desire.

"If you keep looking at me like that, I'm going to kiss you."

My heart pounds in my chest at the thought. I bite my bottom lip to keep from gasping or telling him to go right ahead. That doesn't seem like the smartest idea right now. Because if I give him the go-ahead, I'm not sure I'll ever be able to stop kissing him. And I feel like there are conversations we need to have about what's next before that happens.

"I'm not sure I'm ready for that." The words come out raspy and breathless like I'm laying my cards on the table for him to see.

"I'm here whenever you are." He presses his lips to the crown of my head.

I hum at his touch. "You weren't exaggerating before, were you? When you said that you always looked for me."

Griffin shakes his head. "I told you a long time ago that I don't promise things I can't deliver on. We were talking about endless amounts of snickerdoodle hot chocolate then." He holds up a finger and jogs into his kitchen. When he returns, he has a canister in his hands that, upon closer inspection, is a snickerdoodle hot chocolate mix. "I've bought this from that little café every year, hoping that I would be able to find you and fulfill that promise I made to you." He sets it on the coffee table and turns his body sideways on the couch, taking my hands in his. "I never gave up hope."

Griffin lets go of one of my hands, reaching up and swiping his thumb under my eye. It's only then that I realize I'm crying. I'm not sure when I started, but it's like his words released a dam of pent-up emotions and feelings.

"I hate seeing you cry." He wipes away another tear. "Is it something I said?"

I shake my head. "You didn't do anything wrong. I was hurt by you back then, and I've held this resentment toward you inside for so long." I release a shaky sigh. "It feels good to let it go."

Griffin sits with me in the silence, rubbing small circles on my back. Giving me space to process things on my own. Not forcing me to say where this leaves us or what this means for our relationship. It makes me appreciate him all the more.

"I'm still figuring out what this is and what a possible future could look like between us," I say. "But please know that I am thinking about it."

He smiles. "That's all I could ask for. Like I said, take all the time you need. I'm not going anywhere."

Without giving myself a chance to second-guess my actions, I lean forward, pressing a kiss to his cheek. Griffin's whole body tenses as if one small move will ruin the moment or make me run away. His scruff tickles my lips, sending a tingling awareness throughout my body. I need to figure out my feelings soon, otherwise my body is going to choose for me.

I pull back and clear my throat. "So, did you have any shirtless scenes in any of your movies?"

Griffin laughs. "Yes. What made you think to ask that?"

"The tattoo."

"Ah, they have people on set to cover them up. Sometimes it requires digital manipulation or actual prosthetics, but because mine is small, I only had to work with a makeup artist on set to cover it up any day we shot a shirtless scene."

I nod slowly. "You learn something new every day."

He smiles. "Do you want dinner? We can order in or see what I have in my fridge."

I look out the window at the heavily falling snow. It's coating the roads enough that I can't see any evidence of the pavement. "I would feel bad ordering in, so we could just whip something up?"

"Sure." Griffin grabs the canister of hot chocolate mix and moves into the kitchen. After a few minutes of hearing cabinet doors open and close, he sighs. "I was supposed to go to the grocery store today before Karina set up that call with us, and I forgot. I'm down to bare essentials here. But I do have hot chocolate and popcorn."

"Movie food it is," I call back. "Can I help?"

"I've got this. Just give me a few minutes."

When Griffin returns to the living room, he sets a bowl of buttered popcorn on the table and heads back to the kitchen, returning with two mugs.

I gladly take one of the cups from his hands, bringing it under my nose and inhaling the scent of warm chocolate mixed with cinnamon. My heart flutters in my chest.

Griffin winces. "I forgot you haven't had it after our whole...situation. I can get you some water if you prefer."

"No." I pull the mug closer to my chest. "It smells great. I want it." If this isn't my whole healing process coming full circle, I don't know what is.

Griffin looks at me for a long moment, his eyes turning glossy as his lips slowly tilt up at the corners. The way he's staring at me makes me feel emotionally naked, like he can see everything I'm feeling inside just because I told him I'd drink the hot chocolate. Although I suppose we both know that my willingness to drink it again means a lot more than that.

Sticking true to his promise to give me more time to think things over, Griffin sits beside me and pops a handful of popcorn into his mouth. "What do you want to watch?"

"Only the greatest winter movie of all time." I grab the navy blanket from the back of his couch with my free hand, pulling it onto my lap.

"We'll say it together?"

I nod. "Three. Two. One."

"*Home Alone*," we say in unison, and both smile.

"I'm really glad you said that because I don't know if I could date someone who doesn't think that's the best winter movie." I grab the remote from his coffee table, turning on the television.

Griffin scoots closer to share the blanket, causing my body to lean into his. "So, you admit we're for real dating now?"

I pull the blanket up to my chin, trying to hide my blushing face. "If that's what you want."

He wraps his arm around my shoulder, tucking me into his side. "It's all I've wanted."

CHAPTER TWENTY-TWO

MALLORY

THE WARM MORNING SUN streams through the window, casting a golden hue on my body. Wanting to soak in the rays, I attempt to turn onto my side, but my body doesn't budge. I glance down at my waist and spot a very muscular arm draped over me.

I look around, trying to remember what happened last night. There's an empty bowl of popcorn on the coffee table with two used mugs beside it. Right. I got snowed in at Griffin's. We watched *Home Alone* and then put on *Home Alone 2*. I remember my eyes getting heavy during the second movie and mumbling something about being cold. That's when he pulled off the sweatshirt he was wearing for me, leaving him in only a fitted shirt.

I snuggle deeper into his hoodie and pull the collar up to my nose, inhaling his eucalyptus scent. If he weren't already a world-famous actor, he would still draw in all the ladies with his pheromones.

I tilt my head to take him in. His black shirt is deliciously taut across his chest, and he's half-smiling, like he's in the middle of a dream he doesn't want to wake up from. It's not fair that he's still just as handsome even when sleeping.

I don't know how someone as incredible as Griffin is interested in me.

Worry makes my stomach sink like an anchor to the ocean floor. How will I ever be his first choice when there will always be another movie taking him away from me? I want to date Griffin for real. But I don't know how to move forward with him when I can't help but think about the distance that will be between us when he leaves for LA once his granny's recovered. What's the point of opening my heart and letting him fully in if he's going to break it by leaving?

I burrow deeper into Griffin's hold, and he nuzzles me close. There's no use thinking about him leaving when I have him beside me right now. I need to enjoy the moment while I have it, because I know how quickly it can slip away.

———— ♡ ♡ ♡ ————

I'm supposed to be having a fun night with my friends, but I still can't get Griffin out of my mind. Maybe I need to push all my worries aside and kiss him. But I don't know how I'll ever be able to move on if I kiss him and fall for him, only for him to leave again.

The constant knocking has me shaking my head. "I'll get the door," I call to my roommates. I open it to find Emmy and Connor, my cousin and my brother, standing on our porch. Emmy has never been one to wait for anyone or anything. She's always a spitfire. Maybe it's because of her red hair, but I don't think something as simple as that could define Emmy. She's one hundred percent authentically herself, and I love her for it.

"Finally." She steps past me with a teasing smile.

I open the door wider, waving my brother inside. "Thanks for coming."

"Are you kidding?" Emmy turns on her heels with a smirk. "I'd give anything to spend more time with the Long Live Girlies." Even though she's only two years younger than us, she's always looked up to me and my friends. She moves around us in search of the girls.

Connor's steps falter in the doorway. "Are *all* your friends here?"

"That's what typically happens when you live with people," I deadpan. "Get inside. You're letting all the warm air out."

He sighs as if I'm the most exasperating person on the planet and moves past me so I can shut the door.

"What, are you nervous to be around girls?" I poke his stomach, and he flinches, trying to move away from me. "It's only my best friends. You've known them over half your life, just as long as I have. They're practically your bonus sisters. Well, there's Tyler's sister Tess, too, but she's the best. You'll love her."

Connor's only response is a harrumph.

I follow him into the living room and nearly run into him when he stops abruptly at the sight of Shayna. She stands in front of the fireplace, dancing to "Jingle Bell Rock" in a ribbed cream-colored long-sleeved tee tucked into a baby-blue skirt dotted with a dainty floral pattern. Her outfit is topped off with her pearl-studded headband—I don't think she ever takes that thing off unless she's sleeping. Her outfit screams spring even though we're in the dead of winter, but it's entirely Shayna. And I wouldn't expect anything less from our sunshine girl.

"What are you doing?" I shove Connor lightly on the back to keep moving, but he's immovable, as solid as a tree trunk with deep roots.

Shayna must've heard my question, because she looks up and immediately stops dancing, her cheeks bright pink. "Connor," she squeaks. "I didn't know you were coming."

Before my brother can say anything, my cousin walks into the room with Alyssa, Kelsey, Tyler, and Tess. The moment Emmy sees Shayna, she runs over and pulls her into a hug, jumping and giggling like two long-lost friends finally reunited.

"Restroom," Connor grunts before heading toward our half bath.

I blink. That was weird, but I don't have time to analyze it too much before there's another knock at the door.

"I've got it." Alyssa walks past me and returns a few minutes later with Austin at her heels. He's a giant, making Alyssa look short, even at five feet eight inches. But he's the definition of a gentle giant. Austin is one of the kindest people I know, and I love that he's stayed true to who he is, despite the fame he claimed overnight when he became the starting shortstop for the Mustangs a few years back. I can't help but think that it reminds me of someone else I know. Someone with brown hair and blue eyes who makes women around the world swoon.

Especially me.

"Hey, Austin." Kelsey gives him a side hug. "I didn't think you could make it."

"I was supposed to have a team dinner, but it was postponed due to the weather."

"We Southerners hate driving in ice," Shayna teases before stepping forward and hugging him. "We're happy to have you."

Austin opens his arms to me next, and I give him a quick squeeze before stepping back beside Shay.

She turns to me with a smile. "Lyss was supposed to be your partner, so we need to find someone else"—Shayna shimmies her shoulders—"to fill in."

"Sorry, I messed up the trivia team plans." Austin slings his arm around Alyssa's shoulder. I really wish they'd just date already. They would make the most beautiful children. Aside from how great their genetics would look when combined, they're perfect for each other in every way…if only they'd see it. "I don't have to participate," he says.

"Don't be silly." I pull my phone out of the back pocket of my jeans. "I'll call Griffin."

We planned this before Christmas—before we'd had *the talk*—so I hadn't invited Griffin to our trivia night for obvious reasons, but now I'm buzzing in anticipation at the thought of spending more time with him.

I step into the kitchen and hit the call button next to his name. He answers on the second ring.

"To what do I owe the pleasure of *the* Mallory Porter calling me?" I can hear the smile in his voice.

"Can't I call you for no apparent reason?" I hum.

"You can call me anytime you want."

His words send a chorus of butterflies in my stomach into flight. "What are you doing?"

"Tonight?"

"Right now, actually."

"I just got back from dinner at Granny's facility. She said to tell you hi, by the way."

"That's sweet." My palms get clammy. I didn't think I'd be nervous to invite him over, but this will be our first time being around my friends as a true couple. Er, people dating. I don't know exactly what to call us right now.

Griffin laughs. "Is there something you want to ask me, beautiful?"

"Do you want to come over?"

"Isn't it girls' night?"

I fiddle with the hem of my sweater. "Yeah, we're doing a winter trivia night at home and just realized we have an odd number of people. I need a partner."

"Oh, so I'm the replacement?" His voice is teasing, but I still feel bad.

"We planned it before our talk—"

"I'm just kidding. I'd be happy to partner with you, although I'm not sure how much help I'll be."

I sigh in relief. "Great. How soon can you be over here?"

"Give me ten minutes."

"Sounds perfect."

"See you soon, beautiful," he says, and then the line clicks.

I head back into the living room and rejoin my friends and family.

"Well?" Alyssa raises a perfectly manicured eyebrow.

Shayna rocks on her heels, making her skirt swish around her calves. "Is he coming?"

I nod. "He'll be here soon."

I sit down on the couch, when I hear Tyler say to Kelsey, "It's only a matter of time."

I lean forward and shoot him a look. "A matter of time until what?"

Tyler doesn't even flinch. I don't think he's ever been scared of me, even when I told him that I didn't like him right to his face. It just makes him even more right for Kelsey. "You two realize how in love you are," he says.

"Aren't you already in love?" Emmy plops down next to me. Connor joins as well, taking a seat in an empty chair. Though he doesn't say anything or look our way, I can tell he's listening to the conversation, simply observing rather than participating.

Shoot. I forgot people were here that aren't privy to the details of our "dating contract." I'm not sure if the contract is even a thing anymore now that we're actually dating, but I can't risk that information getting out or breaking my NDA.

I laugh dryly. "You know me. I'm quick to second-guess things when it comes to men. But there's something different about Griffin."

Emmy purses her lips. "You're right. I don't think you've ever introduced a boyfriend to the whole family before him. You must be serious about him."

"That's what they were saying." I gesture to Kelsey and Tyler. "They think I'm in even deeper than I realize."

"Do you agree with them?"

"Let's just say I didn't believe in fate. Not until I met him."

Emmy sighs. "That's the sweetest thing I've ever heard."

When I look over at my brother, his gaze is already on me. For the briefest hint of a second, I think he might smile, but then his features morph back into their perpetually neutral state.

There's a knock at the door. Emmy smiles suggestively at me and says in a singsong voice, "Your boyfriend's here."

I pop up, shaking my head. "I'll let him in, then we can get started if you want to round up the troops."

"Sure thing." Emmy gets up to gather everyone who isn't already in the living room while I head to the front door. I open it to find Griffin's smiling face. He's in dark-gray joggers and a black sweater, but it's the backward baseball cap and the way he's leaning against the wall that sends my stomach fluttering. I get what all the social media girlies meant about the effects of that combination on the female population. It should be illegal to look that good, to be able to cause that instant attraction.

But then again, Griffin's always had this effect on me.

"Are you going to let me inside?" He shoots me his tilted grin. The one just for me. That thought sends the butterflies fluttering again.

I nod, stepping aside so he can come in. Once Griffin has greeted everyone in the living room and I've introduced him to Austin, we sit down on the couch together. With how packed our cozy space is, I end up with my booty half on Griffin and half on the couch. He reaches around my lower back and pulls me fully onto his lap, wrapping his arms around my middle. My legs tangle with his.

If this were happening just a week ago, I would've either jumped right back up or faked a smile for the sake of our audience. But today, I lean into Griffin's touch, resting my head against his. In his arms, I feel safe. Secure. And—dare I say—*loved*. It's scary, but also invigorating.

His thumb brushes across my stomach where my sweater has slid up. I feel that small touch across my entire body. Griffin makes every nerve ending come alive.

When I look at him, I see the same passion and desire mirrored in his eyes.

"If you two lovebirds are done making eyes at each other, we can get started." Kelsey stands in front of the television and crosses her arms, though a smirk pulls at her lips.

I shoot her a thumbs-up while Griffin laughs into my shoulder. She hands each team a whiteboard, marker, and tissue.

"My mom made a slideshow with all the questions and answers. She literally just texted it to me, so everything is fair and square." Alyssa connects her phone to the TV, showing the timestamp of the email from her mom as proof, even though I know she's not the kind to cheat. "Let's get this trivia night started."

We answer questions about generic winter traditions first. Griffin and I successfully guessed that eggnog came from England and that candy canes were shaped to resemble a shepherd's staff, among other questions.

"Next up is Christmas music," Alyssa announces, flipping to the next slide.

I tilt my head back to look at Griffin. "We're going to crush this."

And we do. I mean, who doesn't know that the best-selling Christmas song of all time is "White Christmas" or that Frosty the Snowman's nose is made out of a button rather than the traditional carrot?

All the teams suffer through the winter sports round, except for Alyssa and Austin, thanks to his extensive sports knowledge.

"We are now entering the basic winter fun facts," Shayna reads aloud. "Starting with…" She flips to the next slide. "What is the shortest day of the year called?"

As everyone else starts whispering to their partner, I murmur in Griffin's ear, "It's the winter something."

He laughs and squeezes my side. "I think what you're looking for is Winter Solstice."

"See, I was half right." I write down the answer on our whiteboard. I'm extra thankful he's on my team when everyone else answers that question correctly. I would've looked ridiculous if I had just written down *winter*.

The next slide asks how many sides a snowflake has. I immediately write down *six*.

"How do you know?" Griffin's breath against my skin causes all the hairs on my neck to stand. "Is it something you taught your students?"

"Yeah," I lie. Even with where our relationship is at right now, there's no way I'm telling him that I looked up everything I could about snowflakes after we kissed outside with perfect flurries falling around us. I thought if I learned everything I could about snowflakes, it would help me to focus on those facts rather than the magic of the moment I had surrounded by them with his lips pressed to mine.

Spoiler alert: It didn't work. I don't think there are enough facts in the world to make me forget the feelings I had when Griffin kissed me, but at least knowing this random fact guarantees us another point.

We're the only ones to get the correct answer.

Griffin leans in, kissing my temple. "That's my smart girl."

Normally, I'd roll my eyes if I ever heard anyone say that to their significant other. But I beam under Griffin's compliment. Maybe I'm more of the relationship type than I thought. It just took the right guy coming along for me to realize it.

I nuzzle into him, and he hums happily.

"Y'all are the cutest." Emmy looks at us, doe-eyed.

"Adorable," Shayna agrees.

Alyssa grins. "Totally goals."

"Gross," Connor mutters.

I stick my tongue out at him. "Maybe you wouldn't think it was gross if you ever decided to *talk* to a woman."

"So, I guess you haven't been on any dates lately, man?" Griffin asks with a casual laugh, completely unaware of Connor's nonexistent dating history. He never even took a girl to prom or homecoming. I honestly don't know if he talks to females aside from the ones in our family.

"No." Connor's answer is short and gruff.

Griffin purses his lips, looking at me with confused eyes. I decide to step in and save him, but Shayna beats me to it.

"There's no shame in that." Shayna glances briefly at Connor before readjusting her headband and dropping her gaze. "I haven't been on any dates in a while either. The dating apps are awful, and the only guys I meet when I'm working at the flower shop are there to buy flowers for their significant other."

"Yeah, it's rough out there," Alyssa agrees. "You're saving yourself a lot of heartache, Connor."

Austin laughs and nudges Alyssa with his elbow. "This girl has enough disastrous first date stories for all of us."

"Says the guy who could get anyone he wanted with the snap of a finger," she shoots back at him.

He shakes his head. "I have to be extra careful." Austin turns to look at Griffin. "I'm sure you understand, dude. Most of the women looking to date us are looking for the fame associated with our name, not because they actually like us."

"Right on, man." Griffin nods. "That's why you have to meet someone before you're famous or someone who actually doesn't give a rip about it." He squeezes my middle.

"Exactly."

Tess clears her throat. "Sorry to be a buzzkill, but I need to leave in ten minutes to relieve my babysitter."

"Right, sorry." Kelsey turns the whiteboard with our scores around. "Going into the final round, in last place, we have Shayna and Tess with seven points."

Both girls smile good-naturedly.

"Maybe I should just go home now," Tess teases.

"In fourth place, we have Emmy and Connor with ten points. Tyler and I are currently rounding out third place with eleven points. Mallory and Griffin are in second place with thirteen points. And, with a whopping fourteen points, our current leaders are Alyssa and Austin."

Alyssa switches the slide on the TV. "For the final theme, can I get a drumroll, please?" We all pat our legs as she clicks to the next slide. "Winter movies."

"Boo." Emmy throws a piece of popcorn at the television.

"We know which team is winning now," Kelsey says.

The whole room looks at me and Griffin. He holds up his hands, and I immediately miss his grounding touch. "Hey, I haven't been in any Christmas movies. You all still have a chance."

"Yeah, like we ever had a shot." Tess leans back into the couch, laughing with Shayna. At least they're in good spirits about being in last place.

Despite Griffin saying everyone else had a chance, we don't miss a single question in the round. He answers the ones correctly about *The Santa Clause* and *It's a Wonderful Life*, while I get the responses related to *The Holiday* and *Love Hard*.

"All right, that was the final question." Kelsey looks at the scoreboard. "And we have a tie between Alyssa and Austin and Mallory and Griffin." She pulls out her phone. "That means we need a tiebreaker question." She takes a minute, tapping on her screen and scrolling. "Okay, for the win, what was the highest-grossing Christmas movie of all time?"

Griffin and I look at each other with a knowing smile. It has to be the greatest one of all time—the very one we watched together last night. I write down *Home Alone* and hold the whiteboard to my chest, ready to win this thing.

When the minute is up, we flip over our whiteboard at the same time as Alyssa and Austin. They wrote down *Elf*.

"We've got this in the bag, beautiful." Griffin hugs me.

Kelsey looks between our whiteboards and smiles. "The correct answer is...*Home Alone*. That makes our winners Mallory and Griffin."

I hop up from his lap, jumping like we just won a real award rather than the trivia champions of our friend group. But Griffin matches my energy. He pops up from the couch and lifts me into the air, placing my butt on his left shoulder. I duck to avoid hitting my head on the ceiling as everyone congratulates us. He carefully puts me back on my feet.

I'm in a daze, overflowing with the adrenaline of his closeness all night.

Everyone says good night and heads out, but my steps are slow toward the front door as I walk Griffin to his car.

"Thanks for a fun night. I couldn't have won it without you," I say, trying to delay him leaving. It's crazy how only a few weeks ago I could barely stand listening to him talk for five minutes, and now I'm sad that he's leaving when I've seen him the past four days in a row. But we don't have any plans together again until New Year's Eve.

"I'm glad I could help you get the win, but I like spending time with you more."

A bitter wind rustles my hair, and he brushes the curl flying into my face back.

"I've actually been meaning to ask you something." He pulls his hand back, rubbing it along the scruff on his chin. "It's kind of last minute, but I'm flying to LA in a week for an influencer event for *Accidentally in Matrimony*."

"That sounds fun." I swallow down the sadness threatening to take over at the thought of him leaving for LA again. This isn't like the last time. I know he's coming back, but it still stings.

"It would mean a lot to me to have you there."

I blink. "Oh, right. I forgot that attending a more public event was in our contract."

Griffin steps closer, cupping my cheeks with his hands. His palms feel warm and strong against my skin. "I don't want you there because of a stupid contract. I want you there because I can't imagine enjoying the night without you." He tilts my head back, making me meet his eyes. "I want to show you off to the world, so every single person in it knows you're mine."

It's official. I'm a gooey, melted puddle on the floor, because what kind of man says things like that? It's no wonder his latest movie did so well. I think I need to watch it now. For research purposes only, of course.

"When would we be gone?" I ask. "School starts back up on the sixth."

"The premiere is on the fourth, so I thought we could fly in on the third and fly back on the fifth." He runs his hand along my hair. "I understand if that cuts it too close to school—"

"No," I cut him off. "I'd love to go support you."

Griffin's mouth tilts up into the lopsided grin I've come to love. "I'll arrange a dress shopping trip for you in LA on the third, then."

My eyes go wide. "Oh, you don't need to do that."

"Let me spoil you, beautiful," he croons, his voice as silky and smooth as the hot chocolate he made me last night.

There he goes, melting my heart again. "If you insist."

"I do."

As I lie in bed that night, those words seem to stick with me for reasons I'm not ready to think about just yet.

CHAPTER TWENTY-THREE

GRIFFIN

IT'S ONLY BEEN FOUR days since I've seen her, but they've left a Mallory-shaped hole in my heart.

She's been preparing things for her classroom before school starts back next week, but today she's all mine. Then I get her all to myself this weekend in Los Angeles. I'm glad she agreed to go with me to the movie premiere because I'd be devastated to miss the last few days with her before school is back in session. I know I'm going to see her less once she's back to teaching, but I'm choosing to live in delusion until then.

There's still plenty of time left for us to spend together while Granny recovers. Until I have to return to LA, to my career. I shake my head. I refuse to think about the distance that will separate us when I still have time with her here. Plus, there's a lifetime together to look forward to. I know that's wishful thinking, but, like I said, I'm choosing to live in delusion.

My phone buzzes in my pocket with an incoming text.

RHETT

Did you persuade Mallory to come to the showing with you???

Granny has always called me a golden retriever kind of guy...but if I'm a golden retriever, what does that make Rhett? A Labrador? A poodle? Or maybe one of the little goofy dogs spinning in circles at your feet. Yeah, I think it's that one. Rhett never runs out of energy, even when touring nonstop. And he's the most enthusiastic guy I know.

ME

Yes, you'll get to meet her this weekend.

RHETT

gif of minions cheering

I can't wait!

You better warn her about my charm, or I might just steal your girl *winking emoji*

ME

Have I told you lately how insufferable you are?

RHETT

It's been a while. Thanks, I needed that to come back down.

Save me a seat by yours.

Most of these events have assigned seating, but I don't bother telling him that. The only reason he was initially invited was because we used his hit country song "Forever, For Real" as the promotional song with the trailer and at the end credits.

I likely would've ended up inviting him anyway because he's usually my plus-one to these things. It takes the pressure off having to take an actual date and the media frenzy that always follows whenever I'm pictured with any woman. Instead, the paparazzi have a ton of photos of me talking to my best friend. It's a win-win.

Another text comes through.

RHETT

> Better yet, I'll see you on the carpet! *man dancing emoji*

Oh boy. Once he sends that man dancing emoji, it usually means he's just getting started with all his over-the-top exuberance. If I don't end the conversation now, he'll never stop. I thumbs-up Rhett's last message and slide my phone back into my pocket just as I hear a car pulling into the driveway.

I pop a stick of cinnamon gum into my mouth before grabbing my coat and gloves. I head outside, lifting my pointer and middle fingers in a wave to Ted through the window before hopping into the backseat beside Mallory. She's buckled into the middle seat, so my leg presses against hers as the car starts to move. It might mean nothing at all, but I'm taking it as a good sign that she chose to sit there, closer to me.

I lean over, pressing my lips to her cheek. "It's good to see you, beautiful. It's been too long."

She smiles. "It's good to see you, too."

I love that she genuinely smiles at me now, like it's effortless. A smile she can't contain because she truly enjoys being around me.

"Are you ready for our date?"

Mallory nods. "Can you tell me where we're going, or is this another surprise?"

"I can tell you, if you really want to know. But I think it will be more magical if it's a surprise."

She loops her hand through my arm and rests her head on my shoulder. "Okay, I trust you."

Hope bubbles up inside me like a pot on the stove that I can't keep from boiling over. Joy is my new resting state. I'm not sure I'll ever be able to wipe this grin off my face.

When we arrive at our destination, I open the door and step outside before helping Mallory get out of the car. "Give me just a second," I tell her and move to the driver's side.

Ted rolls down the window. "What can I do for you, Mr. Reynolds?"

"For the millionth time, you can call me Griffin." I smile. "But you can go ahead and take the rest of the day off once you drop your friend off. I've arranged another way to get home."

"You're sure?"

I nod. "Go enjoy New Year's Eve with your family."

"Thanks, Mr. Re— Griffin."

I shake my head as I wave goodbye and return to Mallory's side. I take her hand and lead her from the parking lot into an opening in the woods surrounding us.

"Why are we in the middle of a forest? Why did you say Ted had to drop his friend off?"

Wrapping my gloved hands around her upper arms, I say, "Close your eyes."

Mallory narrows her eyes at me playfully before closing them. Ted's friend pulls the surprise up behind her. It's probably already obvious with the sounds of the hooves crunching the snow.

I let go of her arms and say, "Your chariot awaits, beautiful."

Mallory turns around and opens her eyes, gasping when she sees the horse-drawn carriage. She launches herself at me. I barely catch her in time as she throws her arms around my neck and wraps her legs around my waist. With my hands cupped under her thighs, my heart races, but I try to control it before it makes me do something I might regret. I'm not going to do anything to mess this night up. Even if her lips are in the perfect position to be thoroughly kissed.

I avert my gaze. Nope, we're not thinking about her perfect mouth. Fish lips. That's what I'll think of. Gross, stinky fish lips.

"Thank you." Mallory's words draw my eyes back to her beaming face. "I've always wanted to go on a carriage ride through the snow."

"Really?"

She nods. "It may seem like I'm not into all the romantic things, but I think every girl has at least one princess moment they dream of. This is mine."

"Then let's make your dream come true, princess." I carry her over to the carriage and carefully place her in it. I offer her an exaggerated bow that makes her blush before hopping up into the carriage and sitting beside her. There's a plush cream-colored blanket that I pull up over our laps.

"Do you have everything you need, sir?" Ted's friend—the owner of the horse and carriage—asks.

"This is great. Thank you. I'll return it later, where we discussed."

"Great, you kids have fun." He walks off in the snow toward the car.

I pull my phone out and prop it up on the railing with a timer set. "We need a picture first."

I lean my head against Mallory's as we cozy up under the blanket and smile at the camera. This is a moment I never want to forget. After she approves the photo, I slide my phone back into my pocket and grab the drinks I had prepared for us in to-go cups.

Mallory takes the one I offer her, smiling when she sips the contents. "Snickerdoodle hot chocolate?" I nod. "You're the best."

There's no holding back my smile as I take the reins in one hand while carefully holding my drink in the other. I make a small clicking sound, and the horse pulls us forward.

She raises a brow. "You know how to drive a horse-drawn carriage? Is there anything you *can't* do?"

I laugh. "I had to learn for my role in *A Chance Romance*." Thankfully, Ted's friend owns one of the carriage ride businesses in town and allowed me to borrow it for the evening.

"Of course, you did." She takes a sip of her drink, leaning back and looking at the scenery.

We move down the middle of the forest, rows of pine trees on either side, covered in a dusting of snow. It looks ethereal.

"I think we've been dropped into the middle of a fictional winter wonderland." Mallory looks around in awe. "It looks like a scene from Narnia." She tilts her head back and forth. "Or a horror film before all the murdering happens."

I laugh. "I didn't take you to a murder forest."

"That's a relief." She pats her gloved hand on my chest, and my heart immediately picks up pace, a rhythm it only adopts around her.

I look down at her. "It really is beautiful. More than I could've ever dreamed of."

"Are you saying you didn't orchestrate for there to be snow covering all the trees and fresh snow along the path?" She glances up at me and blushes when she realizes I was already looking at her.

"I'm saying the view from where I am is the most stunning one I've ever seen." I press a kiss to her temple. "Nothing else could ever compare."

The color on her cheeks deepens, almost matching the pink of her coat. "So, should we go ahead and post the picture?"

"I don't see every time we hang out as a photo op." I pull the horse to a stop, set my drink down, and lean closer. A snowflake falls on my cheek, but I don't bother brushing it away. Nothing could pull me from this moment. I'm completely locked in on Mallory. "Maybe I want pictures of us all to ourselves. Or maybe I just want to see you."

"Is that so?" She tilts her chin, giving me the perfect access to her lips—an invitation.

"Mm-hmm," I hum. If she truly was my girlfriend, I'd kiss her without fail, but I don't want to make a move too quickly and lose all the progress we've made.

Thankfully, I don't have to worry about that because Mallory closes the remaining distance between us, pressing her lips to mine. It's nothing like the kisses we've shared before. Our first kiss was tender and sweet, while the one for the photographer was quick and staged. But this one is filled with all the passion I've been holding back since I found her. One that comes from thinking love was forever lost, but it's finally found again.

No more holding back.

I put my all into each press of our lips, telling her everything I can't say with my words yet. Not until I know for certain how she feels.

Your laugh is my favorite sound on the planet. I'd do just about anything to hear it for the rest of my life.

I can't get you out of my mind.

You're slowly becoming the very air I breathe.

Every minute I spend with you is my new favorite.

I don't want this to ever end, because I don't think I'd be able to handle losing you a second time.

I'm falling in love with you as quickly as the snow is falling around us.

I tilt my head, and Mallory deepens the kiss, tasting like sweet cinnamon. A deep sound comes out of my throat, making me sound like a man who's been starving for affection. But I would wait my whole life for this kind of connection. One where it feels like our lives are so irrevocably intertwined that you can't call it anything but fate.

My gloved hands move to the back of her neck. This kiss feels special. Like we're on the precipice of a real future together. Who needs food, water, and shelter when I have her? Every moment spent together—every touch, every kiss, every shared word—makes me feel alive.

When I feel her shiver, I reluctantly pull back. "Cold?"

Her cheeks are flushed from our kiss, but she still wraps her arms around her middle, huddling under the blanket. "Yes and no." She laughs.

I reach down and pull out the thermos I had the owner stow under the seat. "How about more hot chocolate?"

Mallory's eyes light up as she nods. "You thought of everything."

"Only the best for my girl." I open the thermos and pour the steaming drink into her cup.

"Thanks." She sips on it before snuggling back into my side.

We're quiet for a while as we take in the beautiful scenery around us. It smells like the epitome of winter—the scent of pine trees in the air mixed with the sweet cinnamon-sugar of her drink.

"Griff?" Mallory's voice pulls me out of my daze.

"Mm?"

"Thank you."

I laugh, pulling her closer to my side. "You already said that."

"I'm not talking about the hot chocolate, even though it's amazing." She licks her lips and looks around like she's searching for the words. "Thank you for not giving up on me. For pursuing me and showing up, even when I was being…difficult."

"Like I've said, you're worth the wait," I reassure her. "But I think I'd like a repeat of that kiss every day for the rest of my life." I watch her, waiting to see how she'll respond to such a bold statement.

Mallory smiles, her eyes taking on a teasing glint. "I think I could be convinced." She looks down at her cup, then back up at me. "Does this mean we can tear up that contract now?" She leans over and presses a kiss to my cheek. "I don't want your money or anything else between us. I have all I need right here."

I lean into her touch. "So do I."

"Does this make us officially official?"

"Absolutely," I say, even though this has been the real deal for me from the start. "I think you just gave me a new favorite word."

"What's that?"

"Us."

Mallory leans her head on my shoulder. "I like the sound of that, too."

CHAPTER TWENTY-FOUR
MALLORY

I'M ON A JET.

Scratch that.

I'm on a *private* jet.

The kind where we're the only people on it except the flight attendant, a bodyguard, and pilots. The kind where everyone keeps referring to me as "Ms. Porter." I don't think I could ever get used to anyone besides my students calling me that.

Griffin sleepily readjusts in the luxury recliner across from me. There's a small circle of drool on his shirt where his mouth meets his shoulder, and I can't help but find it adorable. He looked perfect when I woke up next to him on his couch after our movie marathon, so it makes me feel better knowing that even celebrities drool in their sleep. That's a win for normal people everywhere. A way of knowing we're not alone in our plebeian ways.

He looks incredibly handsome in his white button-down and khakis. The top two buttons of his shirt are undone, and let me just say, even drool can't take away from his attractiveness.

I feel completely underdressed in my matching pink sweat set. But Griffin said I looked adorable when he picked me up, and I've learned he's the type of guy who only says what he means.

"Ms. Porter?" The stewardess stops beside us. "We'll arrive in Los Angeles in about thirty minutes."

"Thank you." At the thought of landing, my eyes go wide. Will paparazzi be there to greet us? There's not much I can do about my outfit, but I can at least let my hair down and freshen up my curls before we land.

My hair is currently up in a pineapple—not the actual fruit, but a pineapple bun where all my curls are piled on top of my head and secured with the perfect scrunchie. I usually only wear it like this at night to protect my hair, not to be seen getting off a private jet with my movie star boyfriend.

I let out a dreamy sigh at the thought of Griffin. I can hardly believe that he's my boyfriend, and not the fake kind. My feelings for him have been confusing to put it simply. From our explosive chemistry the first time we met to waiting weeks for a call that never came, to seeing his interview and thinking I meant nothing to him. Then running into him again three years later and reliving our first meeting. From fake dating to real feelings to real dating.

Our relationship is tough to describe, and we still have things to figure out if we want a future together. But to end up right here in the arms of a handsome man who truly sees me and values me for who I am, well, I wouldn't have it any other way.

I stand, careful not to wake Griffin, and make my way to the bathroom. My jaw drops when I open the door and see how much larger it is than the ones on the planes I usually fly on—no expert maneuvering to touch the toilet as little as possible is required.

I gently pull out my favorite scrunchie and fluff my hair. A few sections of it look wonky, so I wet them and do my best to finger-curl them back into place. When I emerge from the bathroom, Griffin's gaze is locked on me as I walk back to my seat. I feel like I'm dressed for the red carpet already with the heated way he's staring at me.

"Have I ever told you how much I love your hair?" He stands and kisses me, soft and tender. "And your pink outfits." His lips hover near mine, teasing me, making me want *more*. "Really, it's just you."

"That you *love*?" I pull back, raising a brow. The blush that covers his cheeks feels like a first-place trophy—I'm the winner of our teasing game.

Griffin stutters. "I— Uh— That's not what I meant to say. I just meant that I like everything about you." He rubs the back of his neck.

"I'm messing with you." I nudge him with my elbow. "I like you too, Mr. Razzle-Dazzle."

He groans. "We're still not past that?"

"Never." I grin. "It helps me fall asleep every night."

Griffin squeezes my side, and I can't help but squeal. I try to wiggle away from him, but he grabs my hips and pulls us both onto his leather recliner. I end up on his lap, facing him.

"At least I know my voice is soothing, if it lulls you into a deep slumber." His stubble grazes my face as he moves his lips close to my ear. "Maybe I need to film a different commercial that won't make you fall asleep."

"I can think of *other* ways you could keep me awake." I press my lips to the corner of his mouth, taunting him with the thought of more.

His cheeks tinge pink, giving me another win. He shakes his head. "I thought I knew who you were, but I think I underestimated you."

"I don't know what you mean." I flutter my lashes, playing coy.

Griffin's lips pull up into his signature grin—the one for me. "Oh, I think you know *exactly* what you're doing to me, Mallory Porter." He readjusts my body so I'm facing away from him, then wraps his seatbelt around both our laps before clicking it into place. Griffin takes my hands, intertwining our fingers and resting them in my lap as the plane descends.

I know I should probably move back to my own seat, but for once, I'm exactly where I want to be.

———— ◦ ♡ ◦ ————

I've now learned that a perk of arriving somewhere in a private jet means a private runway, which also means no paparazzi. I planned on changing into something nicer before dress shopping, but Griffin's driver pulls to a stop in an alleyway.

I look around, spotting a few doors but no signage. "Um, where are we?"

"The fancy gown store I rented out for the morning." Griffin turns to face me. "I've already arranged everything with the owners. Pick whatever you want. Nothing is too much. Get yourself some heels and accessories while you're at it."

"Are you trying to spoil me?"

"Now that you're my girlfriend…" Griffin leans in and presses his mouth to mine, parting my lips and getting my heart racing. He pulls away with a knowing smile; he definitely just got a point in the game. "I plan on giving you anything your heart desires."

"Anything?" I move closer, brushing my lips against his.

He laughs. "There will be more time for that later. For now, I want you to feel as beautiful as you are, so pick whatever dress makes you feel like that."

A few weeks ago, I would've thought his words were crap. But now that I know that his intentions are true, they leave me feeling warm. Something akin to love swirls inside, though I'm hesitant to call it that when he hasn't shared those words with me yet.

It takes a minute for everything he said to sink in. "Wait, you're not coming in with me?"

"Karina wants to meet with me in person while I'm here. Besides, I want to be surprised when I see you on the red carpet tomorrow. I'll have a driver here to take you to my apartment when you're done."

"Okay." I scoot away, trying to sound more confident than I feel. I'm in a pink sweat set, about to shop in what I'm sure is not a sweats kind of store. I open the car door and step outside. When I turn back to him, he's smiling widely.

"I'll see you soon, beautiful."

I wave goodbye and open the shop door, making the bell chime. After taking a steadying breath, I walk inside. A tall middle-aged woman with a pinched expression immediately walks over. She's in a tight dress that looks like it would cost more than my monthly salary. "Hello, I'm Serafina. Feel free to browse and bring me any gowns you'd like to try on. I'll be just over there if you need anything." She points to a counter before moving that way.

I clasp my hands behind my back and begin perusing the racks at the front of the store. There are no windows in here—likely for privacy reasons— but there are enough bright lights to make me feel like I'm in a spotlight center stage.

There are so many options, I honestly don't even know where to start. Do I look for high necklines or a low back? Straps or strapless? What kind of material says high-end so I don't end up being listed as the worst-dressed guest in articles? I'm sure many of Griffin's fans already think I'm not good enough for him. I don't want to give them more reasons to think they're right, but I'm way out of my depth here.

I pull my phone out of my pocket, ready to call Alyssa and get her fashion expertise, when the bell on the door chimes again.

"Sorry, I'm late."

I turn and watch as the woman removes her large designer sunglasses, slipping them into her purse. My mouth falls open as she approaches me with an outstretched hand. "I'm Brit—"

"You're Brittany Clearwater." I stare at her as if she's a figment of my imagination.

Brittany tosses her long blonde hair over her shoulder. "Did Griffin not tell you I was coming?" When I shake my head, she sighs. "That's men for you."

"You've got that right." But that still doesn't explain why Griffin sent her.

"When he mentioned that he was setting this shopping spree up for you, I offered to come help," she clarifies. "I remember how overwhelming it was when I had to dress up for my first Hollywood event."

I immediately decide that I like her. For someone so famous, Brittany seems down-to-earth. "That was really thoughtful of you. Thanks for taking time out of your busy schedule to be here. I could use all the help I can get." I let out a nervous laugh.

"You're so welcome." Brittany smiles, and it lights up the whole room. She gestures to the racks of dresses. "Are you ready to shop until you drop?"

I'm not sure that my petite body type is built for all these long, glittering gowns, but I nod anyway. "Let's do it."

"What style of dress are you typically drawn to?" Brittany peers at me over the rack. She's tall and slender, a true model figure. I'm sure she'd look stunning in any style of gown. As for me, I could only dream of looking good in a handful of these.

"I was just asking myself what kind of dress I should look for." I place my hands on my hips, my cheeks warm as I admit the truth. "I have no clue. I never wear long dresses, let alone evening gowns meant for the red carpet. It's always been hard to find ones that work for me." I shrug. "Short girl problems."

"That's where the fabulous Helen comes in."

"Helen?"

"She's the in-house seamstress who'll have any dress you want fitting you like a glove in no time."

"She sounds more like a fairy godmother."

Brittany steps in front of me with a smile. "Let's let her work her magic, then. Do you have a color that you feel most confident in?" She takes a step back, eyeing me up and down. "I'm thinking reds or pinks would look best with your skin tone and hair, but it's up to you."

This is the question I was born for. "Pink," I answer without hesitation.

She leads me to the back of the store. It's intimate, but in a way that feels high-end. I'm sure the dresses are supplied by only the best designers. I don't even want to look at any of the price tags. Griffin told me there's no spending limit since he's footing the bill, but I'll feel like I'm taking advantage of his generosity if I go overboard.

"This section has the evening gowns for special events." Brittany gestures to the space behind her. The racks are color coordinated to perfection. Not a single dress is out of place in the rainbow array of gowns. I head directly for the pink section.

"Come to mama." I run my hand along the dresses, internally melting at the feel of the luxurious fabrics that I'd never be able to afford on my own.

Brittany snorts. "You're hilarious." She thumbs through the dresses beside me. "I can see why Griffin fell for you."

"Do you—" I swallow, struggling to get the words out. "Do you know Griffin well?"

She smiles, and my heart drops. Maybe there was something more between them than Griffin let on.

"Better than any other male costar I've ever had." Brittany pulls out a coral dress and holds it up in front of me, pursing her lips. With a shake of her head, she puts it back on the rack. "He was truly the most thoughtful man I've ever worked with in Hollywood. It was refreshing."

"He shows me every day how thoughtful he is," I agree. The next dress I look at is so silky, there's no way I can pass up the opportunity to try it on. I pull it off the rack and drape it over my arm.

"He's kind, too. He really got to know me and always made sure I was comfortable on set. I felt so safe in every scene." She presses her lips together. "And, trust me, that's not always the case."

"I'm glad he was able to make you feel that way. You deserve to feel safe at work, *especially* when you have to occasionally kiss your coworkers."

Brittany snickers. "You're so right. And just so you know, Griffin and I were never anything beyond coworkers. It was strictly business, though I'd like to think we're friends. I'd work with him again in a heartbeat." She nudges my hip with hers while she pulls a blush-colored dress I wouldn't normally pick for myself. "You landed yourself a good guy."

Relief floods my body. Deep down, I knew that Griffin didn't lie to me—it's not who he is. But it still feels good to have that validation from Brittany, too. "I really did." I accept the dress she hands me and continue perusing the rack. My fingers trail across a magenta gown covered in little sparkles. Upon closer inspection, I think those are, in fact, diamonds. I'll try it on just for fun.

Brittany hands me a bubblegum-pink dress with a plunging neckline, and I add it to the pile on my arm. "I don't know if I could pull this off. You obviously could." I gesture to her perfect figure. "I mean, look at you."

"Me?" she scoffs. "Look at you. I'd kill for hair like yours. There isn't a perm out there that would give me perfect beach waves like that."

"What is it about women that we always want something someone else has?"

"Insecurity? Society? The media?" Brittany shrugs. "At least we can always uplift each other."

"Amen, sister." I pull another two dresses off the rack. "I should try these on."

As if out of nowhere, Serafina appears, taking the dresses from me. She holds them above her head as she leads me down a hallway into a giant room with an ornately carved wooden room divider and a half-circle wall of mirrors.

Brittany sits in a chair by the mirrors while Serafina hangs the dresses up on a rack behind the divider. I thought I would try these on by myself, but she waits for me to undress and then helps me into the first gown. You learn something new every day. Apparently, famous people have someone help them try on their gowns. I've only ever heard of that being done at wedding dress boutiques.

I step around the divider in the first gown, a blush-pink number with a high neck and short train.

Brittany immediately shakes her head. "You look great, but I think this one is a little too understated for your features."

I look at myself in the mirror and completely agree with her assessment. It's pretty, but I don't think it's red carpet worthy, at least not for me. "On to the next one."

I try on the remaining dresses we grabbed and finally walk out in the last one. Brittany's tight smile immediately lets me know this will not be my dress of choice. Looking at myself in the mirror, I place my hands on the bright-pink fabric and let out a small huff. "They're all beautiful, but none of them feels like *the one*."

Brittany taps her bottom lip and suddenly stands, the chair making a screeching sound as it scoots against the marble floor. "I know just what you need. I'll be right back."

Serafina helps me get out of the dress while we wait. Right when we've finished, Brittany returns, holding a dress behind her back. "Don't peek. I think this is it."

I close my eyes as Serafina helps me into the mystery dress. She slides the zipper into place and escorts me around the corner. Brittany gasps and claps her hands.

"Can I open my eyes?" I ask.

"Yes."

When I look at my reflection in the mirror, I'm rendered speechless. The gown is a dusty rose color that's more muted than the shades of pink I normally wear, but it's utterly stunning. I run my hands along the luxe material. It's an off-the-shoulder dress that perfectly emphasizes my collarbones. It accentuates my every curve with expertly placed ruching and a fitted silhouette that makes me feel feminine. Once I have heels on, the dress won't even need to be hemmed.

"For the final touch." Serafina pulls out a matching strip of fabric, wrapping it around my neck and letting both ends fall behind me, like a backward scarf. It ties the whole look together, making me fall in love with the dress even more.

"What do you think?" Brittany leans forward in her seat.

I didn't realize that I hadn't said anything. "I feel sophisticated." I turn to look at the back before facing her with a wide smile. "And beautiful."

She pops up, moving to stand behind me with a smile. "You should. Griffin won't be able to keep his eyes off you."

I can't wait to see the look on his face tomorrow night. Just the thought of it sends a shiver down my spine.

CHAPTER TWENTY-FIVE

GRIFFIN

My pulse skitters as Mallory's car pulls up to the red carpet. She insisted that we take two cars so she could surprise me with her outfit. The anticipation is killing me, especially since Brittany texted me yesterday and told me that I will *die dead* when I see Mallory tonight. I don't exactly know what that means, but I understand enough to know she'll be stunning. Although she looks amazing in anything she wears.

There's also something that happened yesterday while she was dress shopping. Something I need to tell her about, but am terrified to. It all happened so fast that I'm still trying to get a grasp on it myself, but I know the longer I wait, the longer it's going to eat away at me. I'm just not sure how she's going to react to the news.

The car rolls to a stop, and my heart thumps loudly in my chest. The driver rounds the vehicle, opening the back door as the paparazzi push closer, clicking their cameras incessantly and shouting questions as I step closer, not wanting any of them to get too close to my girl.

I offer my hand into the open door, and Mallory grasps it like I'm the only thing saving her from falling off a cliff.

One leg slowly follows the other as she emerges from the car.

The corner of my mouth tilts up in a smile. Stunning isn't a strong enough word for how she looks tonight. "I— Wow, you look—" I shake my head with a laugh.

Mallory smiles, and I hear more cameras click around us, trying to capture the beauty that is her to live for eternity in a photo. "Cat got your tongue?" she teases.

I rub the back of my neck. "What can I say? You've rendered me speechless." My eyes roam over her, drinking her in. Her gown is long and muted pink. It goes off her shoulders, and she has this long piece of matching fabric around her neck and floating behind her like she's some type of goddess.

The dress reminds me of her usual pink outfits, but more upscale with a restraint and subtlety that make her even more captivating.

Rather than make a fool of myself by trying to say all this out loud, I offer her my arm. She wraps her hand around my bicep in a death grip, and we walk down the red carpet, stopping to pose for photos along the way.

"You look pretty dapper, yourself," she whispers as I wrap my arm around her waist.

"Thank you." I dip my chin, trying to hide my goofy grin from the photographers. "How do you feel about all this?"

Mallory smirks. "Right now, I feel like an animal in a zoo. All eyes on me."

We smile for another picture.

"I know one set of eyes that is definitely on you." She spins to me, and I wink at her, trying to ease her nerves. A blush blossoms on her cheeks as the sun sets behind her. Mallory is radiant.

I might be the Hollywood star, but she is the sun I revolve around.

"Griff." She pats my chest repeatedly, then points behind me. "It's Rhett Hayes." She says his name like one would say Taylor Swift or Morgan Freeman, in awe that she's in the presence of celebrity royalty.

"There's Hollywood's power couple," Rhett says in his southern drawl.

I turn just in time for him to pull me into a crushing hug. After a few pats on the back, he moves toward Mallory, his bare arms wide. The sleeves of his white shirt are cut off, and it's tucked into denim. I shake my head. This isn't the Country Music Awards. Only Rhett could pull off jeans and a bolo tie at a fancy red-carpet event without making anyone bat an eye.

"The woman of the hour." He extends a hand to Mallory. I assume he wants to shake hers, but no. Rhett twirls her around, showing off her dress and giving me the perfect view of the way the fabric of her gown dips low on her back.

Have freaking mercy. She's trying to do me in. I'm going to be gawking at Mallory in all of tonight's photos, and I don't even care. Some guys might say I'm *whipped*, but I say let the world know I'm completely, unashamedly smitten with Mallory Porter.

"I'm hardly the woman of the hour." Mallory laughs.

"Have you seen you tonight?" Rhett tilts his head, and she blushes. If it were anyone else besides Rhett telling her this, I would be burning with jealousy, but I know how harmless my best friend is.

"Do you have a sister?"

Mallory laughs. "A brother."

"Darn." Rhett presses his lips together. "What about a cousin? Or a really young aunt?"

I clap him on the shoulder. "Why don't we talk more about her available family members inside?"

"Right." He wraps Mallory's arm through his and walks toward the building. I follow close enough behind to hear their conversation. "I have so many questions for you."

"Is that so?" She sounds intrigued. "I have a lot for you, too."

I quicken my steps, coming up to Mallory's side. "Do I want to know what these questions are?"

"No," they say simultaneously, then burst into laughter.

Having them meet was either the best or worst idea of my life. I guess I'll find out by the end of the night.

⎯⎯⎯⎯⎯ ♡ ♡ ♡ ⎯⎯⎯⎯⎯

It turns out I'm thankful Rhett is here tonight. While the movie director is walking me and Brittany around, introducing us to many of the influencer attendees, Rhett has been able to keep Mallory company.

Anytime I catch sight of them together, they're talking or laughing, so I'd say they're getting along well. I don't think Rhett would ever *not* get along with someone, but it feels good knowing I have my best friend's stamp of approval on my relationship, nonetheless.

When I glance at the time, we're only a few minutes out from when the showing starts. I've never been so thankful. Small talk has never been my thing, but I've had to do a lot of it in this line of work. It seems like it's practically all I do when I'm not on set. I've learned to appreciate it more in recent years as it's helped blossom my career, but right now it feels like pure torture.

Anything that's keeping me apart from Mallory—especially when she looks like that—would feel like torture. She deserves all my time, and I plan to give it to her. One day.

"All right, it's almost show time." Our director rubs his hands together. "I'll have you both come up on stage with me while I make a few quick remarks, and then you can sit with your guests during the movie. I will need you for the Q&A afterward, but other than that, enjoy the rest of your evening."

We follow him down the aisle to the stage. Brittany leans close and mutters, "What rest of our evening?"

I cough to cover my laugh. "I was thinking the same thing."

Once we're on stage, our director taps the microphone. "Hello, everyone. Thank you for attending our special screening of *Accidentally in Matrimony*. We're amazed by the positive reception we've received. Tonight, we're honored to have both our leads, Brittany Clearwater and Griffin Reynolds, with us. They'll be available for a special Q&A after the showing. Thank you all again. Enjoy the movie." He waves to the crowd while Brittany and I walk to our seats in the second row.

Once the spotlight no longer shines on me, I immediately spot Mallory and head her way. Rhett extends a closed fist when I walk past him, and I bump it with mine before moving past them both to take the open seat beside Mallory.

I wrap my arm around her out of instinct. My fingers brush her exposed back, and my pulse becomes erratic at the smooth feel of it. We're in public. I'm at a work event. I can't have my hands all over her. She crosses her legs, the movement causing the slit of her dress to open, showing off skin from her heels to her upper thigh. I want to write *mine* right there—to let everyone know this gorgeous woman is spoken for. My cheeks warm. I really need to stop thinking about her legs.

I drag in a long breath and blow it out slowly through my mouth. I clear my throat, then say, "I just remembered you haven't seen this movie."

"I've been looking forward to watching it since meeting Brittany. She's sweet."

My jaw drops. "Because of Brittany, not your handsome boyfriend?"

She smiles softly, looking playful. "I thought you didn't want me to see you kiss another girl on-screen?"

If she's going to tease me, then two can play that game. I lean across the armrest, brushing my lips across her cheek, then the soft spot between her neck and ear. "What if I told you that I was thinking of you—of our first kiss—when I was kissing Brittany's character?"

Mallory inhales sharply. "*Me?*" She pulls her head back, her eyes searching mine. "But you filmed this a while after we met."

I reach over and intertwine our fingers, the touch immediately grounding me. "That's right."

"Well, if you were thinking of me while filming the kiss scenes, maybe we could recreate them later." She trails a finger along my chest where my dress shirt is unbuttoned.

I have to bite my bottom lip to keep from making any sounds. I'm using every ounce of restraint to keep from pulling her into my arms and recreating them right here, right now. Give this audience a real show.

She presses her lips to the corner of my mouth. "You know, for research purposes."

I pull away, taking a long, shallow breath as the lights dim. "You're lucky there are a lot of people around."

"Why's that?"

"I would tickle you so hard right now."

Mallory laughs, and her eyes go wide as she slaps a hand over her mouth. People turn to look at us as the opening credits play on the screen. "I can't believe you just made me do that." She shoots me a look and pinches my side.

"You started it with all your talk of kissing."

"Stop distracting me." She presses her pointer finger to her lips, mirth glimmering in her eyes. "I'm trying to watch the movie."

"Whatever you say, beautiful." I squeeze her hand and turn my attention to the big screen.

I try to focus on the movie, but every small laugh Mallory makes draws my gaze to her. I know rom-coms aren't her first choice in film, so the fact that she's here supporting me and seemingly enjoying the movie means more than words can express.

When the end credits start to roll, Mallory leans over and kisses my cheek. "That was great."

"You liked it?"

"I didn't like the kissing scenes for obvious reasons. But knowing that you were thinking of me while filming them makes them tolerable." She smiles at me. "In all seriousness, your acting was refreshing. I could tell that you put your all into becoming your character, and it shows."

I stare into her light-brown eyes, losing myself in them. "If I wasn't already falling for you, that would've done me in." I press my lips together as I realize what I just said. I told Mallory I was falling for her as casually as I talk about the weather with a stranger. But I honestly don't care, because it's the truth.

I only hope she returns my feelings…and that she'll still feel the same way when I tell her my big news.

CHAPTER TWENTY-SIX
MALLORY

GRIFFIN'S PERFORMANCE IN *ACCIDENTALLY in Matrimony* was incredible. But it's the words he just said off-screen that steal my breath.

"You're falling for me?" The words barely come out in a whisper, making me sound as stunned as I feel.

"I th—"

"Sorry to interrupt," the movie director says, "but I need you and Brittany for the Q&A session."

Griffin turns to me, rubbing his hand up and down my arm. "I'm sorry."

"Go." A smirk tugs at my lips. "Besides, I have more questions for Rhett."

"Of course, you do." He kisses me, soft and slow. "I'm yours for the rest of the night."

I pull back, smiling at him. "I like the sound of that."

Griffin leans in close, his lips brushing my ear. "We'll continue our conversation then, too." He walks away but glances back over his shoulder, shooting me the crooked smile I've come to love.

I sigh dreamily as I step closer to Rhett. "He looks good tonight." I've seen Griffin dressed up in photos, but seeing him in a suit *in person* is a sight to behold. "I mean, the way the top of his shirt is unbuttoned." I fan my face. Rhett laughs, and I grimace. "Sorry, I shouldn't talk to you like you're one of my girlfriends."

He extends his elbow to me, leading me to a bar table. "I'm always down to yap. At least, I think that's what the teens call it these days."

"I appreciate you standing in." I clasp my hands in front of me, twiddling my thumbs. "Can I ask you a question?"

"Shoot."

"Is it possible to settle down in this industry?"

Rhett nods. "Lots of people do."

"Successfully?"

"I guess that depends upon what you consider success-ful." He blows out a breath. "I think a relationship with a celebrity is just like any other. The falling in love part is easy. Exciting. The staying together and putting in the effort to make your relationship work is the hard part." Rhett leans his elbow on a bar table. "Then you add in the paparazzi taking pictures of you wherever you go, and everyone speculating about your relationship. It just means you have to work harder for it. But if you find the right person, the effort is worth it."

My chest constricts. I never thought I'd be considering signing up for a life in the spotlight. I'm just a teacher. Heck, I wasn't even on social media before this. But if I choose a future with Griffin, I'm in for a life where we'll always be stopped in public. Where people will always speculate about our relationship if we aren't seen together often or posting pictures frequently enough for their liking.

I swallow down the lump in my throat. "What about when he's filming a movie? Or flying to events like this? How do you survive everything the media is saying when you're apart for weeks or months at a time?"

I don't know how often my teaching schedule would allow me to visit him while he was filming or in LA for events. Would I even be allowed to visit him on set? I don't know how this kind of thing works. I don't know how anything in the *movie* industry works.

My palms turn clammy as I think about all the roadblocks ahead if Griffin and I decide to try to make a future together work.

"I'm not speaking from experience here, but from what I've witnessed, it all boils down to two things: trust and love. If you trust and love each other, you're going to do just about anything to make the relationship work. And you can weather any storm together because of the foundation you've built your relationship on."

Rhett makes it sound simple. But the thought of spending months apart from Griffin at a time feels anything but that.

I cross my arms on the table, ready to change the focus of the conversation to him. "You seem to know a lot about making relationships work for someone who doesn't have a girlfriend. Why doesn't some lucky girl already have you locked down?"

He runs a hand through his dark-blond hair, making it stand up in a messy way that somehow doesn't look bad. "I was focused on getting my music career started, which didn't leave much time for relationships. Once I made the time to date, most of the girls I went out with only did it to make a name for themselves, get their five minutes of fame. I want someone who wants me for me, not my fame."

"You deserve that." I grab a dumpling from a passing waiter. "I can only imagine how amazing the love song album you'll make will be once you've found your person."

"Does that mean you like my music?" Rhett pops a bacon-wrapped shrimp into his mouth.

"I may be a Rhettinator."

"No kidding." He smiles. "I'm honored, thank you."

I shake my finger at him. "We're going to find you a girl so you can write the best country love songs of all time."

He shrugs. "I'll take any help I can get."

We talk until Griffin is finally done with all his obligations and rejoins us. He kisses my temple. "What do you say we get out of here? I know it's been a long two days."

I yawn. "Sounds good to me."

Rhett closes the distance between us and pulls me in for a hug. "It was wonderful *finally* meeting you after how much Griffin has talked about you for the past three years. You always have a place to stay if you visit Nashville."

"Thanks." I squeeze him back. "The same goes for you in Louisville."

He moves to Griffin next, pulling him in for a bro hug. "Don't mess this up, dude. You found yourself a good one."

Griffin smiles at me over his friend's shoulder. "I know I did."

We say our final goodbyes and head out the back door to the car. Brittany is standing on the sidewalk and waves when she sees us. "It looks like we had the same idea."

"Avoiding the paparazzi?" Griffin gives her a side hug.

"Exactly." Brittany opens her arms to me, and I fold into them like we're old friends. "How'd you enjoy your evening?"

"It was fun to see Griff in his element." I run my hand along the side of my dress. "And to feel like a princess for the night."

"What'd I tell you?" She smirks. "He couldn't keep his eyes off you all night. I've never seen that man so distracted."

"Hey," Griffin cuts in. "You're giving away all my secrets."

"If the fact that you find your girlfriend attractive is a secret, then you have bigger things to worry about."

He shakes his head, stepping closer and settling his hand on my lower back. It's starting to get chilly as the weather drops into the high fifties, though it's not even close to the kind of winter temperatures I'm accustomed to. But Griffin's hand feels warm and sure.

"Mallory knows just how gorgeous I think she is." He brushes his free hand along my chin, turning my head to face him. "Don't you, beautiful?" His eyes dip to my mouth. I bite my bottom lip, and his hand on my back draws me closer. The romantic tension between us hangs in the air like a thick fog, palpable and unignorable.

Brittany looks between us with a grin. "You two have a fun car ride." She winks at me. "And a safe flight home tomorrow. Griffin has my number. Let me know if you're ever back in the area, and we'll get brunch or something."

I wave to her, unable to find words with Griffin looking at me like that. After she leaves, Griffin's driver pulls up. We slide into the car, and Griffin slides up the divider between us and the front seats.

The moment we're fully alone, he turns to me. He trails his fingers along my ankle, my calf, and thigh before settling them on my hip. He reaches over, cupping the side of my face with his other hand.

The way his eyes soften as he looks at me makes me feel like I'm precious. Not an object to be won, but the prize he'd spend his whole life striving for. "To answer your earlier question, I think I've been falling for you ever since I met you." His voice is low and husky. "I never had a chance of stopping it."

My heart pounds in my chest. I'm still process-
ing my own feelings and what a future between us
would look like. But there's one thing I know for
certain: hearing him say he's falling in love with me
makes me happy. Like front-row-at-a-Taylor-Swift-con-
cert-with-my-besties kind of happy.

"Griff, I—"

He presses a finger to my lips. "You don't have to say
anything. I didn't say I'm falling for you because I needed
you to say it back. I said it because it's become such a large
part of me that I couldn't *not* say it. It's like going up to
someone I just met and not telling them that I'm Griffin
Reynolds or an actor or falling for Veronica Mallory Porter.
It's just who I am."

A tear leaks from my eye at his last words. I never knew I
could be loved so deeply by someone. Sure, my friends and
family love me, but this kind of love feels different. I feel
pursued, understood, and cherished on a level that no one
else has ever shown me.

He wipes away the tear with the pad of his thumb. "Don't
cry, beautiful."

"It's the good kind," I assure him.

Griffin wipes his brow. "That's a relief. Because if I told
you I was falling for you and you were crying sad tears…I'd
probably become a hermit or an old man who sits on his
front porch yelling at the neighborhood children to stay off
my lawn."

"How would you become an old man so quickly? Is there
a Hollywood secret to aging that fast?" I laugh.

"I don't know, but I'd find a way." He smirks.

"Well, then it's a good thing I wasn't crying sad tears,
because I'd hate for you to deprive the world of your
handsome face in many movies to come."

His smile falls, and he sits back in the seat.

"Did I say something?"

"There's something I need to tell you." Griffin clears his throat. "I wasn't planning on telling you so soon after saying I was falling for you, but I need to be honest."

I lean forward, bracing for whatever bomb he's about to drop.

"You mentioned seeing my face in many movies to come, and that might be a little sooner than expected."

I blink. "What do you mean?"

Griffin's eyes are full of pity. "Yesterday, when I was at my meeting with Karina, the director of *The Heartless Prince* called."

"Griff, that's great," I exclaim, squeezing his arms. "Did she want you to audition?"

"I actually auditioned for her yesterday. It was all very spur of the moment."

My mouth drops open. "Seriously?" He nods, and I pull him in for a hug. "Congratulations! I know this is your dream role."

"It's everything I've been working toward." Griffin presses his lips into a firm line.

"Then why don't you sound excited?"

"Because if I get the role—and according to Karina, I'm at the top of a short list—it would mean leaving Louisville sooner than expected."

I take a deep breath, finally understanding his hesitation. "Leaving *me*."

He winces. "Yeah. They won't start filming until summer, but I would have to go to LA for strict physical and combat training for the movie."

"I'm so happy for you." I am, even if the thought of him leaving makes me heartbroken. Even if all I want is for him to tell me that he wants me to come with him, or that he still will prioritize our relationship.

But why would he do that when I can't even admit that I think I'm falling for him too?

CHAPTER TWENTY-SEVEN

GRIFFIN

I WALK TO MALLORY'S front porch, eager to see her for the first time since we've returned from LA. Telling her about my audition for the fantasy movie was both relieving and terrifying. I felt so much better not holding that information back from her, even if it was only for a day. But talking to her about the potential of leaving in the next few weeks physically makes my heart ache.

We ended the conversation with her telling me she was happy for me and that she wants me to pursue my dream, but it still makes me sick to my stomach. I already left her once for an audition, and it took me three years to find her again. We're officially dating now, but it doesn't seem wise to start our relationship by spending months apart, where I'll have very little time to talk to her, and be three hours behind her, thanks to time zones. I don't want this to be something that ends up coming between us.

I inhale a deep breath and release it slowly through my mouth. I'm getting ahead of myself. I haven't even been offered the role. There's still time to figure it out.

After my heart returns to a normal rhythm, I raise my hand and knock on the front door. I offered to help Mallory bake cookies for her upcoming school fundraiser, and I figured it could be a fun activity for us to get a few photos or videos to post together.

It's refreshing being able to post footage together for real, like the ones we shared on social media from the red carpet. Although I had to stop reading the comments on that one before I started to track down and punch every man leaving comments about how hot Mallory was.

The door opens, and Kelsey's dog, Winston, runs to me, licking any stretch of visible skin. Once my ankles and hands are thoroughly slobbered on, he seems appeased. I ruffle the fur on his head. "Hey, buddy."

Mallory laughs, and I move my gaze up, finally getting a good look at her. Her hair is up in a messy bun with a few wavy hairs framing her face. She's in a magenta long-sleeved shirt and jeans with a lacey blush-pink apron over her outfit. And she's just as gorgeous in this as she was at the movie showing.

"Are you ready to bake your heart out?" she asks.

I nod. "Put me to work, boss."

She steps to the side with a raised brow and a smirk, letting me inside. "Boss? I like the sound of that."

"I'll call you whatever you want, beautiful."

I move into the kitchen. Mallory walks to the other side of the kitchen island. Leaning her elbows on the counter, she looks at me playfully. "Boss will do, for now. But I'm sure I can think of some other names." She tilts her head, looking like the sassy girl I quickly knew I needed in my life from the moment I met her. "Well, at least ones I could call *you*."

The suggestiveness in her tone leaves me both wanting to know what names she's thinking of and also slightly terrified of what they could be. My cheeks warm. "I think I'd be interested in hearing those later."

"I'm sure you would." She smirks and throws me an apron. "Put this on unless you want to mess up your fancy sweater and jeans."

"I got these from the clearance rack at Kohl's, thank you very much." I pull the white apron over my head and tie it behind my back.

"Does saying that make you feel better about being rich and famous?"

"I've only made *two* movies."

Mallory gets the oven preheating and starts grabbing ingredients from the fridge and pantry. "One of which has made over one hundred fifty million."

"I don't get to keep that money."

"I know that, I'm just saying that I think that makes you famous. And since your salary for the movie is public knowledge, I'd say that makes you rich as well."

I love how she keeps me on my toes, never knowing what she's going to say next. What Mallory doesn't know is how much of that money is now gone. Between what I've donated to charities, my granny's hip replacement and top-of-the-line rehab facility, my house rental here and my apartment in LA, security teams for my rental and Mallory's house, my drivers, the private jet, and all the normal costs of monthly living, I've spent a lot of my earnings.

But I'd do it all over again if it brought me back to her. To end up here in her kitchen with Taylor Swift playing in the background like the soundtrack of our lives.

She snaps her fingers. "Earth to Griffin."

I blink rapidly. "Sorry, what was that?"

"Can you put all the dry ingredients into that bowl?" She hands me a recipe notecard.

I salute her. "Sure thing." I carefully measure flour, baking powder, and salt into a bowl while Mallory beats butter, sugar, brown sugar, and eggs with a mixer.

I use the back of a butter knife to even out my ingredients, wanting these cookies to be perfect. Once I've finished, I pass over the dry ingredients to her. Before I know it, she's worked her magic and is sliding cookie sheets into the oven.

Mallory turns around and walks my way with a playful glint in her eye. "You know, you have something right here." She reaches up and touches my cheek, leaving behind something that feels like dust.

I narrow my eyes slightly. "Did you just put flour on my face?"

"It was already there." She shrugs, feigning innocence.

I grab a small pinch of flour from the container, rubbing it between my fingers before swiping some across Mallory's nose. "Mm-hmm. Just like you already had flour on your nose."

She places her hands on her hips. "Don't start a fight you can't win."

I lick my lips, and satisfaction courses through me as I watch her eyes dip to them. "I'd only lose because I'd let you win. Since I'm a gentleman and all."

"It sounds like we're both winners, then." Mallory goes up on her tiptoes, her eyes still on my mouth. It would be plain rude to refuse an invitation like that. I brush my nose against hers, teasing. Mallory wraps her hands around my neck, tugging my mouth to hers.

It feels like we've done this thousands of times, the way our lips seem to know each other and move together. But it also feels like the first time, passionate and exhilarating.

It's as clear to me as the sky after a huge storm. If it's not Mallory, it's no one for me.

She tilts her head, giving me the perfect access to the hollow spot on her neck. I move my lips there, and she lets out a small sound that I love even more than her laugh because this sound is only for me. I smile against her skin.

I can't help but think that Mallory was right. In this moment, I'd say we're both winners.

———— ♡ ♡ ♡ ————

I've thought Mallory was beautiful since I met her, but seeing her in action with her students at this fundraiser takes it to a new level. Her passion for teaching oozes out of her, and she looks just as at ease and natural with the kids as she does on the ice.

Right now, she's surrounded by a horde of young girls who look like they're trying to convince her to do the inflatable obstacle course they're standing by.

I can't help but smile like a lovestruck fool, watching her in her element. That is, until I see a young boy stomping his way over to me. I readjust my ballcap. This is Mallory's work event, something for her students and school, so I've just been trying to keep the focus off me. It hasn't been entirely effective since parents, teachers, and students in attendance have still asked for pictures, but everyone's been respectful.

But the scowl the young boy walking toward me is wearing makes it seem like that's about to change.

"Hey, you." He crosses his arms like he's trying to look more menacing, even though he's four feet tall. "I've seen you and Ms. Porter all over the magazines at the grocery store. What are your intentions with her?"

"How old are you?" I laugh, thinking he's kidding, but if his eye daggers could kill, I'd be dead.

"Old enough to know how to treat a woman."

I don't know if this kid watches movies that are too mature for him or if his mom reads him romance novels every night. But either way, he seems to think he's wise beyond his years in the romance realm.

I bend down, getting to his level. "I can't tell you that I'll always be perfect, but I promise to always treat Mal—I mean, Ms. Porter—how she deserves to be treated. Like the queen she is."

He narrows his eyes and looks me over like he's Gordon Ramsay and I'm an undercooked risotto. Finally, his gaze softens. "I guess you're okay." He points a finger at me. "But if you don't treat her right, you'll be on my list."

On his list? This kid can't be serious.

"Good to know." I ruffle his hair. "Enjoy the bounce house." I push up on my knees and hightail it out of there. When I see Mallory still standing with the group of girls, I head her way.

She smiles when she sees me approaching and turns to the girls. "I'll go on the obstacle course with y'all after Principal Abernathy's speech."

That answer seems to appease them because they skip away.

Mallory turns back to me. "I saw you were talking with Aiden."

Well, now I know what name to tell Karina to watch out for in my hate mail.

"If you can call it *talking*," I chortle.

"He's a little precocious."

"A little?" I cross my arms. "That kid is either going to be the future president or on *America's Most Wanted*."

"You're not wrong." She laughs. "I hope he didn't scare you away."

I wrap my arm around her waist as we head to the stage set up on the opposite side of the gymnasium. "There's not a single thing in this world that could scare me away."

She beams up at me. "I have to go stand by all the teachers for the principal's speech, but I'll find you after?"

I kiss the crown of her head. "Sounds good."

As she moves to the stage, I head to the back of the crowd, trying to blend in. I came to support Mallory, not to have a spotlight on me. As the principal begins talking, my phone vibrates in my pocket. Karina's name flashes on my screen, and I know that I should probably answer. Peering over the crowd, I find Mallory already looking at me. I hold up my phone, frowning. She gives me a little wave, so I step out into the hallway and answer the call.

"Hey, Karina."

"Do you want the good news or the good news?"

"Give it to me."

I hear a rare smile in her voice. "You got it."

My mouth falls open as her words sink in. "Wait. You're telling me they want me for the lead role in *The Heartless Prince*? I thought they weren't going to decide for a few weeks?"

"After they saw your audition, they didn't want to see any more. They knew they'd found their heartless prince." Karina laughs.

It's so uncharacteristic of her that I can't help but balk. "What's so funny?"

"Thinking of you being heartless." She pauses, and I can hear papers shuffling. "I guess that's why they call it acting."

"Thank you?" My voice rises, making my statement sound more like a question as I attempt to process everything.

I'm going to be the heartless prince. It's truly my dream role...so, why am I not excited?

I run my hand along my chin, the feel of the scruff against my fingers bringing me back to reality. "You said there was more good news?"

"Oh, right. They want you here next week for a chemistry read."

I wouldn't consider that good news when it means leaving Mallory sooner than expected. I swallow hard. "Then after that?"

"You'll begin your extensive physical training. They mentioned that you'll need to work on combat skills, weapons training, and potentially some stunt training on top of normal physical training and dieting."

"Okay." I pace the hallway. "Can I get back to you?"

"Get back to me?" Karina scoffs. "You're kidding, right?" She sighs like I'm her most exasperating client. "This is what you've always wanted."

"I just need a day to figure things out here."

She's quiet again, and that scares me more than her screaming at me. Her silence speaks volumes for someone who is always brief and onto her next task. "Is this about Mallory?"

"Yes," I answer honestly. "And Granny."

"If Mallory cares about you, she'll be fine with you leaving to film. She has to know this is how relationships work in Hollywood." The sound of more rustling papers comes through the speaker. "They need teachers everywhere. It's not like she's stuck there for her job."

I would never ask that of Mallory. Not when I know how much her family and friends mean to her.

"And I'm sure Granny will understand," Karina adds. "You have her in a great facility."

I know she's right, but I can't have her tell the director that I'll be there next week without talking to Mallory and Granny first.

"I'll call you back soon, Karina."

"Griffin, I need—"

I hang up. I've never done that to my agent before, but I know Karina will find a way to get me the time I need.

I return to the gymnasium, closing the door softly behind me so it doesn't make a loud sound as the principal finishes her speech. I find Mallory in the crowd again, and I can see the concern written across her face from here.

Is everything okay? she mouths.

I nod, shooting her a forced smile. There's no use ruining her work event. My dilemma will be the same in a few hours as it is right now.

"Please make sure to check out the sweets table and silent auction." Principal Abernathy clasps her hands in front of her. "Now, we don't usually include sweets sale items in our silent auction, but this year we have a real treat. There are a dozen cookies baked by the actor Griffin Reynolds and our very own Mallory Porter."

A few excited squeals sound from the crowd, and a large group of moms rushes to the side of the room where the auction is set up to bid on my cookies. Seeing as I only measured the dry ingredients, I wouldn't classify them as *my* cookies, but as long as it brings in money for the school, I don't care what they label them.

I dip my chin as they run by, hiding my face. Thankfully, most people who have recognized me have been pretty quiet about me being here. I want this to remain a school fundraiser, not turn into a Griffin Reynolds event.

The principal watches the mass exodus with wide eyes. "Thank y'all for supporting our school. Enjoy the festivities, and go, Wildcats!"

Mallory quickly makes her way to me once the crowd disperses. "What's wrong?" she asks.

I purse my lips, not wanting to lie to her. "We can talk about it later."

Her forehead creases with worry. "I can leave early if—"

"Go spend time with your students. Everything will be the same in a few hours as it is now."

I only hope that's still the truth after she finds out I might be leaving next week.

CHAPTER TWENTY-EIGHT
MALLORY

"Okay, what's wrong?" I ask as Griffin pulls his car to a stop in front of my house. He's been eerily quiet the entire drive back from the school fundraiser. "Your silence is freaking me out."

Griffin puts the car in park and turns to me. His tense jaw and furrowed brows send my stomach swirling with concern. "I need to tell you about the call I got during the fundraiser."

"Whatever it is, you can tell me." I unbuckle and slide my leg under me, turning sideways to look at him better, before reaching over and interlacing our fingers. "Who called?"

"Karina."

I squeeze his hand. "Did you get the part?" He nods, and I lean forward, wrapping my arms around his neck. "Griffin, that's amazing." I pull back, narrowing my eyes. "Then why do you look like someone just poured pickle juice into your hot chocolate?"

He grimaces. "That sounds disgusting."

I can feel the tension radiating from him, and I subtly brace myself for whatever bad news he has yet to tell me. "Exactly, so what's with your face? Why aren't we celebrating?"

He lets out a long breath. "They want me there next week for a chemistry read."

"English, please?"

That finally brings a small smile to Griffin's face. "They want me to sit down with the actresses they have in the running for my love interest to read through scenes with them. They want to make sure we'll have good on-screen chemistry."

"That makes sense." I bite the inside of my cheek, trying not to get emotional at the thought of him leaving. I'm not even going to think about the fact that he's going to test his chemistry with other women. I understand it's only acting, but I'm only human. The thought of him kissing anyone else stings.

But I trust him. If he's all in on me, I know Griffin wouldn't stray. That doesn't take away the fact that he's leaving, though. That he's choosing this movie over staying here with me.

No. That's not fair. I can't blame him for doing his job. But I don't know if our relationship is strong enough to withstand the distance. I thought we had a few more months until he'd have to leave. It's like Rhett told me—we need a firm foundation to fall back on with being in the public eye.

I clear my throat. "And you'd leave for the chemistry read next week?" When he nods, I ask, "How long will you be gone?"

Griffin worries his bottom lip. "This movie requires extensive physical training. I don't know how long that will take. It could be until they start filming."

I bite my cheek harder to hold back my tears. I never used to cry. I hate showing emotion and looking vulnerable.

But Griffin had to go and make me fall for him, which apparently has turned me to mush.

"You'll be gone for a few months, then?" I will my voice not to crack. I have to be strong for him.

"Yeah, it would be a few months of training and then however long filming takes." He sounds as heartbroken as I feel. "Do you think I should take the role?"

My eyes go wide. "You haven't accepted it yet?"

He shakes his head.

"Why not?" I rub circles on the back of his hand. "It's your dream role."

"But you're my dream girl. I could never accept it without talking to you first. You'll always be my top priority, Mal." Griffin looks at me, his eyes earnest and full of hope. "I thought this movie was everything I ever wanted. That being offered a role I really wanted was going to make me feel like I had made it in life. But all of that means nothing if I don't have you."

"Griffin, you already have me. You can't give a movie up for me."

He flinches slightly, but I see it.

"What was that?" I point at him.

He presses his lips into a thin line. "I don't know what you're talking about."

"Your face did something." I tap his chest. "Come on, we said we'd always be honest with each other."

Griffin lets out a resigned sigh. "I didn't tell you because I never wanted you to feel bad. This was fully my choice, okay?"

"Okay…" I draw out the word, nervous about where this is headed.

"I may have already given up a movie for you."

"*Griff.*" My eyes go wide. "Why did you do that?" I reach over and dig into his jacket pocket, trying to find his phone. "I'm going to call Karina right now and tell her you made a mistake. You have to be the lead in *The Heartless Prince*. I'm not letting you give up your dream."

He gently takes my hands, stopping my frantic movements. "I haven't given her an answer on this movie yet. Not until I talked to you."

"What movie are you talking about, then?"

"The one I was offered right before coming to Louisville. It was another rom-com. I think they wanted to piggyback off the success of *Accidentally in Matrimony* by pumping out another movie with me. But I would've only been able to stay here long enough to make sure Granny was settled in her facility. I already told Karina I didn't think I could accept it because I wanted to be here for Granny, and then I ran into you." He lets out a breath through his nose, tilting his head. "There wasn't a chance I was going to leave after that."

My heart stutters in my chest. Before I'd even given him the time of day again—back when I still thought this was all pretend—Griffin gave up a movie. For me. I always worried I would be second to his career. He's shown me otherwise in our time together. But hearing him say that I'm his priority and that everything else means nothing without me is like the final stitches healing up my past wound.

"Like I said." Griffin holds one hand up and says, "My career." He raises his other hand up until it touches the roof of the car. "You."

His words settle deep in my chest, making me feel a deep sense of belonging. The more I think back on the last month with him, everything becomes clear. He's left a trail of memories and whispered promises, showing me how much he cares. The signs have been there all along, pointing to him. I was just so scared that I wouldn't allow myself to believe it.

Knowing that Griffin wants me—blunt honesty and all—over anything else in his life brings a rush of tears to my eyes.

"What is it, beautiful?" Griffin leans forward, pressing his forehead to mine.

"I can't believe you'd pick me over a movie."

"Well, you better believe it." He kisses my temple. "I'll do it again, if you want me to stay."

He's already given up one big opportunity. I refuse to let him give up another.

There's no sugarcoating, a long-distance relationship with Griffin would be hard, a trial to put our relationship to the test. Being apart from him would feel like death by a thousand cuts—every part of me raw and aching for him. It would suck not being able to see each other every day and to miss important events. The thought of not being able to drive over to his house after a hard day and be wrapped up in his strong, safe arms is gut-wrenching.

But if he feels as strongly as he's said and as his actions have shown, then we just might have a shot at this.

At love.

At a future together.

"You have to accept this role." I pull back, squeezing his hands. "This is everything you've been working toward. I want you to achieve your dreams, but—"

Griffin has repeatedly reassured me of his feelings this past month. He even told me he's falling in love with me. But I've been holding back, terrified that I would tell Griffin that I'm falling for him only for him to turn around and leave. I'm done holding back, though. He deserves to know my heart and receive validation, too.

I take a steadying breath, preparing myself to put my heart on the line. "I want you to achieve your dreams, but I want to be part of them too."

His eyes turn glossy, filled with tears that could only be described as happy because of the tilted smile on his face. "You do?"

I nod. "I don't know what life looks like dating Hollywood's hottest actor. Or how we'll handle living over two thousand miles apart. But there are things I do know. I love how you go all in, like getting a to-go cup of hot chocolate tattooed on your ribcage when you didn't know if our paths would ever cross again. I never want to go a day without seeing the adorable, goofy smile you get whenever you're around me. I love how generous you are. I think you're truly the most selfless man I've ever met. You don't do things for recognition, but just because you care."

A tear drips from his eye onto his cheek, and I wipe it away. "I know I used to call you Mr. Razzle-Dazzle as a joke, but it's the truth. All of the goodness that's in you shines through in your words and actions."

Griffin blows out a breath as more tears fall. "Are you trying to make me cry here?" He laughs.

I smile. "I just want you to know that you're worth it all. The long-distance. Dealing with the paparazzi. Upending my life as I know it to trade it for a new one—a better one—with you."

He stares at me for a beat before unbuckling his seatbelt. Before I can ask what he's doing, Griffin is out of the car, jogging around to my side. He opens my door and lifts me out of the car, enveloping me in his muscular arms.

"Thank you," he whispers into my ear. "I think I needed to hear that you choose me, too. That you choose this life. I never wanted to force you into the public eye."

I pull back just enough to press my lips to his. The kiss is gentle, but filled with desire and anticipation. A kiss to remember this moment by for the rest of our lives. "If I wasn't already clear, this is me choosing you."

His mouth tilts up at the corner. "Does that mean I get the honor of having you on my arm at every red carpet and gala?"

"As long as you don't mind taking me dress shopping."

Griffin chuckles. "Deal."

I run my fingers along the hair at the nape of his neck. "Does this mean you'll finally call Karina and tell her you're accepting the role? I bet she's freaking out."

"As long as you're sure that you're okay with me taking it." He sighs. "I hate the thought of leaving you and Granny so soon, and I could never ask you to come with me. I know how much your job, friends, and family mean to you. But we'll be in completely different time zones."

"It's only for a season," I say, trying to give him every reason to pursue his dream, because I want that for him. And I want to be right by his side, cheering him on as he achieves them.

"Whenever you're filming, I could fly out during my school's spring and summer breaks to be with you. And if you ever have a free weekend, you could come visit." I press a kiss to his cheek. "We'll make things work for this movie once you get a better idea of what your schedule will look like, then we can figure out what we want to do moving forward."

"I'll happily limit the number of projects I take on each year."

"You don't need to make any promises like that now, Griff. The only promise I want you to make is that you'll always come home to me." I move my fingers up into his hair, trailing them along his scalp. He closes his eyes and leans his head into my touch.

"Always." Griffin's voice is low and raspy, his eyes focused on my lips. He traces the outline of my jaw from my ear to my chin.

I inch my mouth closer to his, our breath intermingling in the air between us. "Good, because the truth is, I'm falling for you, too."

Griffin closes the remaining distance and shows me how deeply he cares about me with every press of his lips to mine.

CHAPTER TWENTY-NINE
GRIFFIN

IT'S BEEN A WEEK since Mallory told me she was falling in love with me, and I still haven't come down from the feeling. I've been walking around with my head in the clouds, a permanent smile pasted on my face. One that I never want to fade.

But I have a feeling it will after today. I don't think it's possible to leave Mallory behind tomorrow and still wear a grin, even if I'm excited about this movie. Saying 'see you later' to her is going to be the hardest thing I've done.

One thing at a time, I remind myself. I have to say my goodbyes to Granny first. Today is a whole day of mixed emotions, so I'm going to embrace them. I can feel both joy and dread at the same time.

Ted drops me off and I head inside, waving hi to the receptionist as I pass by. When I arrive outside Granny's room, I'm greeted with a flood of memories from when Mallory came here with me. With a deep breath, I knock on the door.

"Come in," Granny's gentle voice calls out.

I walk in with a forced smile and pull her into a hug. She presses a kiss to my cheek before pulling back.

"You're feeling a little thin." Granny pats my stomach. I can't imagine I've lost much weight since I saw her last, but it's her job to worry about me. "You need some sweets. The dining hall has the best banana pudding. I could get you some." She gestures to the door, and I shake my head.

"Thanks for the offer, but I can't stay long." I help her back into her recliner and sit on the edge of the coffee table across from her.

"I know, I was just trying to prolong our goodbye." Her smile is as warm and sweet as a chocolate chip cookie straight out of the oven. "I'm so proud of you, Griffie. This role is going to open even more opportunities for you. I know it."

Her words bolster my spirit. "Do you think the Griffies will jump from the rom-com to the fantasy train?"

"They will if I tell them to," she tuts.

I raise my brow. It's taken over two years, but I caught her red-handed. "Ha! You finally admitted you're the creator of my fandom."

Granny's mouth drops open, and she sputters. "I— You— I did no such thing."

"Sure." I'm not one to second-guess her intentions, so I let it slide. Even though we both know the truth. "I know you've said you'll be okay, but I feel awful leaving you here alone."

Granny waves off my comment. "Oh, don't fret about me. I've made a few friends to keep me company. And, like I said, the banana pudding really is something to talk about."

"Well, I just can't compete with banana pudding."

She shakes a finger at me. "Don't go twisting my words, Griffie."

"I'm just kidding." I wrap my hand around her dainty, wrinkled fingers. "I'll miss you."

"Me too, but I refuse to be sad when I'm so excited for you." She squeezes my hand with surprising strength. "I do have a question, though."

"Yeah?"

"How are you feeling about leaving Mallory?"

I lean back in my seat and sigh. "I've been trying not to think about it."

"Lucky for you, there are cell phones now and the fancy video calls."

"It'll be hard to talk as much as I want with the time difference and demanding schedule." I inhale a shaky breath.

"How does that make you feel?" Granny asks.

"I feel horrible complaining since I know how lucky I am to have my Mallory and my career, but it feels like I'm going to be leaving half of my heart behind tomorrow."

"It's okay to be excited about the movie and also sad about leaving the girl you love behind." Granny pats my arm. "I've seen the way you two look at each other. And, trust me, she'll still feel the same way when you get back. Feelings that deep don't change in a few months. You two are meant for each other. Just like your grandfather and I were."

I didn't know my grandpa well. He died when I was ten, but every story I've heard about him has made it feel like he's still here, still part of me. I think that's the best we can hope for when we're gone—that our legacy will live on through our loved ones from the impact we've made on them.

Granny always called Grandpa her soulmate. She said she'd never love anyone the way she loved him. And she's stuck true to that promise. Even though she lost him young, she never considered remarrying. I've always dreamed of a love that big, so hearing her compare me and Mallory to them is the highest compliment.

She smiles, making the wrinkles around her eyes and mouth deepen. "A little distance won't change that."

"Thank you. I love you." I pull her into a hug, careful not to squeeze too hard.

She sniffles. "I love you, too. Now, go leave that sweet girl with something to remember you by until the next time you're able to visit."

I laugh and press a kiss to her wrinkled cheek. I think I'll do just that.

--- ♡ ♡ ♡ ---

"I'm going to miss you, beautiful." I run my hand over Mallory's hair, trying to memorize the feel of each strand. Now that I have the honor of calling her mine, I don't know how I'm going to leave her tonight. There will be plenty of time to miss her in the coming months, but I want to be present while she's beside me.

Mallory snuggles deeper into my side, resting her head on my chest and her legs across my lap. "I'll miss you, too."

I lose all sense of time holding her, soaking in the scent of her tropical shampoo and the way she fits perfectly in my arms. I'm about to ask her what she's thinking, when my shirt begins to feel damp. I rub Mallory's back in small, soothing circles and press a kiss to the top of her head.

I clear my throat as Mallory's breathing steadies. "What are you thinking?"

"Your arms feel like home." The words come out raw, filled with emotion. It was hard to leave Lover's Grove, to leave my parents and Granny behind for my career, and LA has never felt like home to me. I haven't had that settled sensation since leaving Tennessee, not until I found Mallory again.

Tears sting my eyes, and pain twists my heart like a sharp knife. I truly consider calling Karina and telling her this is a huge mistake, that I don't want to go because I've already found what I was looking for.

I keep telling myself that this distance will make our relationship stronger. We'll grow our communication skills and not take a minute of time together for granted. Plus, Mallory would never let me give up the movie. But it doesn't mean that I don't think about how different life would be if I were a normal person able to find a new job to be near the woman I love.

Because I do love her. More than acting. More than life itself. More than I ever imagined possible. But I can't imagine telling her that now. It sounds ridiculous, like, *Hey, I love you. But now I'm gonna hop on this plane, and I won't be back for months. Okay, love you, bye.*

Yeah, that's not going to fly.

I run my hand along her back, settling it on her hip. "I haven't had a true home since I left Lover's Grove for LA, but I found it in you."

She lifts her chin, leaving our lips a breath apart. "That sounds like it should be a line in a movie."

"What can I say?" I press my mouth to the corner of hers, teasing. "You inspire me."

Mallory closes her eyes and murmurs, "Does that make me your muse?"

"My muse." I kiss her cheek. "My girlfriend." I move my lips to her forehead. "My favorite person." I kiss the tip of her nose. "My beautiful girl." I lower my head, dragging my lips along the hollow of her neck.

Mallory huffs impatiently, grabbing my stubbled cheeks. My laugh is swallowed by her mouth covering mine. Our lips move together in a flurry of passion, every tug and graze filled with the words we're unable to say—the *see you later* we don't want to speak aloud.

There's no feeling that compares to this. This connection is greater than anything I ever dreamed of experiencing in my lifetime. Better than any screenwriter could come up with. It's the kind that comes from knowing each other deeply, growing together through trials, and coming out stronger on the other side.

I tug her closer and deepen the kiss. My fingers graze the soft skin of her back, under her sweater. She sighs against my lips and moves her hands to my hair, tugging at the strands. I tilt my head back, craving her touch.

"I've been meaning to ask you…" Mallory kisses the soft spot under my ear. "How do you always taste like cinnamon?"

I wasn't even sure she noticed before, but now that I know the truth won't scare her away, I say, "I started chewing cinnamon gum after I met you, since you loved the snickerdoodle hot chocolate so much."

She scans my eyes. "Why?"

I kiss her lips, slow and flirtatiously. "So that I would taste like your favorite flavor if I ever found you again."

"That's the most thoughtful"—Mallory leans in and grazes my lips with hers—"and hot thing I've ever heard."

I lower my mouth to hers again, and we continue to kiss and talk until the sun starts setting.

"Are you all packed and ready to go?" Mallory plays with the hair at the nape of my neck.

The truth is that I'm not ready for any of this. But is anyone ever prepared to find their person and leave them for the second time? There's no amount of preparation that will make me feel ready to leave Louisville. To leave Mallory. But I have to.

"For the most part." I sigh, glancing at the time on my phone. "I should probably get home and finish packing since I have an early morning."

"What time does your flight leave again?"

"Eight."

Mallory pushes up from the couch and extends her hands to me, helping me up. "At least you don't have to be there too early since you're leaving from that private airstrip."

I walk with her to the front door. She stops and turns to face me. Tears brim in her eyes, and I hate that I'm the cause of them. I open my arms and she falls into them, her head fitting perfectly under my chin.

"I'm only a phone call away," I say, my voice thick with emotion. "And we'll figure out a schedule for visits and video calls as soon as I know what my schedule looks like."

"I know." Rising onto her tiptoes, Mallory presses her lips to mine. "I'll be here cheering you on."

After squeezing her tight one more time, I offer her as encouraging a smile as I can muster. "I'll see you soon, beautiful."

She nods and opens the door for me, leaning against it like it's the only thing holding her up. "Bye, Griff."

I move past her into the cold and walk to the waiting car. With my hand on the door handle, I look back, and my heart tugs in my chest when I see Mallory still standing there, watching me leave. I wave and blow her a kiss. She reaches her hand into the air like she's catching it before holding it close to her chest.

If I don't leave right now, I don't think I'll ever be able to. I open the door and slide into the backseat, feeling a heavy weight in my chest. Not just because I'm leaving Louisville. No, I'm leaving my heart behind with it.

CHAPTER THIRTY

MALLORY

As I watch Griffin drive off into the distance, a piece of me goes with him.

I take a shaky breath and head inside, locking the front door before moving to the couch. My friends walk out of the kitchen with a platter of bonuts like they knew I'd need them and some sugar therapy tonight. I'm not sure if cinnamon-sugar biscuit donuts will help my heavy heart, but they certainly won't hurt.

Shayna sits beside me and rubs soothing circles on my back, reminding me of the way my mom used to help me fall asleep when I was younger. With a gentle voice, she asks, "How are you holding up, Mal?"

"It feels like my heart is breaking." I take the tissue Kelsey extends to me and dab under my eyes.

Shayna gives my arm a reassuring squeeze. "Sometimes things need to break in order to shine."

"Like what?"

"Glowsticks, for one." She pauses. "Oh, and that thing where they take broken pottery and repair it with gold."

"*Kintsugi*," Alyssa says, like it's a normal piece of information to know.

"Exactly." Shayna makes a clicking sound with her tongue. "That's all I can think of right now, but I'm sure there's more."

Alyssa takes a bite of a bonut. "Is it just that things feel more real now that Griffin's leaving tomorrow? Or is there another reason your heart is hurting?"

I purse my lips. "I think a part of me wishes I could go with him."

"Then go," they say together, as if it's the obvious solution.

I stare at them, slack-jawed. Is it that simple? Can I leave my life behind and go with Griffin? These are my girls, my soul sisters, but I know they'd gladly make room for Griffin and welcome him into our friend group with open arms. It's a leap of faith, leaving everything I've ever known, but now that I've found the man that I want by my side forever, I think it's a leap worth making.

"I think we broke her," Kelsey mutters out of the side of her mouth.

I throw a decorative pillow at her head.

"But the kind of breaking that leads to something beautiful." Shayna smiles.

"*Kintsugi*," Alyssa says again, making me snort.

"I can't just leave. I have my job."

"Girl, you never take a personal day." Kelsey grabs a bonut and drags it through the berry sauce before popping it in her mouth.

"Exactly." Shayna nods. "Use up your vacation time and go be with your man."

"You could stay out there with him for a little bit and then take some long weekends off to spend with him every few weeks." Alyssa pulls her knees to her chest, wrapping her arms around them.

"What about y'all and my family?"

Kelsey pats my arm. "We'll still be here when you get back. We're talking seven days, not seven years."

"And your family loves Griffin." Alyssa offers me a bonut, and I nibble on it. "I ran into your mom at the grocery store this week, and she couldn't stop talking about him."

"Really?"

She nods. "I think Mrs. Porter would be mad if you *didn't* go."

They're saying all the right things, but there's one major piece of information we haven't discussed.

"Okay, I get what y'all are saying, but Griffin didn't ask me to go with him." I purse my lips. "Well, I guess he told me that he wouldn't ask me to come with him—he knows how much y'all, my family, and my job mean to me."

"See." Kelsey nudges my knee. "He *wants* you with him, but he'd never ask you to sacrifice your life to be in LA because that's not who he is."

"He loves you too much for that," Shayna agrees.

They're right. Griffin has done so much to show me how much he cares. I think it's time that I show him just how much he means to me.

I jump off the couch and grab the bonuts.

"What are you doing?" Alyssa asks.

"I'm going to get my man."

"Yeah, you are," Shayna cheers.

"Why'd you take the bonuts?" Kelsey stands and grabs another one from the platter.

I head upstairs with my friends trailing behind me. "I'm going to need sustenance tonight if I'm going to stay up packing, emailing my principal, and preparing lesson plans for a sub."

When I walk into my room and flick the light switch, I look around with wide eyes. A warm vanilla-and-lavender-scented candle is burning, and there's a bouquet of vibrant pink blooms on my nightstand next to a large Dr. Pepper from McDonald's. My pink suitcase is lying open on top of my bed, already half-filled with clothes. Every little detail is a reminder of how well my girls know me and how lucky I am to have them as my best friends.

I turn around to find Shayna, Kelsey, and Alyssa wearing matching smiles.

"When did y'all do all this?" I ask.

"We divided and conquered while you were saying goodbye to Griffin," Kelsey says.

Alyssa points to my laptop bag. "There's a draft email in your notes on your computer for your principal, too."

They spill into my room, pulling me into a group hug. I squeeze them tight. I'm not sure I've ever loved them more than I do at this moment. My girls. My family. They have been there for me through thick and thin, and I don't want to think about what life would look like without them.

Speaking of, there's also a certain man I can't imagine my life without, and I can't wait to see his face when I show up with my luggage tomorrow.

——— ◦ ♡ ◦ ———

"Come on." I grit my teeth and press my foot harder on the gas pedal as I tap the call button on my car dashboard screen again. "Pick up."

The call to Griffin goes straight to voicemail. I huff as I press the end button on my steering wheel.

I didn't account for rush-hour traffic when I set my alarm this morning. And I definitely didn't account for construction flaggers on the side road I tried to take as a shortcut. It seems like the whole world is against me this morning, trying to ruin my grand gesture, but I refuse to let it. I'm going to make that plane.

A quick look at the clock says I might be too late. 7:58. He's probably boarding the jet, if not already in the air.

I press my foot down harder, going well over the speed limit as I get closer to the private airstrip. If I get pulled over, hopefully the police officer will be understanding of chasing down true love. Maybe they'd even give me a police escort.

The stoplight I'm approaching turns red, and I hit the brakes.

"Shoot," I hiss and tap my fingers against the steering wheel. "Come on. Come on."

The second the light turns green, I hit the gas, speeding ahead. When the airstrip comes into view, I see a plane on the runway and my heart skips a beat. I wish with everything in me for it to be Griffin's.

When I pull up to the gate, a man working the booth looks at me as I roll down my window. "Name?"

"Mallory Porter."

His neutral expression flickers with something like surprise. "Can I see your ID?"

I glance at the plane, relieved to see it's still there, before reaching over to the passenger seat and grabbing my wallet from my purse. My hand trembles as I pull out my driver's license and hand it over.

He glances at it, then at me, before handing it back with a nod. The gate opens, and I fling my ID and wallet onto my passenger seat before speeding onto the tarmac. I'm almost to the jet when I see a figure move onto the plane's airstairs.

A smile tilts my lips when I realize it's Griffin. The kind of smile that hurts my cheeks, but I don't care because I'm so happy.

I pull the car to a stop, hop out, and run toward him. As I approach the airstairs, he shouts three words: "Say 'don't go.'"

I stop at the bottom of the stairs, staring at Griffin. "This is supposed to be *my* grand gesture moment," I huff.

But here he is, begging *me* to tell him not to go.

Griffin jogs down the steps to me. "You came." His voice is husky and riddled with emotion.

"I couldn't let you leave, not without me."

Griffin takes a step closer, taking my hands in his. His eyes are alight with hope. "You're coming with me?"

I nod. "But I have a question for you first."

"Anything, beautiful."

"Were you trying to make me admit that I love you by shouting Taylor Swift song lyrics at me?"

"That depends." He shoots me a lopsided grin. "Did it work?"

"Mm-hmm." I rise onto my tiptoes and give him a whisper of a kiss to leave him wanting more. "I love you, Griff." My heart skips a beat as I wait for his response.

He cups my face in his hands, stroking a finger across my cheekbone. "I love you, Veronica Mallory Porter. More than I ever thought was possible to love another person. I can't imagine a future without you in it."

Griffin pulls my lips to his in a heated kiss. One that comes from knowing him. *Loving* him. One that ignites a fire in my belly and leaves me feeling lightheaded.

When I pull back, I'm lost in his eyes. "When did you know?"

"You had me at hello."

"You've loved me since you met me?"

"Maybe love isn't the right word." Griffin's eyes are full of desire, locked on my lips, but they become clearer when he meets my gaze. "But I felt a pull toward you from the moment we locked eyes and first said hello. It was this innate feeling that you were meant to be part of my life, and now I know why." He kisses my temple. "Everything we told that magazine was true. You're my soulmate, Veronica Mallory Porter. Meeting you was inevitable. Kismet. Destiny. Fate. It was always going to be you and me in the end."

"That sounds like a love declaration in a rom-com."

"Except it's better than any line that could ever be written." He kisses me, pulling me into a love-induced haze.

I kiss Griffin back with all the fervor and love I feel for him. When we pull apart again, I put on a reporter voice. "Griffin Reynolds, what will you do now that you've got the girl?" I hold my fist out to him like it's a microphone.

"I'm going to get on this jet with the woman I love and fly off into the sunset." He wraps his arms around my waist and smiles that tilted grin I adore.

"It's eight in the morning." I laugh.

Griffin squeezes my side, making me giggle. "You know what I mean."

After we park my car and load my luggage on the plane, I find myself once again sharing a leather recliner seat with Griffin.

We're exactly where we want to be.

Wrapped in each other's arms.

Irrevocably in love.

And I wouldn't change a single thing about our journey because it led us to this moment. To each other. To a love that's as sweet and steadfast as the man in front of me.

He was right. This feeling is better than anything that could ever be written or dreamed up.

Because this love is ours.

EPILOGUE
GRIFFIN

Two Years Later

Every minute spent with Mallory since we said "I love you" has only made our relationship stronger and our love grow deeper.

Don't get me wrong, it hasn't always been easy. Living apart for the months I was filming was the hardest test in our relationship. There were days we didn't talk other than a good morning and good night text, and others where we were disheartened by the distance. But we made it work because we're a team with the same end goal in sight—a future with each other.

We've split our time between Louisville, Lover's Grove, and Los Angeles. Each city we occupy time in has become home in a way, because wherever she is feels like home to me. Mallory is my safe place, my confidant, my biggest fan, and my favorite person all wrapped in one. Some people spend a lifetime looking for a love like this. I don't know how I got so lucky to have found Mallory not once, but twice. I guess that's what happens when two lives are intertwined. When something is meant to be.

These past two years together have been incredible as we've built our lives together. I've wanted to drop to one knee countless times throughout our relationship. Between filming *The Heartless Prince*, attending events and interviews to promote the movie, and starting to film the sequel, I've been working endless hours. Mallory has also been busy teaching and beginning her own side business for ice skating lessons. Little does she know that tonight is a night I've been looking forward to for a multitude of reasons.

"Are you ready, Griff?" Mallory whispers in my ear.

I lean back and smile at her. "Yeah." With her by my side, I already feel like a winner tonight. Mallory's hair is pulled up in a twisted updo with strands of her curls hanging around her face. She's in a wine-colored dress with a plunging neckline that's been distracting me all night long.

"Your category is next." She reaches over and straightens my tie before pressing a kiss to my cheek. "Time for you to win that Oscar."

We're currently sitting in the audience at the Academy Awards. I've been fidgeting all night. The only thing that's been able to calm my nerves is Mallory's hand in mine. Her steady presence grounds me. However, she doesn't know that I'm more nervous about what I'm planning on doing *after* the ceremony.

I feel the outline of the small box inside my jacket pocket and smile. I'm hoping to get two wins tonight, but if I just get one—a lifetime with her—that will be more than enough for me.

"And the nominees for best actor are…"

The faces of actors I've looked up to throughout my career appear on the screen. Some of them I've even revered since I was a kid. Finally, my picture pops up, and Mallory leans over and kisses my cheek.

"Griffin Reynolds. *The Heartless Prince*."

The next and final face to appear on the screen of nominees is Glen Powell for his lead role in the action movie, *Brink of Oblivion*. Mallory looks over at me with a devious smirk as she wiggles her brows. I know that she and her roommates love him and his acting from their constant teasing about Mallory's obsession with that movie, or should I say *all* Glen Powell movies.

But I'm the one who gets to take her home tonight.

"And the Oscar goes to…"

Mallory squeezes my hand as the presenter opens the envelope.

"Glen Powell. *Brink of Oblivion*."

I thought I'd be let down not hearing my name called. But I'm not. I'm proud of my acting in the movie. Simply being nominated was a huge honor, especially since it was only my third major movie. I have my whole life and acting career ahead of me, and I'd rather cheer on others in my community than feel like I'm competing with them.

Mallory squeezes my hand and leans over, whispering in my ear. "You're still a winner in my book."

On his way to the stage, Glen stops to shake my hand and smile at Mallory.

She clutches my arm as he accepts the award. "Did that really just happen?"

"Yes, it did," I whisper.

She lets out a dreamy sigh. "I think tonight might be the best night of my life."

With the plans I have in store for her later, I think it will be.

———— ◦ ♡ ◦ ————

After the ceremony is over, I answer questions for a few press interviews before we load into the back of a black SUV.

Mallory slumps in the seat, obviously exhausted, since this is much later than she's usually up. She turns to me, running her hand up and down my arm. "How are you feeling?"

I know she's talking about not winning the best actor award. Reaching down, I grab her hand and interlace our fingers. "I'm great. I was nominated for one of the highest awards alongside the greats of Hollywood." I lick my lips as I drink her in. "I have a beautiful woman that I love beside me in a killer dress. And now I get to go home with said woman." I kiss the back of her hand. "What more could I possibly ask for?"

I keep the conversation flowing until the car pulls to a stop at our surprise destination.

"Are we already home?" Mallory asks.

I open the car door and grin when I see the setup exactly as I'd envisioned it. Turning around, I reach my hand out for her, and Mallory accepts it, joining me on the grass.

"Where are we?" She gasps when she looks over my shoulder. "It looks like someone's about to propose. We should go."

"You're right, beautiful. Someone is about to propose." I wrap her hand around my arm and escort her through the aisle of tealight candles and rose-petal-covered grass.

At the end of the aisle are large clear vases as tall as us, filled with various shades of pink flowers. Twinkle lights hang overhead between the trees, coating us in a soft glow.

I turn to Mallory, taking both her hands in mine.

Her eyes glitter with unshed tears. "Griff."

My lips tilt up into a smile. "I never thought that I'd meet the love of my life by dropping spare change in her cup of hot chocolate while she participated in an elaborate caroling routine. While I wish there hadn't been a three-year lapse between our first date and when I finally found you again, I'm grateful that you gave me another chance. Because there's no one else I'd want to walk through life with than you. I knew you were special from the moment we met, but it's because of the time I spent with you getting to know the real Mallory that I fell in love with you. I love your heart for helping others. I love your sass and blunt honesty. I love watching you teach and live out your passion. I love that you will never be found without at least one pink clothing item on you at all times. I love that you make my friends and family feel like they're yours too. And I love that you make me the best version of myself."

With a deep breath, I drop to one knee and pull out the ring box from my jacket pocket. "I've known that I want to spend the rest of my life with you for a long time, beautiful. And I want the rest of forever to start as soon as possible." I flick the box open, revealing the large oval-cut diamond set on a vintage-inspired rose-gold band studded with diamonds. "Veronica Mallory Porter, will you marry me?"

As soon as the words are out of my mouth, Mallory flings herself into my arms. I'm barely able to keep my balance as she squeals directly into my ear before stepping back and giggling.

"I'll take that as a yes?" I laugh, pulling the ring out of the box.

She nods. "Easiest yes of my life."

Hearing her throw the same words back at me that I used on our first date brings tears to my eyes as I slide the ring onto her finger.

I stand and tug Mallory into my arms, holding both my present and my future. Leaning down, I press my lips to hers. Kissing her after all these years still lights a fire inside that can't be quenched.

While I may not have won the award tonight, I've gained something even more valuable: a lifetime with the woman I love.

And I feel like the real winner.

———— ♡ ♡ ♡ ————

Read a bonus scene about Mallory and Griffin two years in the future when you sign up for my emails at https://dl.b ookfunnel.com/7uj0ma84qv

Keep reading for a bonus epilogue!

BONUS EPILOGUE

SHAYNA

FEBRUARY

There it is. The niggling sensation that I should say something. *Anything.*

All it would take is a quick text message to let him know I'm in the area, but I can't bring myself to type it, let alone send it. If Connor Porter had wanted to say anything to me, he would have done so when he was at my house for our winter trivia night.

But no, he just stood there staring at me as I danced to "Jingle Bell Rock." When I attempted to talk to him, he only mumbled some lame excuse about going to the restroom before scurrying away. Then he avoided me for the rest of the night.

But now I'm in Washington, only an hour and a half from where Mallory told me he lived, at the Northwest Flower and Garden Festival. The seminars have been great. I've learned helpful tips about growing cut flowers, making sustainable centerpieces, and integrating underused blooms into bouquets. And while I love flowers just as much as life itself, I've found it hard to focus, knowing that my best friend's older brother is nearby.

Not to mention, the romantic feelings for Connor I've kept secret for years. Things I've never told a soul. Not even my best friends. I'm not sure they'd even believe me if I did.

My phone screen lights up with a new text, and my heart skips a beat, even though I know there's not a chance it's from *him*.

I unlock my phone and see it's a new message in the "Long Live Girlies" group text thread with my besties.

ALYSSA

How's the flower festival, Shay? *cherry blossom emoji*

We miss you!

KELSEY

Yesss, only one more day until we get to see our sunshine girl again *woman dancing emoji*

MALLORY

We can't wait to hear all about it!

I can't help but smile. These girls have been by my side for years. They're my kindred spirits. My soulmates. Since we've all been roommates for the last few years, I've had the joy of seeing them every day. This week away has been difficult, but I'm doing everything I can in preparation to take over Shirley's Florist once she retires in just under two weeks.

My dream of owning a flower shop will finally be a reality. Everything I've been working toward for six years is finally within reach. So close, I can almost grasp it. But there's a lingering sadness there that I won't have someone by my side to share it with. Of course, my parents and my friends will make me feel celebrated. But for someone who has always dreamed of finding my true love when I was young—to run my shop with them—it's bittersweet.

I type out a quick response to my friends before tucking my phone back in my flower-shaped purse.

ME

> It's been amazing! I've met so many wonderful people and learned so much. Can't wait to see y'all tomorrow though *face blowing a kiss emoji* *yellow heart emoji*

I shake my head as negative thoughts begin to spill in. No stewing in sadness when there's so much to be grateful for in this life. No more thinking about my very single status. No more regret over things I have no control over.

And absolutely no more thinking about Connor Porter.

♡ ♡ ♡

You won't want to miss Shayna's book, I'm Only Me When I'm With Him—a best friend's brother, grumpy/sunshine romcom.

ACKNOWLEDGEMENTS

All the glory to God! Thank you for putting a love of stories in my heart and for giving me the words to write this story.

This book wouldn't have been possible without my husband, Wade. Thank you for talking me down when I thought there was no way I was going to finish my edits for this book. Thank you for taking care of me and our home so that I could fully focus on writing. You're the best partner I could've asked for. I love you forever!

As always, a huge thank you to my beta readers, Kathryn, Kimberly, Meredith, Sara, and Steph. It's because of your feedback and suggestions that Mallory's character development and the ending of this book came to be where they are now. Thank you for helping me figure out what this story needed to shine. Y'all are the absolute best, and I never want to write a book without you! I can never thank you enough for your time and feedback.

Annah, your excitement for this book kept me going! Thank you for being the best critique partner and friend. And thank you for always making the time to give me feedback in the midst of your busy publishing schedule. I'm forever thankful for you!

Another shout out to my sweet author friend, Sara. I know I already thanked you for beta reading, but your support for this book went beyond that! Thank you for reading some of the sections *multiple* times and for all your encouragement and support. I'm so thankful that Hailey brought us together and for the sweet friendship I have with you because of it.

Melody Jeffries, you created my favorite cover yet! Your creativity never ceases to amaze me. It's a joy to work with you!

Thank you to my wonderful editor, Caitlin. Your encouragement and kindness means the world to me. I'm so thankful for your attention to detail. Thanks for helping make this story shine.

Thank you to Alicia Whitaker, proofreader extraordinaire. Thank you so much for your attention to detail and thorough feedback. I feel more confident putting my manuscript out into the world because of you.

Thank you to Brittany (@brittanys_bookcorner) for your suggestion that made it into I Knew He Was Trouble! I hope you loved the character named after you in this book.

Thank you to my mom for reading every iteration of this book. I appreciate your support more than you know!

To all my sweet readers, you make every hour spent on writing so worth it. Thank you for reading this book and making my dream a reality!

Finally, thanks to Taylor Swift for writing songs worth writing love stories about.

ABOUT THE AUTHOR

Amanda Schimmoeller is a closed-door romance author who writes sweet love stories for readers who love happily ever afters. Her books are filled with banter, heart, and characters you can't help but love.

She loves Dr. Pepper, salty snacks, and binge-worthy tv. You'll find her plotting her next great love story and living out her own fairytale in Tennessee with her husband and their dog.

Connect with Amanda at www.authoramandaschimm oeller.com